# The Woodhouse Boys

*by*

## Neil Cawtheray

Grosvenor House
Publishing Limited

Neil Cawtheray is hereby identified as author of this
work in accordance with Section 77 of the Copyright, Designs
and Patents Act 1988

The book cover picture is copyright to Inmagine Corp LLC

This book is published by
Grosvenor House Publishing Ltd
28-30 High Street, Guildford, Surrey, GU1 3HY.
www.grosvenorhousepublishing.co.uk

A CIP record for this book
is available from the British Library

ISBN 978-1-907652-85-1

*This book is dedicated to my dear wife Jennifer,
to whom I owe so much, for her patience and
understanding, and also to Barry McDonald,
the dearest and most loyal friend I ever had.*

The author, born in 1939 at the beginning of the Second World War, has lived in Leeds all his life and has never seen any reason to leave. He was educated at Woodhouse Junior School up to the age of eleven before moving on to Leeds Central High School. He married in 1975 and most of his working life has been in the service of British Telecom. He has always possessed a desire to write, but it was not until reaching retirement age that he found he had the time to do so. 'The Woodhouse Boys' is his first book.

# CHAPTER ONE

Billy wouldn't come down from the monkey tree. It was, without doubt, the best tree for climbing on the whole of the ridge, as any ten year old could easily reach out and grasp the lowest branch to haul himself up amongst dozens of others which reached out in every conceivable direction. Despite the fact that he'd been up there for almost half an hour I was perfectly contented to remain stretched out on the warm, grassy hillside, hands behind my head, remembering the great times we'd had during the summer holidays and contemplating the first morning back at school on the following day.

"Fifty-six", said Billy, "I can see fifty-six chimneys. Just a minute, make it fifty-seven. I forgot to count the Destructor."

This comment interrupted my thoughts and caused me to sit up.

"How could you miss the Destructor?" I replied. "My dad says it's the biggest chimney in Leeds".

"Well, it's because it's right in front of me. I bet if it wasn't there I'd be able to see another half dozen."

"That's only 'cause it's Sunday, Billy and there's none of 'em smoking. I bet if it was any other day you wouldn't see half as many. All you'd see is the smoke."

"Superman would. He could see right through smoke, or almost anything. I bet he'd be able to see as far as York."

I wasn't at all surprised at Billy's reference to Superman. It was the serial currently being shown at the Electra Picture House, a different episode every weekend (fifteen in all) and Billy and I never missed.

"You're not Superman though Billy", I replied. "Anyway, I'd rather be Captain Marvel than Superman. When Clark Kent wants to turn into Superman he has to look for a telephone box to get changed in, but when Billy Batson wants to become Captain Marvel he just shouts SHAZAM."

"It doesn't have to be a telephone box. It just needs to be somewhere where no one sees him. Anyway, he flies a lot faster than Captain Marvel."

"What about that Kryptonite, though. Every time Superman gets near any he loses all his powers."

"I think I'd rather be Batman anyway", said Billy. "I know he can't fly but I bet he could climb to the top of the Destructor before Captain Marvel could get there. That reminds me", he went on, "Did you know that one of the workmen fall off the top when it was being built? Ernie Peyton told me at school. I bet if he fell from that height there'd be blood and guts all over the place."

"You can't believe everything Ernie Peyton tells you Billy. Just before we broke up for the summer holidays he told me that Len Hutton had been bowled out for a duck and that he'd collapsed and died on his way back to the pavilion. I was upset about it all afternoon, and then when I got home I found out that he'd scored a hundred and twenty-three and was still batting."

"Well, that's what he told me anyway."

Actually, I'd heard the same story about the Destructor chimney myself from a different source, but I had no idea whether there was any truth in it. It was, indeed, a massive construction. Owned by the Council Refuse Department and located in Meanwood Road it dominated the skyline and stood higher than the summit of Sugar Well Hill which formed the other boundary of the Meanwood valley.

"There are some lads on the bottom path," shouted Billy, effectively ending our discussion about factory chimneys and the relative merits of the super-heroes of the cinema serials and the sixpenny comics, "I think they might be the Wharfies."

"How many?" I asked.

"I can see five", he replied. "I'm coming down, anyway".

That made good sense to me. The Wharfies were the kids who lived in a group of streets called the Wharfedales, which led off at right angles to Meanwood Road and they regarded the bottom part of the ridge as their territory. So far Billy and I had always managed to avoid them but we had heard from other lads at our school that they would chase any child they didn't recognize and if they were successful in capturing him he would usually face a beating unless he paid a forfeit such as a few sweets or a couple of taws or anything else that might be of value to a child of our age. Though neither of us had ever seen any evidence to back up these stories we decided not to risk the possibility that they were true. I knew that if we were to avoid detection on this occasion we would have to get moving before we were spotted.

"Let's go back along the Indian War Path", I suggested. "They probably won't see us there. We'll be behind the bushes most of the time."

"I was going to say the same thing," replied Billy, "But we'd better run".

The Indian War Path, as it was known to most of the kids in Woodhouse, was just made for running on anyway. It was a very narrow track that hugged the contours of the hillside. It was much more interesting than the official, wider, concrete paths above and below. It weaved and dipped and meandered in and out of various types of shrubbery and its very nature made it a popular venue for any game of cowboys and Indians. It was so easy to imagine that you were galloping along on horseback instead of running. On this occasion, however, our only reason for using it was to avoid detection. After a short while we both looked back and, as we realised that we weren't being followed we slackened our grip on the reins and continued in a more leisurely fashion.

"Do you think they were the Wharfies?" asked Billy.

"I've no idea. Have you ever met any?

"No, have you?"

"No, but Philip Thatcher at school said he would have been beaten up once if he hadn't have had a packet of fruit gums on him."

"Well, if they were the Wharfies we seem to have got away from 'em now."

As we approached the steps that climbed off the ridge and led into the street I noticed that Billy was looking a little despondent.

"I'm not looking forward to going back to school tomorrow", he said.

"Me neither," I replied. The summer's gone and it's ages to Christmas."

We carried on for a while, each with his own thoughts about the coming term, as we made our way down the steep hill towards home, before Billy broke the silence.

"I've just remembered something Neil. Do you remember what Old Rawcliffe said just before we broke up? He said we were going to start a rugby team this year and that Barnesy would be in charge of it."

I'd completely forgotten about that and it certainly seemed to have cheered Billy up. Mr. Rawcliffe was the headmaster of Woodhouse Junior School and Mr Barnes was one of the teachers there. It might not be so bad at that. I knew my father would be delighted because he was always reminiscing about how he used to play for Buslingthorpe Vale, which was an outstanding local amateur team in his day, though I doubted my own ability to create an impression on him. The Vale had no longer fielded a side after the war, but the ground, just off Meanwood Road, was still used by some local outfits and, for one day of the year, in May, particular interest was created by the seven-a-side competition among various factory teams in the area, and it was always well attended.

"I don't think they said they were definitely going to do it," I replied, hoping I hadn't dampened Billy's enthusiasm," and we're not forced to be picked anyway."

"Race you to Ormond's" said Billy, suddenly changing the subject.

"That's not fair, Billy," I shouted as he went racing off. "You've got a head start."

Ormond's was the sweet shop at the end of our street, and from where we were it was downhill all the way. Mrs Ormond was a pleasant, plumpish lady and was very popular with Billy and me. With sweets still being rationed, despite the fact that the war had been over for five years, she was always willing to let you owe a two ounce coupon until the end of the week. Billy, however, was destined never to reach the designated destination for this particular race. As he charged down the street he momentarily glanced back to see how far behind I was and ran straight into Mrs Chapman's washing line, entangling himself in a large bed sheet. In trying to break free he only succeeded in detaching one end from the peg. He then proceeded to trip over it as it trailed along the floor, tried to get up and in doing so brought the entire line tumbling around him. Billy was struggling, I was laughing and Mrs Chapman was coming out of the house looking very displeased.

"I make no wonder this has happened today," she said, helping Billy to his feet. "Never put your washing out on a Sunday, It's not right. Disrespectful to the church it is. I should have known. No, I make no wonder at all." She looked at Billy. "Are you all right lad?" she added.

"I think so", replied Billy. "I've just grazed my knee a bit, that's all"

"Well I make no wonder, racing down the hill like that. Couldn't you see where you were going?"

"I'm sorry, Mrs Chapman. I just turned round to see where Neil was and I ran straight into it. With it being a Sunday I wasn't expecting a washing line to be there."

"Ay, lad I reckon you're right there. It just serves me right it does. Too disrespectful, that's what. Get yourselves home then. I'll take 'em back in and wash 'em again tomorrow. It's the first time I've ever put a washing line out on a Sunday. Well, it just serves me right, that's all. I make no wonder. I make no wonder at all."

As Billy and I made a more leisurely retreat in the direction of home Mrs I-Make-No-Wonder, to use the name we called her by whenever she wasn't around, still muttering to herself about the evils of hanging her washing out on the Lord's day, gathered up the remnants from her broken line and took them indoors.

"You were lucky there, Billy," I said. "She thinks it was her fault. If you'd have done it any other day you'd have been in bother."

"I don't know about lucky," he replied. "Look at my knee. I wonder if my mam will let me off school tomorrow."

"I know mine wouldn't. I'd have to have measles or something like that."

"Why do they call it measles?"

"I've no idea."

"I mean, you never here of anyone having just one measle, do you? They're spots aren't they? Does that mean that a spot is the same thing as a measle then?"

We both laughed at the thought. "I don't think anyone's ever had just one mump either," I said.

"I bet Superman never got measles," said Billy, thoughtfully

"Anyway," I said. "I don't think you should miss the first day back at school. Don't you want to hear about the new rugby team?"

I never looked forward to going back to school after the long summer holiday, and if Billy wasn't there it would be twice as daunting.

"She won't let me stay at home anyway. She'll just stick a plaster on my knee and tell me not to be so silly.

I bet you want to go just so you can stand next to Susan Brown in assembly."

"No I don't," I said, going red and not knowing what else to say. Fortunately, I was saved from further embarrassment for just at that moment our ears became victims of a very loud and piercing yell lasting a duration of about ten seconds, yet it was a very familiar one, especially on a Sunday afternoon, and was always a very welcome sound to all the kids in the area.

"Oh, great," said Billy, rapidly forgetting about his grazed knee, "It's Tony,"

The object of Billy's excitement was at that moment turning the corner to enter our street, and in front of him was the ice cream cart which was the centre of our attention. Tony was lacking in height but the fact that he had been pushing his cart up and down the hills of Woodhouse for many years had given him muscles that even King Kong would have been proud of. He was well into middle age and had rapidly diminishing eyesight. There was certainly nothing wrong with his voice though, for when he announced his presence in the way just described he could be heard as far away as St Mark's church.

Fortunately it was a warm afternoon and, being a Sunday, Tony's arrival at this particular time was not unexpected and was greeted with enthusiasm by both Billy's parents and mine. A few minutes later Billy and I were seated on the causeway opposite our houses eagerly devouring two large ice creams, a threepenny cornet for Billy and a fourpenny twist for me. Both containers were the same size but for one penny more I could taste the delicious, treacly biscuit flavour as well as its content. Billy didn't care much for it though.

He always liked to break off the bottom of the cornet and suck the ice cream through from the wrong end, but it wasn't as easy to do with a twist

At that precise moment I found myself very relaxed and contented and anxious thoughts about returning to school on the morrow were receding. I knew that Billy was right. I was looking forward to seeing Susan Brown again, but I would never admit it to anybody.

# CHAPTER TWO

I was very lucky in childhood to have loving and caring parents who, despite living on the bread line, could see the value of encouraging their offspring to appreciate the benefits that a good and thorough education might bring. To this end my mother, in particular, was very energetic having begun teaching me to read at a very early age. It was during this time that my father was fighting for king and country. After the war he returned to his job as a leather worker in a factory in Meanwood Road. The amount he earned was just enough for us to live on and, with a bit of luck, have a holiday in August, though this was by no means always the case. Unfortunately, there wasn't enough money to enable my brother Tim, who my mother had also set on the right track, to go to university, which goal he would have been perfectly capable of attaining. He was several years older than I and had just begun his two years' National Service, so there were only three of us (plus a scruffy looking mongrel called Nell) living in the terrace house in Cross Speedwell Street. It was understandable, therefore, that my first tutor in life would be extremely keen to make sure that her protégé had no excuse to be late on the first day of term in a new school year, and to this end she made absolutely sure that I was washed, dressed, fed and ready to leave in time to be one of the first to arrive. She had, though, failed to take into account the fact that Billy's mother was not quite as forceful in this direction and, by the time he was ready and we had run the two hundred yards to the school premises and vaulted over the low wall into the playground, the school bell had already sounded and we hurriedly joined the rest of the pupils lined up into two neat rows, the girls taking the left flank and the boys the right.

We followed Miss Hazlehirst into the assembly hall in a surprisingly orderly fashion, considering it was the first day of term, to find the headmaster, Mr Rawcliffe, already on the platform awaiting our arrival.

"I'm sure old Rawcliffe looks a lot fatter," whispered Billy. At least he thought he was whispering, and as far as the other children were concerned he probably was, but he had obviously forgotten the fact that the teacher who had just accompanied us had, in the service of the school and its pupils, been on so many nature rambles, mostly on Woodhouse Ridge, that she could identify a birdsong from about half a mile away.

"Before I pass you all over to the headmaster", she said, "I think Billy Mathieson has something to tell us."

"What's that miss?" asked Billy looking very uncomfortable.

"I'm sure that what you were saying just now was very important," she went on. "Are you sure you don't want the whole class to hear it?"

Billy turned bright crimson. "It wasn't anything really, miss," he managed to get out.

"And do you often talk about not anything really?" she continued, not wanting to let go.

I wasn't sure how Billy was going to get out of this one but fortune decided to smile on him at that moment as Mr Rawcliffe, obviously aware of his junior teacher's tenacity, decided to curtail the proceedings.

"Thank you for your observation Miss Hazlehirst," he said in a very commanding tone, "But I think it is really time to move on now, and to the child in question I would like to add that, as you are so very keen to exercise your vocal chords that I expect to hear your voice above all the others as we sing ALL THINGS BRIGHT AND BEAUTIFUL. Is that understood boy?"

"Yes sir," replied Billy looking decidedly relieved.

His rendition of the aforesaid hymn, however, was as woeful as everyone else's, which was only to be expected on the first day of a new term, the mood of the pupils being very low with the certain knowledge that it would be ten long months before the start of the next summer holiday period.

With the dreadful singing at an end, Mr Rawcliffe faced the pupils again and delivered a ten minute lecture about the advantages of education and how things were so much better than when he was a pupil, and how there were now so many more privileges than were available to him. He then went on to something more interesting, at least as far as the boys at our school were concerned.

"At the end of last term I stated that Mr Barnes was attempting to enter a Rugby League team on behalf of this school into one of the junior leagues in the Leeds area. I am pleased to be able to report that he has been successful in achieving this end. I shall now hand you over to him so that he can put you in the picture."

As Mr Barnes stepped forward it appeared to me that he was looking a bit gaunt but, having in mind Billy's ordeal of a few minutes previously, I thought it wiser not to pass any comment on the matter.

"As you will remember," he began, "When we broke up for the summer I told you all that I was hoping we would be able to form a Rugby League team to compete in the local schools set-up at the beginning of this term. This was a late decision and I am delighted that, with the assistance of the headmaster, we have managed to do this in the short time-scale involved. We have, however, only three weeks before we are due to play our first fixture, which is against a team of a similar age-group from a school in Armley. Mr Rawcliffe, therefore, has kindly consented to allow all those boys who are interested, and I sincerely hope that is most of you, to leave school an hour early on Friday and to accompany me to Bedford's Field at Hyde Park where we can enjoy a practice session. Hopefully, there will be a few more of these before we have to play our first competitive fixture. Now is there anything in particular that you want to ask before I go on?"

"Can I be captain, sir? I'm good at rugger." This question was posed by Tucker Lane. Tucker, whose real name was Tommy and who lived in what was probably the roughest area of Woodhouse was the cock of the school. He knew it, all the teachers knew it and every other pupil at the school knew it. Nobody ever challenged him to a fight or a good scrap as he liked to call it. However, the knowledge that he couldn't be beaten was never enough for Tucker. I think if he didn't get his daily scrap with somebody he would suffer withdrawal symptoms. He was only average size, but what was there was solid muscle.

"I'm glad you mentioned the question of captaincy, Tommy," said Mr Barnes, (I looked across at Tucker. He was scowling. He hated being called Tommy.)

"Because that is one of the issues to be decided as a direct result of these practice matches, as I believe at the end of them it would be an excellent idea to let all those who have taken part to vote for the person they would like to lead them on the field," He paused for an instant before going on. "With a little guidance from me, of course."

I wondered if it would impress Susan Brown if I were captain, but immediately abandoned the thought as I realised I would be very lucky just to be selected for the team and anyway, if Tucker Lane thought it was his right, what chance did the rest of us have?

"Will we be wearing proper sports shirts, sir?" This utterance came from Ken Stacey, by far the tallest pupil in the entire school. In fact he seemed to have grown even taller during the summer holiday period.

"We will indeed have the proper kit by the time we take the field. The school has opted for very smart shirts consisting of green and white horizontal stripes with a large letter 'W' on the breast pocket, and I think I know lad why you might be a little concerned. However I can assure you that we shall check everyone's size before they are ordered and I am sure we will be able to provide one that fits even you.

"This caused laughter all around the hall, though I don't think Ken appreciated it.

Because of our ages both Billy and I were now in the senior class which was always taken by the headmaster. Surprisingly I found the first lessons of the new term didn't go too badly and having caught a glimpse of Susan seated a couple of rows in front of me, I realised that Billy's supposition of the previous day was correct, but I couldn't do a single thing about it. At ten years old you simply didn't associate too closely with girls, not if you wanted to retain a sense of pride and dignity among the other lads. In the main I suppose I enjoyed school more than most of the other pupils, in particular the history lessons with tales of hero kings and bloodthirsty battles. These battles were frequently re-enacted in the cobbled streets of Woodhouse and I remember in particular how I would find myself in trouble every time I used my mother's posser as a lance. The first day of term, therefore, at least from my point of view, could have been classed as fairly successful had it not been marred by one incident. As I entered the schoolyard with Billy, prior to making our way home, we found ourselves accompanied by Tucker Lane.

"I'm going to be the rugger captain," he volunteered.

"What if you don't get picked?" I asked

"What do you mean, not get picked?"

"Well, it's going to be decided by votes, isn't it?"

"And you might not get enough to win," added Billy.

"But I'm the best player," said Tucker, as if the prospect of not getting enough votes hadn't occurred to him. The fact that no one had seen any of the other lads play seemed of no consequence. It was as if the whole process was a foregone conclusion.

"I'd better have a word with everybody then hadn't I" he went on, "And if they don't promise to vote for me I'll have to fight them in the schoolyard."

"But you can't fight everybody," said Billy.

"Who says I can't, you?" he replied, grabbing hold of his shirt and looking particularly menacing.

I realised this called for a bit of diplomacy. It was just possible, I conceded, that together we might just get the better of him, though that was by no means a certainty. However, such a course of action, even if we emerged as victors, could never be a viable solution to the problem. News of the outcome would certainly be circulated around our school and it was a no-win situation. With regard to school fights two onto one was totally unacceptable. The fact that Tucker was the person outnumbered would have been of no relevance in the minds of the other lads. If we were to lose, the consequences would be even greater. Not only would we lose face but our position in the school pecking order would be seriously challenged. I decided on a less direct approach.

"If you were playing rugby," I said. "How many do you think would get past without you tackling them?"

"None of 'em," he replied, suddenly losing interest in Billy's shirt and turning to face me.

"What, not even Dickie Williams?" I challenged, mentioning the famous Leeds player.

"Oh aye, I suppose he might," he conceded, "but I bet he wouldn't do it every time."

"Where's the best place to tackle anybody?" asked Billy, relieved at having control of his shirt again and beginning to sense a way out of the situation. "I mean would you get them round the legs or what?"

I could see Tucker was getting quite enthusiastic and the confrontational nature of the conversation had almost disappeared. "It all depends," he said. "If you get 'em by the legs they'll fall a lot heavier and it'll knock the wind out of 'em. I've seen it happen at Headingley. Sometimes they manage to pass the ball before they hit the ground. That wouldn't bother me, though. It'd just give me someone else to tackle. If you get 'em round the arms, though it stops them passing the ball and it's a lot more like a proper wrestle."

"If you were captain, then—-", I started to say.

"You mean when I'm captain."

"Er, yes, I suppose so. I mean, what would you have to do that's different from what the other players would do?"

"Well, I'd make sure that everybody was pulling their weight, and I'd tell them what would happen to them if they didn't. Anyway, I'd better be going now, so make sure you both vote for me or the same thing might happen to you."

I was relieved as Tucker headed off towards Woodhouse Street leaving Billy and me to go in the opposite direction, as he was beginning to look menacing again.

"What do you think, Neil?" asked Billy. "Are you going to vote for him?"

"I don't know. Maybe we should see what everyone else is doing?"

"Actually, I wouldn't be surprised if he turned out to be the best player anyway."

"You might be right, Billy. We'll have a better idea on Friday. Whatever happens, at least we'll finish school an hour early."

Tucker Lane as captain? I had the feeling that it would happen anyway. Whatever the situation he was always going to regard himself as the one in charge.

# CHAPTER THREE

As Mr Barnes led Billy and me and nineteen other boys from Woodhouse Junior School onto Bedford's Field my first thought was how little it resembled a training field for a game of rugby, or any other sport for that matter. Admittedly there was a set of goal posts at each end of the field, though one of them had half a post missing, and there was a complete lack of line markings. What was on the ground, however, was evidence that the field had been used by cows for grazing purposes in the very recent past.

"I'm not sure I fancy this," suggested Billy, apprehensively.

Whenever a group of boys gathers in the street or schoolyard for any type of competitive team game the two most dominant or assertive take it among themselves to assume captaincy. This is only occasionally challenged if, for instance, some boy new to the neighbourhood decides to join in. Girls, of course, are automatically excluded, which all the participants know is only right and proper. There then follows a pecking order which invariably follows the same pattern as each leader selects in turn from the remaining players. There is inevitably one boy remaining, usually very timid or very overweight, that nobody really wants and who, in the case of a football match, always ends up in goal. Both Billy and I were usually selected just above the halfway mark in the process. This occasion, however, thanks to the presence of Mr Barnes, was different as he took it upon himself to choose both teams. This was much to the disappointment of Tucker Lane who no doubt felt that the abandonment of the time–honoured traditions and unspoken rules of street play was undermining his role as selector-in-chief. His protestations on this issue, however, were to no avail. The selection process took less than a minute and I was delighted to see that Billy and I were on the same team, but not so pleased that Tucker was on the opposing one. No captains were appointed for this kick-about and, there being twenty-one of us, Nicky Whitehead, who lived in our street but was a year younger than most of us, was told he would have to change sides at half-time.

It was decided that we would play two halves of twenty minutes each and, despite the dubious nature of the pitch, the game began amid much enthusiasm. However, the fact that we were having to play in our ordinary street wear, the new shirts and shorts which we had been promised having not yet arrived, it was difficult to remember who was in the opposing team and Tucker, in particular, was causing much confusion in his eagerness to tackle anybody who happened to have the ball, regardless of which side he was supposed to be on. The first half, therefore, was a complete shambles as Mr Barnes struggled in vain to inject some sense of order into our endeavours. To this end he eventually achieved a modicum of success but not until the interval between the two halves. He decided that one team would roll up its sleeves to make identification easier and the second period began in a much more promising fashion, as it was now possible to see that there were indeed two opposing teams, and even Tucker appeared to be behaving himself. About five minutes in, with no team having scored, an event occurred which was to change the whole aspect of the game and one which was also to get me into a great deal of trouble with my mother when I arrived home. As Johnny Jackson got hold of the ball and passed it to me I set off on what I hoped would be an inspired dash to the line. With my first step, however, I slipped on something and found myself falling and losing control of the ball at the same time. The cow pat that I fell on could quite easily have been one of those firm, hard, round ones that you could pick up and throw like a discus but no, this one just had to be freshly-made, very soft and extremely smelly and I was absolutely covered in it from my right knee all the way up to my hip bone. I picked myself up and was standing feeling very sorry for myself when a cheer went up at the other end of the field. Alan Bartle, on the opposing team had scored a try. I had barely time to adjust to the new circumstances in which I found myself when, from the kick-off, Nicky Whitehead gathered the ball. Just before he was about to be pulverised by Tucker Lane he thought better of the situation and threw it to me. I barely had time to set off in an attempt to cover the remaining thirty yards before I became the sole focus of Tucker's attention. He looked as threatening as I'd ever seen him as he hovered in front of me. My immediate concern was how much this was going to hurt when, all of a sudden he seemed to back off, and almost before I knew it I was past him. Much to my astonishment it didn't end there, however, as precisely the same thing occurred with two other would-be tacklers and then there I was, touching down behind the posts. My state of euphoria was dampened somewhat as Billy came over and made it patently obvious as to the cause of my unexpected heroics.

"Cor! You don't half stink," he said, holding his nose firmly for emphasis.

From that moment on I could do no wrong. I was constantly being given the ball at the earliest opportunity and scored a further three tries before the game was brought to a halt. I was a hero in name only however for, as far as my team-mates were concerned, being chaired off the field of play was never an option. I knew at least though that there was very little possibility of Tucker coming over for a scrap, even if his side did lose. How little my heroics meant was quickly brought home to me when Billy, ever loyal, went over to Mr Barnes.

"Neil played well, didn't he sir?" he said, with a grin on his face.

A scowl came across our trainer's face as he gazed down at him.

"Let's just say that there were extenuating circumstances lad and leave it at that, shall we?"

"What am I going to do now?" I asked Billy, after the rest of the school had departed. "My mam will kill me when I get home."

"I don't think there's much you can do. We could take a bit longer going home by going onto the ridge. At least it might dry a bit and you might not stink as much."

"I wish you'd stop going on about me stinking. It's much worse from where I am."

"Well at least I'm not leaving you to go back on your own. I bet you wouldn't get Susan Brown walking back with you. I think I'll tell her about it on Monday. We can have a good laugh."

"It won't make any difference. All the school will be laughing about it anyway."

I decided to accept Billy's suggestion regarding the best route home. The ridge bordered onto Bedford's Field so it wasn't very long before we were walking along the uppermost concrete path.

"Why don't we hang around Table Top for half-an-hour?" I suggested, as we approached the area in question. "Do you remember that serial called 'The Lost World' that was on the wireless earlier in the year? It was all about dinosaurs on this plateau in the jungle. Table Top can be the plateau and Death Valley can be the jungle."

Table Top was a flat, grassy area about twenty feet above the level where we were standing and could only be reached by climbing a steep path after pushing your way through a very overgrown section of weeds and bushes which certainly did, in our minds, remind us of a jungle. Death Valley was the name by which it was known by all the lads who lived locally.

"Oh, yes, I remember it," said Billy, enthusiastically. It was on Saturday lunch time just after Charlie Chester in that programme called 'Stand Easy'. I'll be Professor Challenger and you can be Professor Summerlee."

"Not likely, I'm not going to be Professor Summerlee. He did nothing but complain all the time. Anyway, I'm going to be Lord Roxton. I bet he was the best shot in the world with a rifle."

We lived in a make-believe world of dinosaurs, fierce natives and brave hunters and became quite oblivious to the lateness of the hour until Billy reminded me that we could be in bother if we were late home for tea. That would be by no means an unusual occurrence for either of us. On countless occasions in the past we had become so absorbed in what we were doing that we had arrived home to a real ticking off. As it was it would take us about another twenty minutes to reach our destination.

"What if they won't let us go to the pictures tonight," I said, suddenly alarmed. "I think we'd better be off, don't you?"

"Your mam might not let you go anyway when she sees what your trousers are like."

That was something I'd completely forgotten about. That would be a double ticking-off to look forward to. My chances of going to the Electra seemed to be rapidly receding.

When we finally arrived in our street it was approaching 6 o'clock and the first to greet us was Nell, who had a good sniff in the area affected by my recent mishap. The expression on her first suggested that if dogs could speak she would have said "Cor! You don't half stink. You'll have to tell me where you got it from."

My father had arrived home just before me and was taking off his coat. My mother, I noticed, seemed to be preoccupied with a letter she had received.

"It's from Tim", she announced, on noting my arrival and seeming too absorbed in its content to give me a ticking off for getting home so late. I wondered if she would fail to notice the other cause of my concern.

"He says," She went on, "That he's not enjoying his————What on earth is that smell?" Putting the letter to one side, she looked down at Nell who had followed me in. "I'm going to stop giving you that new dog food," she said, looking most decidedly stern. "It must be too rich for you."

My canine friend looked up at me with a hurt look of betrayal in her eyes. "Aren't you going to say something?" they seemed to say.

There was of course no way I could get away with it. The evidence was plain to see. Would I have let my faithful companion take the blame if I thought I could? I like to think not, but I can never be sure. I mean how important was a change of dog food compared to missing the latest episode of Superman?

My father was now beginning to take an interest in the proceedings. Before he had time to say anything I decided to get in first. "I scored four tries today, dad."

"Well, lad, did you really?" he said, looking so impressed I began to think I might be rewarded for the day's work rather than be punished for it. Unfortunately, however, my mother chose this moment to notice her mistake regarding the location of the aroma that had assaulted her nostrils.

"What on earth's been happening to you?" she gasped.

"I fell in some cow clap mam. It was on the rugby pitch. I couldn't help it, honest," was all I could splutter out by way of a reply.

At this point my father decided to take command of the conversation.

"Just a minute," he said. "These four tries that you scored, Were they before or after you fell in the cow clap?"

"After. It was in the second half."

"Ah! Well, lad. That just might explain it. Still, it probably got you noticed, eh."

"Never mind 'got you noticed'. It's about time this new rugby kit got noticed. When is it going to arrive that's what I want to know?" said my mother, deciding to take charge again. "You can't keep on playing in your school clothes. See, you'd better get your shirt and trousers off so I can get 'em washed. I've a good mind to make you sit in your pyjamas for the rest of the day."

"Aw, mam, Billy's going to the pictures tonight. Can't I go?"

"As soon as you've had your tea you're going straight into the bath. That's where you're going. If you behave yourself tonight I might let you go with us tomorrow."

I always found bath night to be a humiliating experience. Like all the other houses in the street we only had a tin bath which hung behind the cellar door. Even though now I was allowed to bath myself, my mother still allowed it to be open house for anyone who cared to call and that included, on occasions, a various assortment of aunties who, instead of pretending I wasn't there, would insist on making some remark which only caused me further embarrassment. My greatest fear was that Mary Pearson who lived a few doors away might think of some reason to make an appearance if she were aware of the circumstances. She was two years older than I and, if she happened to see me enter the lavatory yard, she would wait until I entered a cubicle before pushing open the door and standing there chanting "I've seen your willy. I've seen your willy." Billy told me he'd had the same problem.

So I didn't get to go to the pictures that night. However, the likelihood of going on the following night meant that I probably wouldn't have to ask Billy about the latest episode of Superman. The bath was, thankfully, intruder free and I wasn't made to sit in my pyjamas until bedtime. Mam read out the letter from

Tim, and it became clear that he wasn't particularly enjoying the initial training period of his National Service.

"He'll get used to it I reckon, after a week or two," commented my dad. "Everybody's like that at first."

Nell settled down in front of the fire relieved that the threat of a change of dog food might just possibly have receded and I thought all things considered that the day had not gone too badly after all.

I had a dream that night. I was in the Lost World and Susan Brown was running away from a huge dinosaur. Realising that I was armed with a spear I ran fearlessly towards it. Seeing me the dinosaur turned its huge head and said "And just what do you expect to do with that?" I looked down and was horrified to see that the spear had miraculously transformed itself into my mother's posser. I gulped.

"Are you going to eat me? "I asked.

"Nay lad," it replied. "This sort of food is much too rich for me. Let's just say there are extenuating circumstances and leave it at that, shall we?" and so saying it disappeared into the night. Susan started to walk over to me, a look of eternal gratitude in her eyes and, as I waited for my reward, at that precise moment I slipped in something particularly nasty which the dinosaur had left before departing.

Susan hesitated a few feet away, held her nose and said "Cor! You don't half stink."

# CHAPTER FOUR

One of the most satisfying feelings I experienced as a child was the realisation on waking in the morning that the day was a Saturday, and this particular one was no exception. My father worked until noon while my mother usually paid a shopping visit into town. With three aunts residing in our street she was confident that if any unpleasantness occurred due to my being left to my own devices then there was no possibility that she would not hear about it. Within reason, therefore, this usually left Billy and me to indulge in whatever escapade took our fancy. It was an unwritten rule, however, that when the omnibus edition of Dick Barton, Special Agent was on the wireless between eleven and twelve that we abandoned our adventures and retired to our separate houses to listen. On some occasions, however, Billy would come round to my house and we would enjoy it together. I was not unduly surprised, therefore, when he knocked on the door about ten minutes into the broadcast.

"Are you coming out?" he asked.

"But Dick Barton's started," I replied. "Don't you want to listen to it?"

He looked around to make sure that no one else was there. "Well, I did, until I noticed that Helen Thomas is doing handstands against the lavatory wall." Noticing my indecision he added, "She's got pink knickers on."

Now here was a dilemma indeed – Dick Barton against Helen Thomas's knickers. Helen was our age but, living in Meanwood Road, didn't go to our school. She went to Buslingthorpe instead. She was undoubtedly a very pretty girl and it wasn't the first time that Billy and I had received a flash of her underwear in this way. I often wondered why girls were so keen on performing handstands. Were they intentionally providing the local lads with a glimpse of what they would not normally be privileged to see, or was it just the innocent outcome of a genuine desire to perform gymnastics? Either way, we never saw any reason to complain.

"She usually has white ones on," I said, as if that would in some way resolve the conflict that was taking place inside my head.

"Yes, I know," replied Billy impatiently. "Well, are you coming?"

"All right then. We'd better go before she stops doing them, but if she wants us to play 'Houses' I'm coming back in." Girls always wanted to play such soppy games which always seemed to revolve around some pre-conceived idea of domestic marital bliss. It was really all quite nauseating.

True enough, there she was head first against the lavatory wall. When she saw us, however, she immediately got to her feet. "Hello!" she said. "Do you feel like playing 'Mammies and Daddies'?"

Suspecting that this was just another name for 'Houses', we both ignored the question, having half expected it

"I bet you could keep doing that for ages," I said, hopefully.

"Yes I could, but I want to play something else now."

I was beginning to think that this wasn't worth missing the omnibus edition for, but Billy persisted.

"I bet you couldn't even do one more," he suggested. "I bet you're too tired."

"Just watch this then," she replied, and Billy and I were treated to one more sighting of pink underwear. No amount of cajoling, however, could invoke a repeat performance and we decided enough was enough. If she wasn't going to continue, her idea of play was much too girlie for us to be involved in. I decided there and then to call the contest between Dick Barton and Helen Thomas's knickers a draw.

"I'm going back in," I told Billy. "Are you coming? We should be able to catch the end of it."

"No, I think I'll listen to it at home. It'll be dinner time soon, anyway."

I re-entered the house to find that I hadn't switched off the wireless. Nell was stretched out in her usual place on the clip rug. If she had been enthralled by the adventures of Dick, Jock and Snowy she wasn't filling me in on the parts I had missed. "What do you think you're doing?" her eyes seemed to say. "You know we always listen to it together."

After catching the final few minutes I heard my mother enter. "Quick! I want you to go to the fish shop," she said, taking off her coat. I met your grandad after I got off the tram. He's paying us a visit as soon as he's finished his round. We were going to have fish and chips anyway but you'd better get another portion."

I was always pleased to see Grandad Miller. He was a postman but he was due to retire soon. Every time I'd seen him, either at our house or at his in Harehills, I would always discover a threepenny bit in my pocket afterwards, and on some occasions, if he was feeling a bit flushed, it would be a sixpence.

"What shall I get then, mam?" I asked.

"Well, you'd better get fish and chips for your dad and grandad and you can have a piece of my fish. So you can ask for three times and a bag of chips and make sure you go to Jubilee Fisheries and not the one round the corner opposite Doughty's."

It was a very short walk to the establishment in question as it was almost immediately opposite to my school. When I arrived I was surprised to find that the queue almost extended into the street, which was very unusual for a Saturday. I could ascertain immediately, however, the reason for the glum expressions which appeared on the face of each person there. At the front of the queue was an uncouth looking individual in scruffy overalls holding a large cardboard box. While this would not be an unexpected occurrence on a Friday, on this particular day everyone had been taken by surprise. The factory across the road was obviously working all day instead of closing at noon which was usually the case. I noticed that one familiar individual a few places ahead of me in the queue was not taking the situation lying down.

"Well I don't make any wonder that a lot of your customers have started flocking to Craven Road fish shop, Alice," she said, addressing the apologetic looking, but obviously harassed individual behind the counter, but in a voice loud enough for everyone to hear. I couldn't help noticing that she did not consider the one opposite Doughty's as a possible replacement. "No," she went on, "I make no wonder at all. I reckon I'd have been better stopping at home, going to the pantry and getting myself a couple of pikelets. I mean surely you can't be surprised that people are getting fed up waiting the best part of an hour to be served, because I don't make any wonder at it. It's bad enough on a Friday but no one expected it today. I mean twenty-two times and three fish, what's going to be left for the rest of us? I bet you won't even be able to scrape a bag of scraps together."

There were a few mutterings of agreement among some of the others in the queue and the person who was the cause of the unrest, despite his rough exterior was looking decidedly uncomfortable.

"Well we have to serve anybody who comes in. We can't put a limit on how much they want," attempted the proprietor a little unconvincingly. Mrs I-Make-No-Wonder, however, once she got a hold of something was like a terrier. She was never in a mood to let go easily.

"Well I think you'd better give us some indication as to how long we're going to have to wait, though I bet everybody in this queue wouldn't make any wonder if we were all here until the middle of the afternoon. Would you make any wonder Mrs?" she asked, nudging a small, timid looking lady next to her.

"Er, no, I suppose not," she replied nervously.

"There's enough fish cooking for this order now," ventured Alice, "And Eddie's in the back making some more chips. So it shouldn't be anything like as long as you think." It seemed to me that Eddie was always in the back making chips. It wouldn't surprise me if nobody had ever seen him.

"By heck! I make no wonder yon chap with the cardboard box is looking a bit sheepish," said her antagonist deciding to finally call a halt to the protest.

I suppose we'll just have to wait then, but I'm not happy about it, not happy at all."

By the time I arrived home with my precious bundle and explained to my mother the reason for the delay a full hour had elapsed, Grandad Miller had arrived and everyone was extremely hungry. My mother, however, seemed more interested in the argument in the fish shop. "The people in that factory should give plenty of notice if they intend working all day on a Saturday. I remember this happening before, only they ran out of fish that time. There was a real to-do over it."

"Hello, grandad," I said.

Now then, lad, what do you reckon?" he said, by way of greeting.

"I don't know, grandad."

"Well, you must reckon something, surely. This lad don't reckon nowt," he said, turning towards my father.

"Well, he's young yet. Mark my words, he'll reckon all sorts of things before he gets much older."

"Well, I hope you're right. A lad his age should reckon summat."

"Now then, lad," he said, turning back towards me. "What have you been doing today then?"

"Well," I replied, "I was just listening to Dick Barton before I went for the fish and chips."

"You didn't go to the one round the corner opposite Doughty's, did you?"

"No, my mam told me not to."

"Well, I reckon that's as well."

He lowered his voice and spoke directly into my ear. "Now, here's me thinking you were looking at yon lass's breeches and all the time you were really listening to Dick Barton. So I reckon I must be mistaken then.

Best not say anymore about it, eh," and he gave me a wink.

A few seconds of embarrassing silence followed, but I felt grateful that Grandad Miller had made it possible for me not to make any further comment on the matter. I decided to change the subject.

"How long is it before you have to retire, grandad?"

"It'll be next summer, and I'll tell you something, that'll be when things'll start to go downhill."

"What do you mean?"

"Well, you see, I don't know how much longer I've got before I'm called upstairs."

"Now, we'll have none of that sort of talk dad," said my mother as she began to lay out the fish and chips.

"Well, it's true, lass. Nobody knows how long they've got left. That's the trouble."

My father entered the room after changing out of his work clothes and took his place at the table. Nell, having long ago worked out where she was likely to get the most offerings on this sort of occasion took her accustomed place at the side of his chair.

"What do you think it'll be like when you get to Heaven, grandad?" I asked, believing it to be a perfectly sensible question.

"Neil, you mustn't talk like that," admonished my mother. Your grandad will be around for a long time yet.

"Nay, leave him alone lass. There's nothing wrong in talking about it. You see, lad," he said, turning towards me, "How do I know they're going to let me in?"

"How do you mean, grandad?

"Well the way I see it, it's all to do with points."

I still didn't see what he was getting at and I told him so.

"All right then, look at it this way," he went on. "Let's say you do a good deed and you're awarded so many points. Do a bad deed and you get so many deducted. Now that's fair enough I reckon. Then when you're called away God gets one of his angels or whatever to get this 'ere book out and tot up how many points you've been awarded. He'll be too busy to do it himself you understand, what with dealing with earthquakes and tornadoes and things. Now, and this is where the problem is, nobody down here has been informed as to how many points they've got to have to get in and if you don't have enough you could get sent to the other place. Now then, I suppose if I'm lucky, I reckon I might just about be breaking even, but not knowing how much longer I've got left you can see my predicament. Happen I'll get enough and happen I won't."

I'd never thought about the requirements of getting into Heaven in quite those terms but, as always, Grandad Miller talked a lot of sense. However, my mother decided to put an immediate end to my thoughts on the subject.

"Now that's enough talk about dying," she said, turning towards me. "Get your fish and chips eaten and think about something else. It's Woodhouse Feast next week. I thought you'd be thinking about that."

That cheered me up. I'd completely forgotten about it.

"By heck, that seems to have come around again quickly," said Grandad Miller. "I've been to a few of them in my time I can tell you."

"What about Elsie Waterman?" queried my father, holding out a chip for Nell to eagerly devour and hoping my mother didn't notice. "Do you think she'll go this time?"

"Keep your voice down Tom. According to what I've heard I don't think she will."

From that moment on I hadn't a clue what anyone was talking about. It was as if I had suddenly been banished from the room as everyone began speaking in whispers.

"Surely, she's got over it by now," suggested my grandad. "It's been at least two years hasn't it?"

"Well, I was talking to Mrs Up-The-Street the other day and she told me that she'd be surprised if she ever went again." My mother was never very good at remembering names but she had worked out a system that was quite acceptable to her. Sometimes it worked for the listener and sometimes it didn't.

"Well I don't think it could be as bad as she made it out to be," ventured my father, "And it's hardly likely to happen again, is it?"

"Why won't Elsie Waterman go to the feast?" I asked, quite innocently. Three people suddenly stopped eating and stared at me with a look of amazement on their faces. Nell walked out from under the table and stared defiantly at me with her face showing the same expression. It was as if I had suddenly dropped out of the sky.

"That's not for you to know," my mother finally managed to get out. "You shouldn't have been listening."

Every time adults drift into 'grown-up talk' they never tell you in advance not to listen, but always seem astonished afterwards that you have heard anything of what's been said.

"Look, you've finished you're fish and chips," she went on. "Why don't you pop round to see Billy?"

It was patently obvious that, now that the meal was over and the conversation was getting interesting, I was no longer welcome at the table.

"My mam says Elsie Waterman won't go to Woodhouse Feast," I told Billy a few minutes later, "But nobody will tell me why. It's as if it's a big secret. They all talk in whispers about it."

"Why don't we try to find out why?" he suggested enthusiastically. "Surely we'll be able to find out from somebody. I'll start by asking my mam if she knows anything about it." And there and then we made a pact to find out as much as we could before the end of the week.

By tea time I had been re-accepted as a member of the family and that evening my mother kept her promise and we all went to the Electra. So I didn't miss the latest episode of Superman after all. The main picture was an adventure called 'Kidnapped'. At the beginning of the film the hero, a young lad called David, was made to climb a staircase in total darkness by his wicked uncle, unaware that the top steps were missing and that he could have hurtled to his death. He did of course survive, but I remember thinking about it in bed that night along with the remarks my grandfather had made and wondered how many points his uncle might have had deducted for that evil deed. Unfortunately, my thoughts on the matter did not end there as I realised that my own situation in that respect might be a little cloudy. Perhaps I shouldn't have allowed myself to be persuaded into looking at Helen Thomas's knickers.

# CHAPTER FIVE

The new rugby strip arrived on the following Wednesday, much to my mother's delight, as there was to be a second practice match on the Friday afternoon. Mr Barnes had been as good as his word as even Ken Stacey's shirt seemed a good fit. No sooner had we been issued with them than we were out in the schoolyard having a team photograph taken. I was on the front row holding one end of the ball, which had a large 1950/51 embroidered on it, with Alan Bartle holding the other. Surprisingly, this fact didn't seem to bother Tucker Lane who was sitting with his arms folded and an enormous grin on his face. No more mention had been made of the captaincy, and I was beginning to wonder if he might, after all, have decided to let things take their natural course.

On re-entering the building I was surprised to find us being ushered into the hall where all the other pupils were already gathered instead of to our appropriate classrooms.

"What's all this about?" whispered Billy in my ear.

"I've no idea," I replied. "Maybe it's something to do with the rugby team. Perhaps we're going to do the voting now."

"But we've only had one practice match. If it went by that they'd have to make you captain because you scored four tries, though Barnesy didn't seem very impressed did he?"

"It's not likely to happen again is it? I mean I'm not likely to fall in some cow clap every time am I? Anyway, I don't want it to be me. I don't want to end up as Tucker's punch bag."

I needn't have worried, however, as the reason for us all being gathered there had nothing to do with the rugby team. Mr Rawcliffe was starting to speak. "As no doubt you all know, Woodhouse Feast begins on Friday and I'm sure that most of you will be going on at least one day. I just want to make a few points about it before you depart to your various classrooms. Many of you may be under the misapprehension that the minute you leave the school building at four o'clock that what you do with your time is entirely between you and your parents. I must tell you that this is definitely not the case. If any pupil misbehaves in any way while sampling the entertainments on offer it will reflect badly on the school as a whole and on me in particular. If there is any such unpleasant incident you can be sure that word will get back to me and the person concerned will be dealt with in the appropriate manner. Do you all understand what I am saying?"

"Yes sir," came the answers in unison. No one had any doubt about what was meant by 'the appropriate manner', especially where the boys were concerned.

The headmaster hadn't finished, however. "There's another concern regarding visitors to the feast and that is the safety aspect. Some of you may recall that Valerie Trainer's younger sister was injured last year when she fell off one of the high swings. I shouldn't need to tell you that we do not want to be hearing of any similar accident. You must see that it is in your best interests to be very vigilant regarding your own safety. There is one other thing I should mention while on this subject. Be extremely careful, especially if you attend without an adult, about whom you speak to. Try to avoid getting into a conversation with someone you don't know. I remember in particular an incident a while back, about which I do not wish to go into in detail, involving one girl, several years older than the pupils in this school, who is still suffering stressful memories today. What I am saying to every pupil of this school is to go out and enjoy yourselves but be extremely careful. That's all I have to say. You may all now return to your classrooms."

As we started to leave the hall, the same thought occurred to both of us, but Billy got in first. "I wonder if he was talking about Elsie Waterman," he said.

"I was wondering the same thing, but we can hardly ask him can we? He said he didn't want to discuss it." Billy had already told me that his mother had been as silent as mine on the matter and I was beginning to lose interest, but the headmaster had just whetted my appetite. "On second thoughts, though, it might depend on how we ask him."

"How do you mean?"

"Well, if we don't mention any name but just get him to tell us a little bit more about what happened I could then tell my mother what he said and ask if that's what happened to Elsie Waterman."

"I don't think he'll say anything though. He'll just think you're being nosey. You might not have time anyway," and with that statement we both entered the classroom for the remainder of our morning lessons.

I was hoping that Billy and I would get permission to go to Woodhouse Feast by ourselves on the Friday even though I knew there was a possibility that my mother and father would be taking me on the following day. It was with a hint of mischief that Billy suddenly asked "Would you like me to ask Susan Brown if she's going on Friday? I don't know why you don't tell her you like her anyway."

"If you do that," I replied, "I'll tell Sally Cheesedale that you like her."

"I'm not bothered. She's all right is Sally Cheesedale."

"Right, well I'll tell Sophie Morton instead then." That threat seemed to shut him up.

As we were still only a few days into the new term no one had been allocated permanent desks yet and I was disappointed to see that Susan Brown was now sitting in the row behind, but a few desks to the left, and I hoped this was not going to be the situation right through to next summer. For the remainder of the English lesson, however, I succeeded in looking round only twice, but each time I did Billy flashed me a wink which started me blushing. By the time we broke up for lunch I had managed to become absorbed in the lesson and I decided to banish all thoughts of Susan or Elsie Waterman until the afternoon when I knew that Mr Rawcliffe would be taking us for geography just prior to the end of classes for the day.

Both Billy and I were accustomed to going home for dinner and we both felt fortunate to be doing so after hearing so many adverse comments about the fare that was on offer for those pupils who were not quite so fortunate. After giving the matter some thought I suggested to him, as we made our way back to school, that I approach the headmaster just before leaving to see if I could squeeze some more information out of him without appearing too pushy. With this in mind, after the afternoon's lessons came to a close, I deliberately waited until everyone had left the classroom and walked up to him as he was tidying his books and papers.

"Excuse me, sir," I said, rather nervously.

"Yes, boy, what is it?" His rather abrupt manner made me hesitate. However, as I would have to say something anyway, or look incredibly stupid, I managed to stumble out a few words.

"I was just wondering, about that girl sir, the one who went to Woodhouse Feast who you said was several years older than us. What happened to her? Did she have an accident?"

"Were you standing in the hall with the rest of the pupils when I was speaking about it?"

"Yes, sir."

"And did you hear me say that I was not inclined to discuss the matter further?"

"Yes, sir.

"Well, then?"

"I'm sorry, sir. I just thought it might make a difference if I knew what happened." This wasn't going very well and I wasn't sure what to say. I just added, "How long ago was it?"

"You're certainly persistent boy. I'll tell you this much. It occurred two years ago and, as I understand the situation, the poor girl hasn't been back since. And if she does I should imagine she'll steer well clear of the chair-o-planes. Now that's enough. Off you go home."

At least, I now knew something and I couldn't wait to tell Billy. He was waiting for me as I opened the main door which led into the schoolyard. "Did he say anything?" he asked.

"I thought he was going to say nothing at all, he was so grumpy, but he told me it happened a couple of years ago, so it's probably the same person. It's also got something to do with the chair-o-planes. Maybe she just fell off."

"Well, that wouldn't stop me going again."

"Me, neither. But she's a girl isn't she?" Billy fully understood the point I was trying to make and regarded the matter as closed.

Elsie Waterman was in fact now seventeen and, despite living in the same street, her age and gender meant that she could never really be a part of our social circle. Neither of us came into contact with her much, yet we remained intrigued by the question of what occurred at the feast that made such an impact on her, and as we made our way to our respective houses I felt even more determined to solve the mystery.

I had no sooner gone through my front door than I noticed I had been followed in by Mr Senior, who lived a few doors away. He had had a long and active life in the merchant navy but was long since retired and could no longer walk very far. He had entertained Billy and me on numerous occasions recounting his adventures overseas. He often came in without knocking but not without the obligatory 'Are you there, May?' I suppose if my mother hadn't have been there on these occasions he would have just gone back out again.

"How are you today, Mr Senior?" she asked as she approached from the other room.

"Just fair to middling, lass. Just fair to middling, but best not grumble, eh! Nay, what it is, I've just run out of bread, do you see, and I was hoping your lad might nip over to Doughty's and bring me back a loaf. He can get himself a bag of spice as well if he likes. I've got some sweet coupons left."

My face lit up immediately at this suggestion.

"No need for that. I was going to get him to go for me anyway. You never know when you might need your coupons. What about when your grandson calls again?"

Nell looked up at me from the fireside. I got the distinct impression that she was amused by my misfortune.

I returned from the shop with the items my mother had asked for, which did not include a bag of spice as my allocation for that week had already been used up, and walked over to Mr Senior's house to present him with his loaf.

"Here you are lad," he said. "I know you didn't get any spice but here's a glass of Tizer for you. Now sit yourself down for a minute or two."

I thanked him and did as he asked. I sat silently for a while supping the drink he had offered me and wondering if he was preparing himself for another tale from overseas. When it wasn't forthcoming, however, I decided to try a bit of prompting. "Where's the most interesting place you've been to Mr Senior?" I asked.

"Ah, now that's a question. I can tell you the most interesting time, and that was during the war, and I'm talking about The Great War, not that little skirmish that finished a few years back. Didn't even have much time to think in those days. It's difficult to give you a proper answer. I've been all over the world and all the places are so different, yet each fascinating in its own way. What you find happening, though, is that you lose touch with the places nearer home. I've sailed all the oceans except the Southern Ocean and there's nothing down there but

Antarctica. I've been to the far east, India, all over the African and American coast and other places too numerous to mention, but I'll tell you one thing that might surprise you. Despite all this, I've never once set foot in Dewsbury."

"But Dewsbury's only a few miles away. Even my dad's been there."

"Well, lad, that's as maybe but I've spent so much time on board ship, do you see, and when I was a nipper public transport wasn't as good as it is now, but even so my dad would sometimes suggest going on an outing to Otley, Ilkley, Harrogate or some other place close by but he never once said 'By heck, lad, it's a grand day. Shall we go to Dewsbury?' So I never went, do you see. By the time I joined the merchant navy an aunt of mine had gone there to live, but I never got the chance to pay her a visit. Never shall now. She passed over a long time since. Now lad, I can see you've finished your Tizer. Thank you for my shopping but you'd better get yourself home or your mother'll be wondering what's keeping you."

I determined to get in one more question before leaving. "By the way, Mr Senior, do you know why Elsie Waterman won't go to Woodhouse Feast?"

"Well, I should think that's because something nasty happened on the chair-o-planes and I'm not saying any more than that. Now off home with you. I've answered enough questions for today."

That evening my father said it was all right for me to go to the feast on Friday with Billy, assuming he could get permission as well. "Don't expect to have much to spend, mind you," he added. "I'm not made of money."

It looked like being an interesting day. We'd be leaving school early for the practice match and then, straight after tea, we'd be heading up to the moor for the main event of the evening. One thing I was sure about. If I bumped into Susan Brown while I was there I wouldn't be bothered whether Elsie Waterman turned up or not. The thought occurred to me that, as Billy suggested earlier, maybe I should ask her if she was going but deep down I knew that I wouldn't.

# CHAPTER SIX

Friday's practice game, despite having the same venue as the previous one, did not on this occasion allow me to play quite so prominent a part. The arrival of the new playing strip did not really solve the problem of identification until it was decided that players on one side would turn their shirts inside-out. This idea did not really suit Tucker Lane until he realised that he had been selected for the side that didn't need to, at which point he decided that he could not see anything wrong with the idea and was at a loss to understand why some of the other pupils were making a fuss about it. Despite the prestige of playing in more acceptable attire, Mr Barnes was far from happy with the way things were progressing. There just seemed to be no teamwork, but it was difficult playing against people who would eventually be part of the same team. I had to grudgingly admit, though, that Tucker was one of the few who seemed to have some idea, even if he was a little over-zealous. I was beginning to think that having him as captain might not be such a bad idea after all. Before the game ended there was a downpour and the field turned into a quagmire. "We'll carry on a bit longer," suggested our coach. "You won't be able to choose the weather when you're playing against other schools. Anyway, it'll be good practice for you." It wasn't long before you couldn't tell the difference between what was genuine mud and what the cows had left behind. When the game was finally over our coach told us that there would be very few practice matches before we played our first competitive game, but every afternoon during the following week we would be practicing some running and passing in the schoolyard.

"I knew it would rain today," I said as I hurried home with Billy and Nicky Whitehead. "It always seems to be raining for Woodhouse Feast." A sudden thought struck me. "You know how you live next door to Elsie Waterman?" I added, turning towards Nicky.

"Yes, what about it?"

"It's just that people keep saying that she won't go to the feast because of something that happened two years ago. My mam talks in whispers about it. I just wondered if you had any idea what happened."

"We've been trying to find out all week," said Billy.

"I don't know anything about it," replied Nicky. "I haven't spoken to her much. She always seems a bit stuck up to me. I'll see if my mam knows anything though. I'll see if she'll let me go with you tonight as well."

"I'm going round to Billy's straight after tea, so we might see you then," I told him as we entered our street and went our separate ways.

Auntie Molly was in the house when I walked in. I was very embarrassed, therefore, when the first words my mother uttered were "I knew you'd be in that state when you walked in. Get your clothes off straight away and get into the bath with you. The water's nearly ready." In order to satisfy herself that what she had said was correct she walked over to the set pot in the corner of the room and looked in.

Auntie Molly was my mother's sister who lived next door. "You've no need to be shy of me young man. I'm sure you don't have anything I haven't seen before." This, of course only made me go redder still.

My mother laughed. "Don't worry I've put the bath in the other room today. You can get bathed in there."

"There you are then," said my aunt, "Nothing to worry about. I'll wait until you're nicely settled in then I'll just pop in and wash your hair for you, eh." This was one of those occasions when I wondered if aunties were worth all the trouble.

I arrived at Billy's just before Nicky, who proudly announced that he had managed to get permission to go with us. We were surprised at this as nine seemed an awful lot younger than ten.

The heavy rainfall had stopped shortly after I had arrived home, but miraculously started again just after the three of us set off. Woodhouse Feast was an event like no other in the social life of our locality. It would be difficult to find anyone who didn't attend on at least one of the several days that it took place. Even from half a mile away you could hear the noise from the various rides and the excited, joyful shrieks of pleasure emanating from the delighted crowd. You could see the bright glow in the sky illuminating even the darkest night. Even the taste buds came into play in anticipation of the first bite of a toffee apple or a stick of candy floss. The nearer you got to your destination the more your senses were bombarded with missiles of pure delight, and by the time you actually arrived you felt you had been transported to a utopia of pure pleasure.

"Oh, great!" said Billy with unconcealed joy as we reached our destination. "It's on three sides of the road."

I, also, had been hoping that it would be. The September event was always known as the Big Feast and the one held at Easter as the Little Feast. Frequently, it was necessary for the one held in the autumn to overflow to the other side of Woodhouse Street and Rampart Road as the main section of the moor, despite its comfortable size, was not always large enough to contain all the various rides, sideshows and caravans.

"What shall we do first? asked Nicky.

"How much have you got to spend?" enquired Billy. "I've got two and threepence, but I might not spend it all. I might buy a Superman comic tomorrow."

"I've got one and tenpence," replied Nicky. "So I could probably go on seven rides and have a penny left over."

"I've got three and sixpence," I volunteered, "But I might be coming again with my mam and dad tomorrow, and they told me that if I spent it all they wouldn't be able to give me any more. So I'll probably spend about the same as you."

"Right, so what shall we go on first then?" asked Nicky, repeating his earlier question.

"I'm getting a toffee apple first," I said. "My mouth's been watering all day at the thought of it."

"I'm not going to use any of mine on anything like that," said Billy. "I'd rather go on one of the rides."

"Yes, me too," added Nicky.

They followed me, however, to the appropriate stall and watched as I paid for the afore-mentioned delicacy. "By the way," I said, turning towards Nicky. "You said you might be able to find out why Elsie Waterman won't come to the feast any more."

"Yes, and I did find out," he replied, "But I'm not going to tell you unless you give me a bite."

"That cost me threepence," I replied, rather aggrieved "Are you sure you know something?"

"Positive, my mam told me last night."

"Aw, give him a bite," suggested Billy, "Or we'll never find out."

"All right," I agreed, "But it had better be a small one."

After he had taken as large a bite as he could, much to my annoyance, we both leaned forward eagerly in anticipation.

"Go on, then," said Billy. "What happened? Why won't she come to the feast?"

"If I find out you've been kidding just so you could get your hands on my toffee apple," I said, leaving the threat unfinished.

"I bet you don't know anything at all," added Billy.

"Yes, I do. Like I just said, my mam told me all about it last night.

"Well, go on then," I said. "What happened?"

"The reason Elsie Waterman won't come to the feast is because something nasty happened on the chair-o-planes."

A look of pure exasperation appeared on the faces of both Billy and me. "We already know that," we cried in unison. "Didn't you find out anything else?"

"No. She said she wouldn't tell me any more."

"And I've lost nearly half a toffee apple finding out something I already knew," I shouted.

"Well I didn't know that did I?" Nicky replied. "You said you didn't know anything about it."

"Aw, come on," interrupted Billy, attempting to diffuse the situation, "Let's see if we can get out of this rain somewhere. It's getting heavier and I'm soaking already."

"All right then," I agreed but where can we go. We'll get wet on most of the rides anyway, unless we can find out where the dodgems are."

"What about the Haunted House?" suggested Billy, pointing, "It's just over there."

"It's a bit scary in there," said Nicky. "I'd rather go in the Fun House."

"Well I'm not scared," I said as confidently as I could.

"I bet you too scared to go in by yourself," challenged Billy.

"Of course I dare. It's just that it would be much better with three. Don't you want to go in?"

"No, I'm not bothered now, but me and Nicky will wait under this awning until you come out if you like."

"You're both scared, I can tell. Well, I'm not. There's nothing in there that's going to frighten me."

A blood-curdling scream followed by a maniacal laugh chose that moment to make itself heard from within the confines of the Haunted House. I gulped, my bravado rapidly beginning to recede and I realised that I didn't really fancy this on my own, but how could I get out of it without losing face?

"I'll tell you what then," I said. "We'll all go over to the Fun House instead. There's no point in splitting up."

Billy started laughing. "I knew you wouldn't go in," he said before turning to Nicky and saying, "I bet he'd have gone in with Susan Brown because she'd have been able to hold his hand when he got scared."

"Shut up, Billy," I said. "I've a good mind to go off on my own and leave you two to do what you like."

"I'll tell you what then," said Billy, realising that he'd wound me up a little too much, "I think the rain's easing off a bit. Let's all go have a look at the Fun House."

Relieved that Billy was offering me a way out of my embarrassing predicament I accompanied him and Nicky in a search for the location of the construction in question.

"Actually," said Billy as we walked along. "Why don't we stand outside and just watch for a while?"

I knew at once what Billy was getting at, but Nicky apparently didn't."

"Why?" he asked. "What's the point in just standing outside watching?"

"Because something might happen," I replied.

"I don't know what you're talking about," he said.

"Well you probably soon will," said Billy.

As we approached the Fun House it was obvious that several other lads had the same idea

"What are they all waiting for?" asked Nicky.

This time we didn't answer as, at that moment, our attention, and that of the other lads, was drawn to the appearance of a young woman at the end of a platform which crossed the front of the building before disappearing at the other side. As she stepped on to it a sudden updraft sent her skirt flying around her waist, an event which was accompanied by loud hoots and whistles from those watching outside. Scarlet-faced, she dashed along the platform as quickly as she could, using her hands in the best way possible in an attempt to preserve a little dignity.

A voice behind us said "I'd rather pay to stand out here than to go inside, wouldn't you?"

We turned around simultaneously to see a familiar figure who was grinning profusely.

Billy was the first to speak. "Hello Tucker. We thought we might see someone here from school."

My first concern was that he was going to ask one of us for a scrap. I certainly didn't fancy rolling around in the mud. None of us needed to have worried though. "I've come to see the wrestling as much as anything," he said. "The booth's on the other side of the road. Do you fancy it?"

"No we're going to go on some rides now," I said, hopefully on behalf of Billy and Nicky as well as myself. "We haven't been on any yet."

"Are you going to challenge the wrestler?" suggested Billy, mischievously.

"No," replied Tucker, quite seriously. "You have to be at least sixteen to do that."

"I bet you'd be able to beat him before you got to that age," I said, as amicably as possible. I knew from experience that Tucker always responded well to flattery. "I think you get ten shillings if you do. Is that right?"

"No, it's fifteen now. Still, even if I can't wrestle I can pick a few tips, eh. I'll see you back at school then."

I think all three of us were relieved to see him head off towards the wrestling booth. "He doesn't seem as threatening, does he?" I said as he walked off in the appropriate direction.

"That's just what I was thinking," replied Billy. "Maybe he's mellowed a bit. Perhaps he's not bothered about being the team captain after all."

All of a sudden, however, he turned and shouted back. "They'll be voting soon. Don't forget what I told you will you, or there'll be trouble."

Deciding it was about time we spent some of the money we'd brought for the rides we went on the Caterpillar and the Helter Skelter twice before Nicky suddenly announced that he needed to relieve himself somewhere. One thing Woodhouse Feast never seemed to provide was a portable lavatory.

"I could do with going myself," said Billy, "But where can we have a pee around here?"

"What about behind that caravan," I suggested, pointing in the appropriate direction. "Nobody should see us there."

As the three of us stood there seeing who could direct his flow to the highest point of the caravan, Billy said "I keep half expecting Mary Pearson to make an appearance round the corner. She always seems to know when I'm going for a pee."

However, on this occasion it wasn't Mary Pearson who arrived out of nowhere, but one of the roughest looking, hairy, bare-chested men I had ever seen, who had evidently just stepped out of the caravan. He seemed to have muscles everywhere. "Oy, come here you lot," he shouted in an extremely angry, gruff voice. "I've just washed this van. I'll beat the living daylights out of you."

We gave him no time whatsoever to carry out his threat. All three of us shoved our private parts away in mid-flow and set off like bats out of Hell, not stopping to do up our buttons until we hoped we had lost ourselves in the crowd.

"Let's go right to the other end of the feast," I suggested. "I don't fancy meeting up with him again. If he'd have caught us I bet old Rawcliffe would have found out about it somehow."

Once we felt reasonably safe we found ourselves standing alongside the chair-o-planes. Inevitably, our thoughts returned to the mystery surrounding Elsie Waterman.

"Why don't we see if we can work out what might have happened ourselves?" I suggested.

"Good idea," said Billy.

Nicky went first. "She was eating a stick of candy floss and the wind blew it back into her face and some of it got stuck in her hair."

"That's ridiculous Nicky," I said. "That's hardly likely to make her stay away for two years is it?"

"Well you know what girls are like when their hair gets messed up," he protested.

"No it's got to be something much worse than that."

Billy joined in. "The ride was about to start when the man in charge of the ride started to turn into a werewolf, with big menacing fangs."

"That's stupid Billy. That's even worse than what Nicky came up with."

"Well see if you can do any better. What do you think happened?"

"I've no idea, and I don't think I'm bothered any more. The rain's getting worse, I'm soaked to the skin and I'm supposed to be home in half an hour. I think we might as well go back now. What do you think?"

"Yes, "agreed Billy. It's not as much fun with all this rain. The money we've got left we can use for something else."

"Well I'm not staying on my own," said Nicky. So we might as well all go."

When we got home I was subjected to yet another bath. However, because of the lateness of the hour there was no possibility of an intrusion this time. After a warm cup of cocoa I went to bed and was asleep immediately, a sleep which could have been most peaceful if I hadn't dreamt that I was sitting on the chair-o-planes at the side of Billy when all of a sudden he changed into a werewolf.

# CHAPTER SEVEN

"I don't like October," said Billy as we stared into a shop window in Woodhouse Street. "It gets dark too early and there never seems to be much sun."

This particular Saturday afternoon was very overcast and quite chilly and I found I could quite easily share Billy's depression. The feast had departed until Easter, and Bonfire Night was a month away. The last practice match of the rugby team had taken place on the previous afternoon under the same dismal weather conditions that we were experiencing now, and both of us found that our initial wave of enthusiasm was beginning to subside.

"Baggy that Batman comic," he said, suddenly springing into life. "What do you bags?"

Baggying, or bagsing something, usually provided the perfect remedy for boredom, though it was necessary for the afflicted individual to be standing outside a shop window at the time. It could not be any shop window, however. It had to contain items that would appeal to the desires of a ten-year old male, but it wasn't something you could do alone. It was only effective if in the company of a boy or boys of a similar age.

I stared harder into the newsagent's window. "I bags that 'Amazing Adventures' magazine," I replied, enthralled by the fantastic art work on the cover featuring a semi-clad girl about to be devoured by a huge dinosaur while several cave men looked on in horror.

"I wouldn't mind that either," he admitted.

"I bet I know something you don't," I said, deciding to change the subject.

"What's that?" he asked, betraying a slight interest.

"I bet you didn't know that Mr Senior's never been to Dewsbury."

"He must have been. Mr Senior's been all over the world. He's been telling us stories about it for years."

"I know, but he told me he's never set foot in Dewsbury."

"But it's only a few miles away."

"That's what I told him. Anyway, ask him yourself if you don't believe me."

As we made our way along Jubilee Terrace, which was really an extension to our street, the conversation changed to the forthcoming selection of the team captain, but Billy's mood hadn't improved much. "I don't think I'm all that bothered whether Tucker gets picked or not," he said. "I don't enjoy playing much when it's this sort of weather."

The first game would be played at the end of the following week and, with over twenty boys to choose from there was no guarantee that either of us would be selected. Tucker had been even more forceful with his threats over the past few days and I wasn't sure how many of the lads, myself included, would be influenced by them. The truth was that he was one of the best players anyway, despite his over-exuberance. Wouldn't it be much less hassle just to allow him to get what he wanted? I was undecided on the issue and Billy seemed to be losing interest altogether.

"How many games do we have to play before we break up for the summer holidays?" he asked.

"I don't know for sure. About sixteen I think, and they're all on a Saturday morning."

"We won't be able to go to the Saturday matinee at the Electra then."

"We never go anyway, not since we started going on Friday nights. You always said they were too noisy, too many younger kids screaming."

"Well, they are. Saturday matinees are all right if you're about seven or eight, because you get distracted at that age and it doesn't matter if you kick up a fuss because there are no adults to complain, but we're both more grown up now and I don't get bored unless it's one of those sloppy pictures that's always about a woman, you know, like the one we saw last night. Anyway the picture's always breaking down during the matinee."

Billy was certainly right in that respect. It was a rare occurrence for a film to last from beginning to end without a cut somewhere.

"It shouldn't matter if the rugby match stops you from going then," I said.

"Yes, but it's just the thought that if I wanted to go I wouldn't be able to."

"It's the last episode of Superman next week," I said. "What do you think will happen then? I mean, will a new Superman adventure be starting or what?"

Johnny Jackson said he'd heard there was going to be a new serial but it wouldn't be about Superman."

"What if it's about Captain Marvel? I think that'd be all right."

"Well I don't think we'll find out until next week anyway."

As Billy entered his house and I entered mine I was not really surprised to find Grandad Miller there.

"Now then lad," he said, before I had time to take off my coat, "Did you go to the pictures last night, then?"

"Yes, grandad. Me and Billy Mathieson went, but we didn't like it all that much. It was a bit boring."

"Didn't you know it was going to be boring before you went?"

"We thought it might be but we went hoping there might be a Tom and Jerry cartoon on or The Three Stooges, but all that was on was a film with someone talking about sheep farming in Australia. We had to go though or we'd have missed Superman, and it finishes next week."

"Oh dear," he said. "I was going to ask if you wanted to go with me tonight. I thought I might go to the Capitol at Meanwood, but perhaps we should forget it, eh. You might be too bored. It's Abbott and Costello, by the way."

"I think Abbott and Costello are great," I said, eager to get in my response before he changed his mind. I'd no need to worry, however. He already knew what my answer would be.

"We'll have to go first house, though," he went on, "Or I won't have time to get home afterwards. So it means we'll all be having our tea early."

Half an hour after having washed and eaten fried egg and scallops, I was seated next to my grandfather on the number six tram on its way to Meanwood. We had travelled no more than two stops before he gave me a nudge with his elbow. "Do you know yon lass sitting two rows behind?" he asked, "Because I'll swear she's been making sheep-eyes at you ever since we got on."

I turned around to look, not being quite sure what 'sheep-eyes' was supposed to mean and realised that

I was looking at a girl from school who, although quite attractive in appearance, had the annoying habit of seemingly being unable to stop talking once she started.

Yes," I whispered. "It's Lorna Gale. She's in my class at school." No sooner had I said it than, much to my discomfort and embarrassment, I saw that she was coming over.

"Hello Neil", she said. "Is that your father you're sitting with?

Hello Lorna," I replied, knowing that I was not going to avoid what would virtually be a one-sided conversation. "No it's my Grandad Miller."

"Yes, I'm his grandad all right," he said. He then directed his next comments to me. "Now then Neil, there's an empty seat over there. Why don't you and your girlfriend sit together for the rest of the journey?

I could feel the colour immediately rushing to my cheeks. There was only one girl I might not have minded sitting next to and she wasn't there.

"Lorna giggled. "I'm not really his girl friend," she said, then added "Come on, Neil it'll be fun. We can talk about school."

I wondered why she hadn't simply said "I'm not his girl friend" rather than "I'm not REALLY his girl friend" which seemed to suggest doubt. I didn't have time to reflect more on this as, before I knew what was happening, I had been led by the arm to a seat a few rows in front. My grandfather, I noticed, was chuckling to himself.

"Maybe I could be your girl friend if you like," she said after we were seated. "What do you think? Would you like that?"

"I don't really want a girl friend," I managed to get out, immediately realising that I, myself, had used the word 'really' instead of being more forceful.

"Well," she went on, "I might be kidding about being your girl friend or I might not. What do you think? You're not blushing are you?"

This was getting most uncomfortable. I knew other people on the tram were starting to take an interest in the conversation. I wished it had been Billy in this situation. I felt sure he would have handled it much better. I attempted to change the subject. "Are those your parents?" I asked, looking towards the area of the tram where she had previously been seated.

"Yes they are," she replied. "Are you going to the pictures, then?"

A feeling of impending doom swept over me. Surely she can't be going as well. What had promised to be a great night was turning into a nightmare. I had to find out even though I dreaded hearing the answer.

"Yes, my grandad's taking me. Are you?"

"Now that would be really nice wouldn't it?" I mean we could sit together and maybe hold hands while watching the film, and then I'd have to be your girl friend wouldn't I?"

I felt I couldn't bear much more of this. I glanced back and I could see that both of Lorna's parents had huge grins on their faces as, in fact, did many of the other passengers. The prospect facing me was intolerable. The thought of sitting next to Lorna and being subjected to girlie talk through the entire film was an extremely unattractive prospect. I would have rather stayed on the tram at the terminus for the return journey home than tolerate that. My relief, therefore, was immense when she said "No, much as I would like to go to the pictures with you I'm going with my mam and dad to my Auntie Jean's in Church Lane," but it immediately subsided when she added "But you can ask me to go with you again sometime."

I could hear my grandad laughing out loud this time.

Lorna was still talking. "You don't mind if I tell my friends at school that you offered to take me do you? Not many of them have got boy friends. I think Pauline Dixon had one once but she got fed up with him after a while. Which other girls at our school do you like Neil, apart from me I mean? I bet you like Jenny Unsworth and Sally Cheesesdale because they're both very pretty aren't they? Do you think I'm pretty? No, don't answer that one. I'd rather not know what you think, because sometimes I think I am and sometimes I think I'm not."

I just couldn't get a word in to answer any of the questions she was throwing in my direction, but I don't think she'd have taken notice of any of the answers anyway. I dreaded the thought of any of the details of this embarrassing encounter being related at school, but knowing Lorna's enormous capacity for exercising her vocal chords I realised, despairingly, that it was a forlorn hope. I suddenly was made aware that I had stopped listening to what Lorna was saying when she gave me a nudge on the arm.

"What do you think Neil?" said the voice at my side.

"Eh, what do I think about what?"

"Oh, you can't have been taking much notice of what I have been talking about," she said rather indignantly.

I'm sorry", I replied, wondering what I was apologising for. "I was just thinking about something. What did you say?"

"I was just saying that if we went to the pictures together and it was the Capitol, we could maybe have tea at my Auntie Jean's. What do you think about that?"

"I haven't said anything about taking you to the pictures," I finally plucked up the courage to say, aware that all the passengers within hearing range were now in fits of laughter.

"Well I know that you didn't come right out and say it, but then it wasn't necessary because I could see that you wanted to. A girl can always tell if a boy is interested in her. No, it's just that you're too shy to ask me properly. So you've nothing to worry about you see."

I was left feeling total exasperation, but my ordeal didn't end there as she suddenly covered each of my ears and planted a huge kiss on my mouth. As the tram approached the terminus all those passengers who still occupied the upper deck were experiencing a bout of mass hysteria. Lorna, however, seemed to remain totally oblivious both to this and to my own feeling of humiliation.

Eventually, she said "Well, I have to go to my Auntie Jean's now, but I'll ask her if I might bring you round for tea sometime. I hope you enjoy the picture, Neil. No, I don't really mean that, because I know you wanted to see it with me so I hope you don't enjoy it quite so much. Oh dear that doesn't sound quite right either does it? No, what I mean is that I hope you enjoy it but not as much as you would have done if I'd have been with you. There, I think that's all right isn't it? I say things without thinking properly sometimes. Anyway, I'll see you at school on Monday."

She finally turned away from me and I watched her walk towards her parents who had just left their seat to make their way off the tram. Just before going down the staircase she turned and blew me a kiss.

I turned to face the front and remained seated, staring ahead with a dazed expression on my face for what seemed much longer than the few seconds it must have been before Grandad Miller took me by the arm and directed me to the back of the tram. "By heck!" he said, "Yon lass can talk three times as quickly as I can listen. I reckon you've landed yourself in a right pickle there. I bet you're not looking forward to going back to school."

This latter comment did nothing at all to improve my feeling of misery, especially as it was he who had suggested that we sit together, and I was regretting the fact that I had accepted his invitation for an evening at the pictures. "She wants to take me to her Auntie Jean's for tea" I said, despairingly.

"Oh dear," he replied, "You can never tell when life is going hand you a knock down. You can be quite contented with your lot, looking forward to things and minding your own business when, before you know it, you find you've been invited to someone's Auntie Jean's for tea. Well, I must admit it doesn't sound very appealing does it. I don't think I'd fancy it."

As we stepped into the street and began to walk the short distance to our destination he seemed to sense my mood and put a comforting arm around my shoulder. "Now listen here," he said. "I doubt the situation is as bad as it seems. One of the things you need to learn is that women are strange creatures, aye, and lasses too I dare say, because they seem to have developed womanly ways a lot earlier these days. They look at the world in a totally different way to us, and a lot of them are very fickle. Now I was observing yon lass who was making such a fuss over you and I'm pretty sure that she falls into that category. Now I reckon, and I'm not usually wrong in these matters you understand, that you'll suffer a few days of discomfort at school, which is all part of life's learning process, but by the end of the week she'll have forgotten all about today's encounter and moved on to something or someone else. Her mind races ahead so quickly you see."

"I hope you're right, grandad," I said not being totally convinced.

"Now you take your Grandma Miller, God bless her soul," he went on. "Now she was one in a thousand and we had a really good life together and though I could never be entirely sure what she was thinking she never gave me any cause whatsoever to have a minute's regret about having placed a ring on her finger. Do you see what I'm getting at They're all different in their own way, but I'd like to bet a week's wages that I'm right about this Lorna of yours. Anyway, here's the queue so let's forget it for a while, eh, and see if we can have a good laugh at the picture."

Surprisingly, I did manage to shake off my moods at least for a couple of hours. Laughter is an excellent tonic for almost any condition and Abbott and Costello certainly provided it on that evening. In addition to the main feature there was a short film celebrating the first half of the twentieth century and I thought about this on the journey home. I wondered what I would be doing in the year 2000. Whatever it was, it was very unlikely that Lorna's Auntie Jean would still be around.

# CHAPTER EIGHT

I had said nothing at all to Billy regarding my unfortunate encounter with Lorna Gale. In truth, I suppose I was putting off the moment for as long as I could, fearing it would only provide for him a sense of merriment at my expense. As we walked the short distance to school on the Monday morning, however, I realised that it would probably be far better from my point of view if he heard about it before we entered the premises. With this in mind I stepped into the ginnel opposite the Electra and beckoned him to follow.

"What are we stopping for?" he asked. "We've only got five minutes before assembly."

"I want to tell you what happened on Saturday night before we go in."

"What do you mean? What happened?"

As quickly as I could I related the happenings of that very memorable tram journey, leaving out nothing.

"What, you mean she actually kissed you?" said Billy. He said it in such way that indicated that up to that point there might have been some hope but once the kiss had taken place I was, in his eyes, probably beyond redemption.

"Yes, and it was all wet and sloppy and horrible. I don't know what to do Billy. The whole school will hear about it. You know what she's like. I've been trying to think of a way of missing school. I told my mam that

I didn't feel well this morning and started coughing, but she told me I'd probably be all right and to see what I was like at dinner time. She said it was wash day and she couldn't be having me under her feet all day."

"Well, even if you had taken some time off school you'd have had to go back sometime. At least this way you can tell people that what she says isn't really true. Why did you let her kiss you?"

"I didn't know she was going to do it did I? There was no way I could stop it."

"Well you can't undo what's already happened. Maybe there's a way of stopping her from doing it again, though.

"How do you mean?"

"Just tell her that you like someone else and that you'd prefer her to be your girl friend. Well, its true isn't it?"

"Don't you dare tell anybody that I like Susan Brown, Billy, or we won't be friends any more?"

"I'm not sure I want the sort of friend who goes around kissing girls anyway. Only kidding," he added, seeing the look of annoyance on my face. "Don't worry. We'll have to think of something that's all."

At that point we both heard the school bell and I realised that the moment I had been dreading was imminent. My spirits were low as we entered the assembly hall after everyone else, though I was glad that I had confided in Billy first. His reaction could quite easily have been much different. I was grateful, therefore, that he seemed to be showing a genuine concern for my predicament.

After we had all sung the obligatory hymn Mr Rawcliffe, as usual, had the platform. I tried to stare straight ahead listening for the first sign of sniggering. There was complete silence as we waited for the headmaster to speak. Either Lorna hadn't told anyone yet or she had failed to attend, although the latter possibility seemed too much to hope for. He began in his usual pompous manner pointing out how the beginning of a new week was an opportunity for all of us to re-assess our attitude to school and schoolwork in general, how education was a gift not to be squandered and how fortunate we were not to have lived a hundred years ago when scholastic knowledge was a province of the rich. He then asked Miss Hazlehirst to step forward.

"I have decided," he said, "That now we are in the throes of autumn another of Miss Hazlehirst's nature rambles would be of great benefit to you all. This will take place tomorrow, immediately on arrival at the school. However, in view of what occurred on the previous one just before we broke up for the summer holidays involving some of the boys from the senior class I have decided to make some changes. During the walk from the school to Woodhouse Ridge there was much unruliness which resulted in complaints to the school from several of the residents in the area. Now I know that all the boys from that class have now gone on to secondary school, but I have decided to take no chances this time of a repeat performance. I have discussed this with Miss Hazlehirst and I shall now tell you the decision we have reached. In the past the pupils have walked behind the teacher in a haphazard manner. This will no longer be the case. On this occasion we are looking for a controlled and unhurried procession through the local streets. We have decided that boys and girls will walk in pairs in a respectful manner, one couple behind the other. The boys will walk on the outside of the girls at all times as is only right and proper in any dignified society."

Groans could be heard from all the boys that were assembled, but I heard giggles from some of the girls. This seemed to me to be little better than playing at 'Houses'.

"Silence," said the headmaster. "I shall now call on Miss Hazlehirst to give you the details."

"Thank you headmaster," she said as she stepped forward. "I have drawn up a list of which boy shall partner which girl and the order in which they will be walking behind me. I cannot stress too highly that anything less than an orderly procession will not be tolerated. If discipline is maintained up to the point that we step onto the ridge then I may decide that we can proceed in a less formal manner thereafter. Please pay attention now, and anyone making any comment before I have finished will be in serious trouble. The first pairing will be Gregory Sutherland and Dorothy Steedman; the second pairing will be——"

Each pupil was eagerly listening to every name. I had my eyes closed and was silently praying. "Please God, not Lorna Gale. Please God, not Lorna Gale."

Miss Hazlehirst continued speaking. I opened my eyes when I heard Billy's name called out. "Billy Mathieson and Jenny Unsworth; Tommy Lane and Pamela Black."

I looked at Tucker. I knew that from his point of view that having to take part in this humiliating procession was really bad for his ego, but hearing himself called Tommy again was a step too far. I realised that Lorna's name had not yet been called.

"Phillip Thatcher and Pauline Dixon," she went on.

There weren't many names left. I just knew that my worst fears were about to be realised

"Neil Cawson and———-

My heart was thumping so fast I felt sure everyone in the room would be able to hear it

"Susan Brown"

I couldn't believe it. I'd been so obsessed by who I didn't want I'd been completely oblivious to the other possibility.

Miss Hazlehurst was just coming to the end of her list. "———-Which leaves two girls left over, namely Lorna Gale and Eva Bentley who will accompany each other."

I looked at Billy who was standing next to me. He was struggling not to laugh out loud. I spotted Lorna for the first time and she looked absolutely furious.

Our leader for the following morning's ramble was still speaking.

"I expect all those mentioned to assemble in the schoolyard and line up in the order I have just described. I hope that is fully understood by everybody. I shall now hand you back to the headmaster."

"Thank you Miss Hazlehirst," he said. "That brings this assembly to a close. You may now all proceed to your classrooms. School dismissed."

"This might not be so bad after all," said Billy. "I know we'll look a bit soppy walking through the streets like that but at least I'll be with Jenny Unsworth. I mean I could have got Sophie Morton couldn't I? Anyway, you've got who you want haven't you?"

We entered the classroom to discover that everyone had now been allocated permanent seats, all the desks having names on. I was delighted to find myself in the row behind Susan and just one place to the left. As I sat down she turned towards me.

"I hope you don't mind having to walk with me Neil," she said.

Every time she spoke to me I always felt tongue-tied. Yet this never happened if I was in conversation with anyone else. She was like no one I had ever met. Even hearing her voice left me with a warm contented feeling. I was smitten and I didn't know how to do anything about it.

"No it's all right Susan," I managed to squeeze out, but it sounded all choked and flustered.

Billy was on one of the rows behind, so I couldn't see him but if he was in hearing range I could imagine the huge grin on his face. Lorna, fortunately, was on the other side of the room but I could tell she was in constant conversation with those around her and several of them were laughing and kept glancing in my direction. I knew now that the story of the humiliating circumstances of Saturday had begun its journey across the entire classroom. Within minutes the laughs and giggles had reached my side of the room and I knew it wouldn't be long before Mr Rawcliffe, who was spending a few minutes preparing his English lesson while we were supposed to remain silent, became aware of it. I just wanted the ground to open and swallow me up. No sooner had the thought entered my head than he stood up and grimaced at the class.

"What on earth is all this racket about?" he shouted. "I asked everyone to be silent until I had finished my preparation. Well, come on, I'm waiting."

Everyone became silent.

"Right then you, Pauline Dixon, you were giggling louder than anybody. What is the cause of all this hilarity?"

She stood up. "Neil Cawson kissed Lorna Gale when they were on the tram, sir, on Saturday, and he's asked to take her to the pictures and Lorna's taking him to her Auntie Jean's for tea, sir."

She said it all rather hurriedly and quickly sat down again. I sank down into the chair as low as I possibly could. Every eye in the room was fixed on me, but the ones that concerned me the most were Susan's. They indicated surprise.

"I see," said the headmaster in a much quieter voice. I got the impression that he was enjoying this break from the routine of teaching English.

"Well, perhaps then we should hear from the persons in question. So, if Neil and Lorna will stand up we can all hear the story properly and perhaps then we can get down to some proper schoolwork."

As I rose from my seat I felt my legs starting to tremble. Lorna, however, appeared to enjoy being the centre of attention.

"Let's hear from Lorna first," he went on. "Would you like to tell the class exactly what happened?"

She needed no encouragement whatsoever in that respect. "Well, sir," she began in rapid fashion and hardly pausing for breath, "I was on the number six tram with my mam and dad, because we were going to visit my Auntie Jean at Meanwood. We usually go every week but my dad had been poorly for a while so we hadn't been for quite some time. It was during the summer holidays in fact, so it must have been in August. It might have been July though because it certainly seems a long time ago. No, just a minute, it must have been at the beginning of August because my cousin Doreen had just had her ninth birthday. She's my Auntie Jean's daughter and my dad tells me she's spoilt because she always starts crying if she can't get her own way. Anyway, it was after that when my dad got poorly. My mam says it's because of the conditions in the factory where he works, but I remember once that he was poorly when he was supposed to be on holiday, so I wondered if perhaps she might be wrong and that it might be something else altogether that caused it. Anyway, I realised that Neil was sitting a few rows in front. No, that's not exactly true because that sounds like he was sitting directly in front but he wasn't really because he was on the other side of the tram. So he was in front of me but to one side. After a short while he turned round and looked at me and I could tell right away that he was wanting to sit with me, because I could see it in his face and his grandad thought so too because he suggested that we sit together on one of the empty seats. He said they were going to the pictures and that he'd like to go with me sometime and I could see that he wanted me to be his girl friend, and I didn't mind because I hadn't had a real boy friend before, well, not properly anyway. So I agreed and just as I was about to get off the tram he kissed me, and then he said———-"

"Thank you. I think that's enough. I believe I've got the gist of it," he interrupted, probably regretting that he'd got himself involved in the first place. He turned towards me. "And what do you say? Is that what happened?"

"Well not exactly, sir." I replied, in such a way that there was no disguising my extreme discomfort.

"Perhaps you'd better explain yourself, boy."

"I mean I wasn't kissing her, sir. She was kissing me."

"Now what kind of sense is that? I mean if both your faces were in contact then it seems perfectly obvious to me that you must have been kissing each other mustn't you?"

Laughter echoed around the classroom.

"Silence," boomed the headmaster. "I think we've had enough of this delay to the morning's lesson. If there is a budding romance taking place I see no reason to be a killjoy about it, providing it takes place out of school. However, I will have no more mention of it in this classroom." He looked straight at me again. "Who are you accompanying on the nature ramble?

"Susan Brown, sir."

"Well then Master Cawson, just to prove that I have nothing against pupils of this school showing signs of affection to one another I think it would be entirely appropriate if you accompany Miss Gale tomorrow and let Susan Brown change places with her."

"But, sir," I began to say a feeling of absolute despair sweeping over me, but he didn't allow me to protest any further.

"Enough, now boy, I don't require any thanks from either of you. The subject is now closed and it is time to get down to some serious work."

I sat down totally demoralised. Susan turned around and said "I don't mind swapping really. I didn't know Lorna was your girl friend."

I couldn't say anything. I just stared and must have looked incredibly stupid. The remainder of the morning's lesson was a blur and I found myself getting more and more annoyed at the way life kept kicking me in the teeth. By the time we entered the playground for the morning break I was in a furious mood and was ready to take on anyone who said the wrong thing. Billy approached just as I kicked a tin can with such force against the school wall that if it had happened on a football pitch it would have surely broken the goalmouth netting. I wasn't in the right frame of mind even for him. I think the reason no one else was coming up to me and sniggering was because they could see the mood I was in, but I expected Lorna to seek me out at any minute.

"Don't say anything funny Billy," I said, not giving him the chance to speak first, "Because I don't want to hear it."

"I wasn't going to. It seems to me you need a way to get out of this situation, but I'm blowed if I can think of anything."

"Well, I can. I'm going to pick a fight with Tucker Lane. I'm going to call him Tommy and tell him that I think he'd be lousy as captain of the rugby team and that I'm going to vote for someone else. Then when I get beaten up my mam will have to let me stay off school tomorrow."

"Don't be daft, Neil," he said, horrified at my intention. "You can't do that. If you have a proper scrap with him he's going to keep coming back every day." As an afterthought he added, "I think you'll just have to accept the situation for a while until we can think of something."

I was grateful that he was willingly involving himself in my problem and I knew that what he said was really the only action I could reasonably take. I decided to accept his advice but it did nothing at all to improve the remainder of the day. I put up with all the sniggers and comments which came my way and avoided Lorna as much as I possibly could and somehow I survived unscathed until the bell sounded for the end of school. Unfortunately, things did not improve much as I was morose for the whole of the evening, thinking about how miserable I would feel when I awoke in the morning and contemplated the awful prospect that awaited me.

# CHAPTER NINE

After a rather disturbed night during which the few brief periods of sleep to which I succumbed refused to provide a remedy for the dreadful feelings of anxiety which dominated my mind, it was with a heavy heart that I trudged, with Billy, the short distance to school, arriving in time to see the two rows of boys and girls in the process of being formed. Miss Hazlehirst seemed very diligent in ensuring that the pairing she had arranged was strictly adhered to. For a brief instant I clung to the thought that Mr Rawcliffe might have been too busy to inform her of the change, but my hopes were immediately dashed when I realised that even if he had forgotten there would be no possibility that Lorna would fail to notify her. True enough, there was Susan standing at the back alongside Eva Bentley while Lorna stood a few rows in front with a vacant place for me at her side. As I took up my position Phillip Thatcher in the row in front turned towards me and said, "Will you two be holding hands then?"

I barely had time to grimace before Lorna's vocal chords began their frequent exercise routine. "That's for us to know. You keep your eyes to yourself Philip Thatcher. If we want to hold hands we will do. What's wrong with that?"

I decided that if I was ever going to get through this wretched morning I would have to keep as low a profile as I could and give her no encouragement whatsoever. It occurred to me that I didn't recall giving her any encouragement on the tram journey to Meanwood either, but it hadn't made any difference. My only consolation was that at least it wasn't one of the other lads who was accompanying Susan in my place.

The entire sorry procession from school to Woodhouse Ridge remains nothing but a blur in my mind, yet it could all have been so different had the original choice of my companion remained. I would then have been able to proceed with my head held high and possibly revel in any attention I might have received, chiefly I suppose, because the situation would have been thrust upon me and would not have required any embarrassing admission on my part of my feelings. Instead I walked in a slouched, melancholy manner and attempted to remain as oblivious to the occasion as I possibly could. I was aware that Lorna was speaking but was totally unaware of the content of what she was saying. Did she take hold of my hand? I honestly can't remember. As we approached the ridge and I realised that, in all probability, the class would be able to continue in a much less formal manner I began to take more notice of my surroundings.

"I don't know what's the matter with you today," Lorna was saying. "You've not spoken to me ever since we left school and I don't think you've been listening to me either."

I was saved from having to give any acknowledgement to what she was saying by Miss Hazlehirst. As we stepped out onto the ridge she called everyone together. "Now I want you all to pay attention," she began. "We are now well into the autumn season, and as we proceed along the path I expect each of you to be examining your surroundings with a view to noticing the differences that this time of year brings. Make mental comparisons between what you observe now and the things you noticed when you were here in the summer. I have spoken to Mr Rawcliffe and he has accepted my suggestion that he makes the title of your next composition 'Woodhouse Ridge In Autumn - The Things I Saw'. You will be asked to write this tomorrow morning while it is still fresh in your minds."

Several groans could be heard, mostly from the boys. Miss Hazlehirst pretended not to notice.

"For the remainder of this afternoon's ramble I shall allow you to continue a little less formally, at least until we re-enter the streets. That does not mean, however, that you shall behave in an undisciplined manner. Is that clear to everyone?"

"Yes, miss," replied the class in unison.

When we set off again, Lorna said, "I'm going to walk with some of the girls now and I'll see you later on, because I think you might want to be with some of the other lads for a while won't you?"

Lorna's decision to let me off the lead for a while was only in keeping with what the other girls were doing as the class split up again into two more natural groups.

"I didn't mind walking with Jenny Unsworth'" said Billy, as he approached. "She's not as soppy as some of the other lasses. How did you get on with Lorna this time? I could see that you weren't talking so much."

"I wasn't listening so much either. I mean she's quite good-looking really but why does she have to talk so much, and why pick on me for a boy friend? I would have been walking alongside Susan Brown if it wasn't for her. I hate her now, I really do. How do I get out of it Billy? I can't let this go on for weeks."

"I don't know, unless————," he looked thoughtful. "Just a minute," he said, "I've just thought of something. I'll be right back."

He walked towards a group of the girls, one of which was Lorna. I had no idea what his intentions were but I just hoped he wouldn't go back on his promise not to tell her about the way I thought about Susan. Other than that, any way that he could get me out of the situation would be extremely welcomed.

Alan Bartle came over. "You don't really want to go out with Lorna do you?"

I was grateful to be getting what looked like genuine sympathy from one of the other lads instead of the expected jokes and sniggering.

"No," I replied, "But Lorna thinks I do. You know how she is. I just can't seem to get her to think otherwise."

"Well I'm glad it's not me. I haven't much time for girls. They always want to play such daft games, and you can't talk to them about football or rugby or anything important like that."

"I know. I haven't much time for them either," I replied, not mentioning the one exception to that statement. I decided to change the subject. "I think you're one of the best players in the rugby team. Do you think you'll get picked as captain?"

We continued walking and although we could hear the voice of our rambler-in-chief ahead of us making various observations about the things we were supposed to be looking at, we were paying little attention. "I've no idea," he replied. I wouldn't mind being captain but

I haven't a clue who people are going to vote for. I mean, you scored four tries in the first practice match didn't you?"

"Yes, but you know why that was don't you? I haven't scored any since have I? I don't suppose I will until I find another cow pat big enough."

He laughed. I could feel the tension draining away for the first time in three days. It was a refreshing change to engage in a conversation which did not feature Lorna Gale as the main subject.

"I suppose horse muck would do just as well," said Alan. "In fact, I bet any team covered in horse muck would never get beaten. Maybe we should try it."

It was my turn to laugh. "I think it would have its draw-backs though. I bet it would take days to get rid of the smell."

"Perhaps we should just cover Tucker Lane in horse muck and keep passing the ball to him," he suggested.

This time we were both in hysterics. "He wants to be captain you know," I said.

"Yes I think he's threatened everybody. He's a good player though."

Miss Hazlehirst was attempting to take command again. "Right, gather round everyone." We formed a rather disorganised group in front of her, and it seemed to me that perhaps it was not as large as it should have been. "Now, who can tell me anything about this object I am holding up?"

"I think it might be a leaf, miss," came a male voice from the rear of the assembly, followed by a few girly giggles.

"I know it's a leaf, silly boy. I want to know what else you can tell me about it."

"It's green miss," came a voice from the back.

"Yes it is green but one month from now it will be brown. You, Phillip Thatcher, why will it be brown?"

This question and answer session continued for about five minutes, but I was trying to figure out why there seemed to be less pupils than we began with. No one else seemed to have noticed. I nudged Alan Bartle who was still standing next to me. "Some people are missing, "I whispered, "But I can't figure out who."

We tried counting bodies which was not easy as no one seemed to stand still for more than a few seconds and we didn't want to attract our leader's attention. Alan made it 24 and I counted 23.

"I think there were about thirty when we started out," suggested Alan, so who's missing?"

I immediately sought out Billy, and couldn't spot him, nor could I see Lorna

Alan added the names of Leonard Horsey and Tucker Lane. "It looks to me like there could even be someone else but where can they have gone?"

No one seemed to have noticed. "Perhaps we should go back a short way and see if we can find them before our fearless leader becomes aware of it," I suggested.

We started to retrace our steps with the realisation that with two more missing it couldn't be long before someone called the alarm.

A couple of hundred yards further on we saw Billy heading towards us. "Leonard Horsey's stuck in a bog down by the beck," he said. "I was just going for Miss Hazlehirst. He's not sinking or anything, but it's nearly up to his waist and he can't pull himself out."

"I'll go get her," suggested Alan. "Whereabouts is it?"

"Just go a few yards past the monkey tree, and then straight down the hill."

"How did he manage to get stuck in a bog?" I asked, as Billy and I made our way towards the incident and Alan set off running in the opposite direction.

"Well you know how we were talking about how to stop Lorna from thinking of you as her boy friend and I said that I'd thought of something, well it all started when I went over to talk to her and at first I thought I'd just tell her that you liked someone else."

"Billy, you promised me that you wouldn't say anything about Susan Brown."

"I didn't. I mean I wasn't going to."

"Well what then?"

"I was going to tell her that you liked Sophie Morton."

"You were going to do what," I said with as much indignation as I could muster. "Nobody likes Sophie Morton, you know that."

"I know, and she probably wouldn't believe it anyway, so I was about to think of someone else then all of a sudden I remembered something. Before we broke up for the summer holidays I was with a few of the lads in the schoolyard and we were talking about how you never saw girls playing proper games like football or cricket and then we started talking about who were the best looking ones and Leonard Horsey said that he liked Lorna Gale best. Everybody said that she wasn't bad but she never stopped talking, and Leonard said that he hadn't really noticed. So I thought instead of telling her that you like someone else, why not do the opposite and tell her that someone else likes her?"

"Is that what you did?"

"Yes, I told her what he'd said about her in the schoolyard and that he was probably upset because she'd taken you as a boy friend instead of him."

I was intrigued. Could this be a way out? I sincerely hoped so. "Go on," I said eagerly, "What did she say?"

"She said that she hadn't known anything about it and that she didn't want to upset anyone, and straight away she walked over to Leonard and started talking to him. They stood there chatting while everybody else walked on, but I couldn't tell what they were saying. Then suddenly Lorna stepped onto the grass, slipped and started to roll down the hill. It was quite funny because it must have been legs and knickers all the way down because by the time I got to the spot where she slipped she had come to rest against a bush and her dress was around her waist."

"Hey, watch it Billy," I said, my face a picture of mock indignation, "That's my girl friend you're talking about."

We both laughed. "She wasn't hurt or anything," he went on, "But was covered in mud. The thing is when she started rolling down the hill Leonard chased after her but because it was slippy he fell on his backside and ended up in the bog at the bottom of the hill by the side of the beck. When he stood up he was almost up to his waist in mud and couldn't get out. Tucker Lane, Dorothy Steedman and Gerry Sutherland, who were a little farther back from the rest of the class, heard her scream when she slipped and rushed back to see what had happened."

Billy finished his narrative just in time for me to observe the proceedings for myself. Leonard seemed to have stopped struggling and appeared to be waiting for assistance. Lorna was covered in mud from head to toe but it did not stop her from yelling at everyone to do something. Dorothy and Gerry were just standing around, but there was no sign of Tucker at all. I had barely time to take in the scene when the rest of the class led by Miss Hazlehirst appeared on the path above. Our teacher had a look of anguish on her face.

"Better not come down the hill, miss," shouted Billy. "There's a path round the side."

She gave no indication of having heard and immediately stepped onto the hill. She had taken no more than two strides before she was flat on her back. Uttering a shriek she plunged passed everybody and landed in the bog at the side of its other occupant. The only difference was whereas Leonard was standing in it, she was sitting in it with her knees under her chin.

"Get me out," she shouted. "Get me out. I can't move."

The problem had now doubled. The rest of the class arrived via the more sensible route. Some were laughing at the sheer comedy of the scene, but others appeared puzzled with regard to the question of how to provide a solution to the problem. No one, however, was doing anything that could even loosely be termed effective, that is until Tucker Lane appeared, muscles bulging, as he dragged a tree trunk behind him, his eyes briefly taking in the latest addition to the drama.

"Help me spread it across the surface," he demanded. Eager hands strove to oblige, until the trunk rested on the bog passing between its two captives. "Do you think you can stand up, miss?" he asked. "Put one hand on the tree trunk and see if you can pull yourself up." Our distressed teacher did as she was asked, prepared immediately to accept, without any outward demonstration of injured pride, that the role of authority had, at least for the time being, passed to another. With a great effort she managed to get to her feet, but was still unable to move. I realised I was seeing a side of Tucker Lane that I hadn't observed before and admit to being suitably impressed as he kept a cool head while everyone else seemed to be lacking in ideas. Perhaps these were just the talents that the captain of the rugby team should be displaying, but then I recalled some of his more silly antics in the practice games. It was baffling.

"See if you can climb onto the trunk, miss, and we can help pull you back," he suggested.

At first it seemed that she wasn't going to make it, but by leaning as far over the trunk as she could she managed to get one leg over. This proved sufficient for the rest of the manoeuvre to be successful. Before long both she and Leonard Horsey were on dry land, extremely dishevelled but very relieved.

She grabbed hold of Tucker and planted a kiss on his cheek. "Thank you very much Tommy," she said beaming," That was very, very clever." The look on his face suggested that he wished he hadn't bothered.

As an inevitable halt was called to the nature ramble, I saw Lorna approach the hero of the afternoon.

"I thought you were wonderful, Tucker," she said, "Getting Miss Hazlehirst and poor Leonard out of the bog like that. They could have been there for hours if it wasn't for you. I suppose it was my fault really because I fell down the hill. Well, no it wasn't my fault exactly because I couldn't help it could I? But what I mean is if that hadn't have happened then no one would have gone into the bog would they? Oh dear I'm getting everything mixed up again, aren't I? I bet tomorrow everybody at school will be talking about what you did, and if they don't you've no need to worry because I will. Anyway

I think what you did was wonderful. By the way, have you got a girl friend?"

"Get lost," growled Tucker, displaying the sort of charm that only he was capable of, the sort which would have been most useful to me over the past few days if only I had possessed a small percentage of it.

The procession which made its way back to school could not have been more different from the one that preceded it. Miss Hazlehirst was content to hide away in the very centre of the group in order to avoid displaying her dishevelled appearance as much as possible from the eyes of the local residents and therefore save her from even more embarrassment. Tucker Lane, surprisingly, kept a low-profile. I thought he would have revelled in his newly acquired hero status but he acted as if his image had in some way been tarnished. Lorna recovered quickly from Tucker's dismissal and attached herself to Leonard Horsey. He did not seem at all dismayed by the situation though the conversation taking place between them was extremely one-sided. She had said nothing at all to me regarding her change of affection and I certainly did not pursue the matter. I was contented that Grandad Miller's prediction appeared to have been correct. I was aware that the main event of the morning and its fortunate consequences for me in particular had been engineered, albeit indirectly, by Billy and I knew I would be eternally grateful. I looked across towards Susan Brown walking alone and looking very thoughtful and I could not help marvelling at the contrast between her and the person from whom I had had such a narrow escape, and I found myself looking forward to the remainder of the week. At least the following morning's compositions entitled 'Woodhouse Ridge In Autumn - The Things I Saw' should prove very interesting.

# CHAPTER TEN

Thursday afternoon was decision day, the day when the voting for the team captaincy would take place. During the morning Tucker Lane had continued his strategy of threatening anyone who refused to vote for him, despite the fact that after his heroics earlier in the week he had probably emerged as the favourite anyway. During the previous day his endeavours had been officially recognised by the entire school when he had been singled out during assembly in order to earn the gratitude of the teaching staff, though the rather undignified details of Miss Hazlehirst's involvement in the proceedings were glossed over. Tucker might have been happy to accept this accolade of his achievements had he not been referred to as Tommy on three separate occasions.

As the entire school gathered in the hall immediately after dinner, Mr Barnes addressed the pupils. "As you will remember a few weeks ago I mentioned a few things regarding the captaincy of the rugby team, which on Saturday plays its first competitive game against the boys of Armley Church of England School. One of the things I stated at that time was that the person who would lead the team onto the pitch would be chosen by all those boys who have taken part in the practice games. I also said that there would be some guidance from me on this matter. From my own observations I have decided that two pupils have repeatedly stood out above the rest and they are Tommy Lane and Alan Bartle, and it is from these two names that you will be asked to choose. I would like to stress that whichever of the two misses out he should not regard it as a reflection on his ability. The voting will take place by a show of hands immediately following the afternoon break to give time to those of you who will be voting on the issue to reach a decision."

I sneaked a look at Tucker. The smug expression on his face suggested that he seemed to regard it as a foregone conclusion. The speaker, however, hadn't finished. "The person who is selected," he went on, "Will of course be expected to put in more hours at school. He will be expected to remain behind for approximately one hour on each Thursday prior to a game, during which time he and I will consult together in order to choose the team for the following Saturday and to decide on tactics. It will also be necessary for him to stay behind for the same length of time on the Monday following to discuss the game and suggest what, if any, changes need to be made and how to proceed with the training. He may also be called upon to stay behind for a few minutes at any time during the season if I feel there is anything important that needs clarifying."

As Mr Barnes came to the end of his explanation as to how he saw things developing the expression on Tucker's face changed to one that could only be described as panic. Whether anyone else had noticed I couldn't say. It was obvious that the thought of having to put in extra hours had never occurred to him.

Mr Rawcliffe's history lesson leading up to the break did not give anyone the opportunity to discuss the event which was to take place later that afternoon as the headmaster was in one of his stricter moods and allowed no interruption to the teaching of what he regarded as his favourite subject. All the pupils, therefore, had no option but to become absorbed in the story of The Wars of the Roses; all, that is, except Tucker Lane who seemed most uncomfortable and distracted and had to be spoken to on two occasions. When the end of the lesson finally arrived and the pupils headed into the school yard he became quite frantic with activity.

"I bet he's trying to persuade people not to vote for him now," said Billy.

"I think you're right," I replied, "But how is he going to threaten everybody in fifteen minutes? And there are about seven or eight lads in the other class and they aren't even outside yet."

"I've decided I'm going to vote for Alan Bartle anyway," he said.

"So am I, but we've no need to let Tucker know have we? It'll be more interesting if he thinks he's going to be landed with the captaincy and have to stay behind after school at least twice a week."

"It all depends on whether we can stay out of his way for a bit longer."

We went round to the back of the school where the lavatory blocks and the air raid shelter left over from the war were located. Within a couple of minutes we were joined by Ken Stacey.

"I'm trying to stay out of Tucker's way," he announced. "He's trying to get round everybody to tell them not to vote for him now."

"We know," said Billy. "We've decided not to vote for him anyway, but we can't wait to see his face if he wins."

We managed to remain undetected until the bell sounded for the resumption of lessons. Once inside the building all those boys from our class who had taken part in the practice matches plus those from the other class, whose afternoon break had been postponed until the voting process had taken place, were summoned to the hall. Mr Barnes, the only other person there, began to speak.

"I would like to begin by asking both Alan Bartle and Tommy Lane to come and stand beside me."

"Excuse me, sir" said Tucker, looking rather agitated. "Could I just say something?"

"Not at the moment, Tommy. We have to get this over fairly quickly so we can all get back to the afternoon's lessons."

"But, sir," he persisted.

"There's nothing to worry about boy. I know how much you want to be captain. You made it very clear on the first morning back at school after the holidays, and the fact that you were willing, even at that early stage, to accept such a responsibility was noticed by me and I have not forgotten it. However, I promised everyone a vote and that decision will be strictly adhered to."

That statement suggested to me that, at least in our coach's mind, that Tucker was the hot favourite. The person in question though looked decidedly unhappy about it as he made his way along with the other contender to his designated position. Mr Barnes touched Alan Bartle on the shoulder. "All those voting for this candidate please raise your hands," he said. I looked around the hall and could see that the result was going to be close. I think Tucker would have had his arm raised too if he thought he could have got away with it. "I make that sixteen," he announced. "Now, all those voting for this candidate, please raise your hands. I make that seventeen," he went on. "Therefore, I declare that the new team captain will be —-. Just a minute, how can that be right? That makes thirty-three and there aren't that many people in the room. Some boys have been voting twice. Hands up anyone who's voted for both candidates." Of course, no hands were raised, but there was quite a lot of sniggering.

"Very well," said Mr Barnes. "It is quite obvious to me that some of you are totally incapable of voting in the traditional manner which has, up to now, been a perfectly acceptable way for English gentlemen to express their preferences. We will, therefore, resort to a more foolproof method. Now, I want no one to move while I'm counting." A few seconds later he proudly announced that there were twenty-seven pupils in the room who were entitled to register a vote, at which point he promptly sent one of the boys to the classroom with instructions to return with twenty-seven pieces of blank paper. It must be exactly twenty-seven, no more and no less.

"Now then," he said after this particular exercise had been completed to his satisfaction, "I shall give each boy a blank sheet of paper. On this paper I expect to see the name of one candidate only. Is that perfectly understood?"

"Yes sir," was the unanimous reply.

I wrote down the name of Alan Bartle realising in the process that, had everyone known that the ballot would ultimately be performed in this fashion, it would have made Tucker's threats completely pointless as he would have had no idea who anyone had voted for anyway. I wondered which pupils had voted twice. I certainly wasn't one of them.

Mr Barnes gathered the completed papers, studied them carefully and began to speak.

"That is more like it," he said. "I shall now announce the result of the ballot. The number of votes cast for Alan Bartle is fifteen and the number cast for Tommy Lane is twelve. Alan Bartle, therefore, will captain the team for the coming season."

He turned towards the victor and patted him on the shoulder. "Well done, lad. I feel sure you will lead the side well."

I looked across at Tucker as the result was given. He immediately gave a huge sigh of relief, an emotion which was betrayed on his face to all those facing him. Within seconds, however, his demeanour changed as he realised that he ought to be displaying a more mournful expression. He managed to achieve this just as his coach touched him on the shoulder.

"I'm sure we would all like to commiserate with Tommy and I would just like to say to him that I am sure you would have made an excellent captain but someone has to lose on these occasions, so I urge you not to be too down-hearted about the result no matter how disappointed you must be feeling at the moment."

After he had finished, Tucker began his speech.

"No, sir, well, yes, I suppose I am disappointed sir. I was really looking forward to being captain, but it's about what's best for the team sir, isn't it? I mean the vote has been fair and square with nobody interfering so I've nothing to complain about. I'm ready to support Alan in any way I can, sir to help this school to be the best one in Leeds."

I couldn't help admiring his acting performance. It was worthy of an Oscar.

"Well, Tommy," said Mr Barnes, "That was very well said. You could not have given a better or more unselfish response to the circumstances you have found yourself in. Now that's two occasions this week that you have been a credit to this school and demonstrated to the other pupils the type of behaviour that they should be trying to emulate."

"I just try to do my best, sir," added Tucker. "That's all it is really."

Billy whispered in my ear. "I don't think I can take much more of this. He's going to end up getting a medal."

The team coach continued his accolade. "I must admit, Tommy, how impressed I have been with the way you have handled your disappointment and I have come to the conclusion that the way you have spoken today has made me realise that it would be an excellent idea if I allowed you to stay after school with Alan and myself in order to make your own input into the affairs of the team, three heads being better than two, so to speak. What do you think of that?"

I knew immediately what the rest of the lads thought about it. It would be a fitting retribution for all his threats over the previous few weeks. They had been worth it just to see the expression of horror on his face. I couldn't wait to see how he was going to talk his way out of this one. Billy could hardly prevent himself from laughing out loud.

"But sir," he started to say. The remainder of his statement, however, was garbled as he visibly struggled to find the right words to extricate him from the pit he had dug himself into.

As Mr Barnes continued to talk about the merits of allowing Tucker Lane to have some input into team selection and tactics by putting in extra hours after school, I suddenly realised that, despite the undoubted attraction of seeing him suffer for all the hassle he'd been causing, perhaps it might not be such a good idea after all and I briefly explained my reasoning to Billy. "I think we should try to get him out of this," I said. "Much as I'm enjoying his discomfort, think what he's going to be like for the rest of the year if he's prevented from leaving school at the usual time. Apart from that, if he's helping to select the team while he's in this disgruntled mood he could cause all kinds of mischief. I'd rather it be left to Alan Bartle and Barnesy, wouldn't you?"

"Even if you're right," Billy replied, "I don't see what we can do about it now."

Tucker was looking more and more despondent as I attempted to make some input into the proceedings.

"Excuse me, sir", I began. "I was just wondering if perhaps what you're suggesting might not be a good idea, you know that Tucker, er, I mean Tommy, should be involved in the process.

Tucker became immediately alert, his eyes betraying a flicker of hope.

"I think, perhaps, you'd better explain what you mean boy."

"Well, sir. It just doesn't seem right to have two people deciding things. I mean they might disagree every time and then where would we be?"

"Are you suggesting then that I shouldn't be involved either?"

This was getting difficult.

"No sir, of course not; you're the team coach so you have to have a say."

"I agree with him, sir," piped up Billy. It just seems to make more sense, that's all."

Tucker joined in, hoping to push the escape door a little wider.

"I think Neil's right, sir. I'd very much like to be playing a part in things." He paused momentarily. I could see that he was remembering how he'd talked himself into this situation in the first place and he didn't want to make the same mistake twice. "Well, what I mean really sir is that, despite that, I don't think I should be involved in team matters. I think it should be between you and Alan Bartle, sir, because he has been voted team captain and I think I can help him out best when we're playing on the field."

"I see. Very well, then, I suppose I can see some merit in your argument. We'll revert to the original decision of the team captain and me selecting the team and deciding tactics. Now, the day is not yet over, so if there is nothing else there remains the small matter of schoolwork so I would be obliged if you would all return to your lessons."

Alan Bartle came over as we returned to the classroom. "I'm glad you spoke up in there. I didn't really fancy having a difference of opinion with Tucker twice a week. It's bad enough having to stay behind, but that would have made it ten times worse."

"I bet he's not too unhappy with the situation either. It was funny watching him squirm though." We both laughed.

Tucker didn't approach us until we were leaving school at the end of the afternoon. "I want to thank you two for helping to get him to change his mind," he said. "I didn't manage to get round to you earlier to tell you to change your vote, but it doesn't matter because it's all worked out O.K. No, it's definitely thanks to you.

I certainly didn't fancy staying behind after school. I couldn't see any point in it anyway."

I couldn't believe my ears. Any kind of thanks from him seemed so out of character. Billy looked astonished too. Had we perhaps misjudged him?

Tucker paused for a while with a thoughtful look on his face before continuing. "Mind you, I'm not in any real hurry today. We can have a scrap if you like. Which do you prefer, one at a time or both at once?"

# CHAPTER ELEVEN

"Thirty-six nil", said Nicky Whitehead with disbelief in his voice. "How could we lose thirty-six nil?"

"Because every boy on the pitch was bigger than us, that's why," explained Billy. "Even Ken Stacey looked smaller than he usually does."

As we were seated on a wall waiting for the bus to take Mr Barnes and his team back to Woodhouse I knew that Billy's observation on one of the reasons for our defeat was correct, though there were certainly other factors involved. All the players on the opposing side were supposed to be nine to eleven year olds, yet it was as if we had been in conflict with a team of giants. Once again Alan Bartle, as captain, and Tucker Lane were really the only two who made any sort of an impact. Tucker, in particular, was well able to hold his own when it came to a crunching tackle. He just got back to his feet immediately and continued playing. The fact that his assailant was probably several inches taller didn't mean a thing to him. As far as the rest of us were concerned, however, it was obvious that a lot more training would have to be performed. I wasn't too sure either about the commitment once the first two tries had been scored. One thing that struck me quite forcefully after the match was how much I would rather have been playing football. "Rugby is a man's game," my father had always said. He never actually expressed the opinion that football was for cissies, but the implication was there. When he was my age he had been a pupil of Buslingthorpe National School which was, at least according to what he told me, to be constantly winning awards for the sport. The bruises I had sustained that Saturday morning bore witness to the fact that it could indeed be a rough game, especially so if you were on the wrong end of a thirty-six nil score line. I was just grateful for the fact that my father did not finish working until midday. I would not have wanted him to witness the debacle that had just taken place. Our team coach attempted to make light of the affair, though he must have been bitterly disappointed. "I suppose this was always a possibility on our debut in this league," he had told us. "At least we know now what sort of challenge lies ahead of us."

There was little conversation on the bus taking us back home, even Tucker seemed to be lost in his own thoughts, and it was obvious when we disembarked at the terminus at Hyde Park that the mood hadn't changed. Mr Barnes caught the tram to his house in Headingley, telling us again not to worry unduly about the heavy defeat and that things would seem a lot better on Monday morning. The rest of us were left to continue on the short journey home, and as the unhappy band trudged down Woodhouse Street it gradually fragmented into smaller groups. By the time we entered Johnstone Street and said farewell to Ken Stacey, there were four of us remaining and we began at last to discuss the events of that miserable morning.

"I think this has been one of the worst Saturdays I can remember," said Billy.

"Not for me it hasn't," I reminded him. "Last Saturday was far worse."

"Yes, I suppose it must have been for you. Some of us thought it was quite funny though. Anyway you seem to be rid of Lorna Gale now," he pointed out. "She's still insisting that Leonard Horsey's her boy friend, but he doesn't seem to be too bothered about it."

I know, but it was a lucky escape."

"This morning was horrible though," said Billy, reverting to his earlier theme. It certainly wasn't worth missing Dick Barton for."

"I don't think it makes much difference now," suggested Johnny Jackson. "It's finishing soon anyway. My dad told me. He said it was mentioned in the Daily Herald. They're going to replace it with a serial about a circus called 'The Daring Dexters'. I don't think I'll bother listening to it, though."

"I don't think I will either," replied Billy. "What are they taking it off for? Dick Barton's been on the wireless for as long as I can remember."

"Superman finishes at the Electra next week as well," I said, "But I don't know what'll be on instead."

"I heard it's going to be a jungle picture," said Nicky Whitehead, "And that there'll be fifteen episodes like there were with Superman."

"I wish we'd have had Superman in our team," I suggested, "Then we wouldn't have lost thirty-six nil."

"Are we supposed to be playing again next week?" asked Billy.

The answer was provided by Johnny Jackson. "I think most of the games are every two weeks. So there should be plenty of time to get some training in."

Billy moaned. "If it's going to be anything like it was this morning," he uttered, "I don't think I'm bothered about playing any more."

As we passed the bottom of Ganton Steps, Nicky suggested that we hung around for a while and did somersaults on the bars that lined the steps on either side.

"It's too near dinner time for me," said Johnny. "I think I'd better be getting back."

"He lives somewhere near Cocoa House Hill, doesn't he?" asked Billy as we watched him walk towards the far end of Johnstone Street while we contemplated a few minutes of amateur gymnastics on the bars of Ganton Steps.

"I think so," I replied in answer to Billy's question.

"Did you know," said Nicky, as each of us took hold of the rail and performed a somersault, "That Cocoa House Hill isn't its real name? It's actually called Speedwell something or Melville something."

The street in question ran from Melville Road down towards the tram stop in Meanwood Road opposite the Primrose public house, or the Primmy as it was known by all the locals who frequented it. If you boarded a tram in the town centre with the intention of alighting at that stop you would just ask the conductor for a ticket to the Primmy. He would always know where you meant.

"Why does everybody call it Cocoa House Hill then?" I asked.

"I've no idea" said Nicky. "I've always known it as that."

"It's the best street in Woodhouse for sledging on anyway," suggested Billy, forcefully, as if he was daring someone to contradict him."

Neither of us did as we knew that it was probably the steepest slope in the area.

"I don't think I'd like to live in that street," observed Nicky. "I bet Tony never pushes his ice cream cart up there."

"That doesn't mean he doesn't go there," I said. "I bet he comes up Speedwell Street and pushes his cart down Cocoa House Hill on the way back to his yard."

"He won't have much ice cream left then," said Billy, "If he's on his way back home after being all round Woodhouse. If it was me I'd sit on it and ride back down."

"You'd kill yourself if you did that Billy," said Nicky. "You'd have no way of stopping it. It wouldn't be like being on a bogie, and you'd probably end up on the tram lines in Meanwood Road."

"Why don't we find out why everybody calls it Cocoa House Hill?" Suggested Billy.

"I don't think I could be bothered," I replied. "We spent ages trying to find out why Elsie Waterman wouldn't go to Woodhouse Feast, but we never did. Anyway, I'm getting hungry now. I think I'll go back home. It might be fish and chips today."

"I don't know what we're having," said Nicky as he gathered up his rugby kit, "But I'm starting to feel hungry as well."

"Me too," said Billy. Anyway, I want to see what my mam says when she sees how mucky my shirt and shorts are."

"Well, they can't be any worse than mine," I said.

Ganton Steps was one place where we didn't mind if there were a few girls swinging on the bars as it could be as entertaining as watching them perform handstands. However, despite it being a Saturday morning this added attraction was not in evidence, so we all decided to make our way home. As we set off downhill it started to rain so that we had to finish the journey in a canter.

"Watch out, Billy," I shouted as he sped off in front. "Remember what happened last time. Mrs I-Make-No-Wonder might have another washing line out."

Fortunately, his way was clear this time and all three of us disappeared indoors just as the rain got really heavy.

My father hadn't arrived home, which was a relief in a way, because I was dreading having to tell him the score, but I knew he would ask as soon as he came through the door.

"Your Auntie Molly fancies some fish and chips," said my mother, as she disapprovingly examined the contents of my duffle bag, "And as we were going to have some anyway, I said you could get some for her and your Cousin Raymond as well. He can't go for them because he doesn't finish work until half past twelve."

I always liked Raymond. Even though there was a six year difference in our ages and he'd left school during the summer, he often spoke to me as if we were the same age. He was very interested in football and I learned a lot from him about the various Football League teams and what part of the country they came from.

My mother resumed speaking. "How on earth have you got these things in this state?" she asked. It's a good thing you weren't playing in your street clothes."

She didn't bother to ask me anything about the game, and I didn't volunteer any details.

"I heard from Mrs At-The-Other-End that the factory's working all day again so you'd better not go to Jubilee Fisheries or you'll be as long as you were last time it happened. Don't go to the one round the corner opposite Doughty's though. I think you'd better go to Craven Road. Let's see if it stops raining first though shall we?"

I presume Mrs At-The-Other-End was the lady who lived at the end of the street. I assumed she meant the end near the Electra as Mrs Ormond's sweet shop occupied the other extremity.

As the door opened I expected it to be my father, but at the same time a voice asked "Are you there May?"

"Come on in, Mr Senior," she replied.

"Sorry to disturb you," he said. "I was just wondering, do you see, if your lad was going for some fish and chips today."

"Why would you like him to bring you some?" she asked.

"If it's not going to be too much trouble," he replied, thought about it for a moment, then added "He won't be going to the one round the corner opposite Doughty's, will he?"

"No, as soon as the rain eases a bit he's going to the Craven Road fish shop, because the factory on the Jubilees is working all day again. So I think they'll be too busy."

"Aye, lass. I reckon you're right there. I've known 'em run out of fish many a time when that happened."

"What would like him to bring for you? Is it just fish and chips?"

"It is now," he said. "I was expecting our Doreen and her husband down this morning with my grandson and I was going to get him to go for 'em, but Phillip, that's her husband do you see, rang to say that she was full of cold and that they'd better leave it until next week."

I noticed that he had made no mention of a bag of spice on this occasion and that my mother had not even given him the opportunity to say that he was 'fair to middling'.

"Well," she said. "It's the time of year when people start coming down with something. It's certainly turning a lot colder lately."

"Well. I'd best be getting back then," he said. "Thank you very much May. It's very good of you."

"Not at all," she said. Any time we're having any just ask. By the way, I never asked you how you were feeling today."

"Oh, I'm just fair to middling lass, just fair to middling."

"Mam, did you know that Mr. Senior's never been to Dewsbury?" I asked, after he left the house.

"Mr. Senior travelled all over the world when he was younger. He used to be in the merchant navy you know."

"Yes, I know that, but he's never been to Dewsbury. He told me himself."

"Well, fancy that now," replied my mother, rather disinterestedly. "Who'd have thought it?"

Within a few minutes of his departure the rain stopped and I was able to go on my journey. The queue on this occasion was fairly small and I arrived home with my bundle shortly afterwards, only to be scolded for not having asked for them to be wrapped separately. "I'll have to sort them all out now," chided my mother. By the time I had visited my Auntie Molly and Mr. Senior the fish and chips were already on the plate and my father had arrived.

"I can't believe your mother never asked you how the game went," he said.

"I was too busy, Tom. I never thought to ask," she offered by way of explanation.

"Never mind," my father went on, "You can tell us now, eh"

I explained to him in great detail the way the morning's fiasco had progressed, placing heavy emphasis on the fact that all the lads on the opposing team were much taller, hoping it would lessen the impact of the margin of the score line and our own lack of ability and experience as the primary reason for the heavy defeat. I was very surprised to see him take the same optimistic view of the situation as Mr. Barnes.

"You can't expect too much from your first game," he said.

"A letter arrived from Tim this morning," said my mother. "He's finished his initial training and he says he's settling in to things a lot better and that he'll be home on leave for a few days soon, but he doesn't know the exact date yet."

"I knew it'd be hard for him on the first few weeks," said my father, "But I reckon he'll be all right now. After all he wasn't very happy at the place where he worked before being called up, was he?"

There was an age gap of several years between Tim and me so I suppose we didn't have a lot in common, but I was looking forward to his being a part of the family again for a while and, as my mother and father continued their conversation, I looked out of the window and noticed that the damp atmosphere appeared to have gone and that the sun had started to shine. I went outside closely followed by Nell and the two of us sat on the causeway immediately opposite the house. I thought again about the game that had taken place during the morning and I realised that only two players would be sure of their place for the next one, neither of whom would be Billy or me. What I wasn't sure about was whether I was bothered or not.

# CHAPTER TWELVE

As the month of October plodded its weary path the nights grew darker and the weather became perceptibly cooler. For Billy and me it was a gloomy time, brightened only by the prospect of Bonfire Night looming on the horizon. Tim arrived home on leave for a short visit which, though over all too quickly, was very worthwhile as it gave everyone at home the opportunity to see that army life, now that his initial training period was at an end, seemed to be suiting him better. At school there was more intensive training for those involved in the rugby team. It did not, however, prevent us from losing our second fixture by a score of twenty-seven points to three. All that could be said was that it was an improvement on the first game. Billy and I had both been selected, but I had serious doubts about whether that would continue. Billy, in particular, was becoming most disillusioned and Tucker Lane was beginning to get rather aggressive with those he considered had not been pulling their weight which, in his eyes, was just about everybody except him. Lorna Gale detached herself completely from Leonard Horsey and announced to anyone who could spare long enough to listen that she had finished with boys altogether as they kept letting her down. My feelings for Susan Brown were the same as ever, but I still found it practically impossible to say anything to her that made any sense. A new serial had begun at the Electra entitled

'Nyoka, The Jungle Girl'. It wasn't Superman but it was starting to get interesting. At the same instant, however, 'Dick Barton – Special Agent' disappeared from the wireless, changing Saturday mornings forever.

The Monday following our second fixture was the first of several days when, much to the dismay of most parents, we did not have to attend school because of what was commonly, though perhaps erroneously, known as 'Teacher's Rest'. Billy and I had been looking forward to it for several weeks and only a few days previously had suggested that it was the perfect time for us to go chumping as the big night was rapidly approaching. With this in mind, and not wanting to be anywhere near the house on wash day, I decided to raise the issue immediately after breakfast.

"Is it all right if me and Billy go chumping today, mam?" I asked, as the theme music to 'Housewife's Choice' could be heard emanating from the wireless set which always heralded the beginning of my mother's household chores.

"You can this afternoon if you like," she replied, "But I've got an errand for you this morning. I want you to go see the Shoddy Man."

At these words Nell let out a large yelp and immediately crawled under the table.

"Aw, mam, do I have to?" I pleaded, a look of horror on my face. "Can't I go to the dentist instead?"

"Now stop being silly," she said. "I've got a few rags here that I want you to take down to him and I expect you to get at least two shillings mind. Don't be coming back with less. She paused briefly before adding, "On second thoughts you'd better give me that old cardy back. I'd forgotten that your Auntie Eileen wanted to know if I'd got anything she could use to make a clip rug. You should still get one and ninepence though. So don't let him fob you off."

I hated coming face to face with the Shoddy Man. He had a rag and bone yard just off Meanwood Road and he was the meanest, roughest and scruffiest person I had ever encountered. If my mother wanted to squeeze one and ninepence out of him it would have made more sense for her to send in an elite unit of commandos. I'd heard that the only person who seemed to be able to get the better of him was his mother, the actual owner of the business if such it could be called, though she was supposed to look every bit as fierce as he did. The thing was that if he could his rags for next to nothing he would do everything in his power to do so.

"I think I'll take Nell with me mam if I have to go," I suggested, hoping it would give me some bargaining power once I'd entered the yard.

The object of my suggestion crawled further under the table and began to whimper and shake uncontrollably.

"No you won't," replied my mother. I'm not having her roaming around in that filthy yard. She'd be in a disgusting state when you got back, and be careful what you come into contact with as well."

Nell stopped shaking and left her refuge to sit at the side of her rescuer and stare defiantly at me.

As I reluctantly accepted my fate and left the house with the bundle of rags under my arm I knocked on Billy's door hoping I could get him to accompany me.

"Right, are we going chumping then?" he asked, as he opened the door.

"I've got to go see the Shoddy Man," I said. "Will you come with me?"

"I don't want to go down there," he replied. "He's real scary is the Shoddy Man. Every time I've taken anything down for my mam he always tries to cheat me."

"If you're my best friend Billy you'll come with me," I pleaded in the hope that his strong sense of loyalty would come to the fore. "I've to get one and ninepence for these rags."

"You've no chance Neil. You'll be lucky to come away with a balloon." He thought for a minute before saying, "I'll come with you but if he starts swearing and shouting I'm not stopping."

I had little choice but to accept Billy's terms and we set off down Speedwell Street towards Meanwood Road, neither of us inclined to hurry. As we neared my Grandma Cawson's house close to the Old Carr Nursery School I suggested to Billy that if we called in for a while we might get a glass of lemonade, which I suppose was really just an attempt to delay the inevitable. He welcomed the suggestion, though I suspect his reasons were probably the same as mine.

Grandma Cawson was a widow, my grandfather having died two years previously, and I was always a welcome visitor though I was usually scolded for not going more often. "Well, it's about time I saw you again," she said on opening the door. "I was beginning to think you'd forgotten where I lived especially now that you don't seem to go to Sunday school much." The establishment she referred to was almost opposite her house. Billy and I always thought of it as a waste of a Sunday afternoon and we got out of going whenever we could. "You had to go when I was your age," she continued, "And quite right and proper it was too. There was no staying away just because you felt like it and preferred to be outside playing. My parents would never hear of it I can tell you."

I stayed silent not wanting to say anything on this particular issue. The truth of the matter was that it was only recently that my mother and father had become less insistent as to whether I went or not and I didn't want anything to alter this state of affairs.

"Now who's this then?" said my grandmother, having exhausted her opening remarks. She stood with her hands folded eyeing Billy up and down. "I bet you never go to Sunday school either."

"Me and Billy are on our way to see the Shoddy Man with these rags but we got a bit thirsty so I suggested we call here and ask for a glass of water," I said, hoping that something a little more appetising than water might be in the offing.

"I see," she said, a thoughtful look upon her face. "So it's not really me you came to see then is it? Well, you'd better both come in then hadn't you?"

As we stepped inside Grandma Cawson pointed to the couch and told us to sit down. "You can have some water if you like," she said, smiling, "But I've some Dandelion and Burdock left. Are you sure you wouldn't prefer that?"

"Yes please, Mrs Cawson," said Billy eagerly.

"Yes, me too please," I added, rather hurriedly.

She went into the small scullery and returned a brief moment later holding two glasses, each containing the rich, dark liquid. She was about to hand one to Billy when she suddenly paused and gave him a thoughtful, yet suspicious look.

"Just a minute," she said. "Didn't I see you making a mischief of yourself on the nursery roof a few days ago?

I knew I'd seen you somewhere before. I had to chase you down didn't I? Yes, I'm sure it was you."

Actually we had both been up there but only Billy had been spotted, yet I knew he wouldn't give me away. I was aware, however, that my grandmother's only concern about children playing on the roof was purely an altruistic one. She dreaded the thought of any child being injured as a result of a fall. Billy, though, looked crestfallen as he realised that the Dandelion and Burdock he had been eagerly anticipating might be under serious threat.

"So you're going to see the Shoddy Man," she went on, deciding not to berate Billy any further and handing each of us our drink. "Let's see what you've got then."

She examined the bundle of rags. "Well, I reckon you might get about one and sixpence for those. Mind you that's only if you take them to a decent rag and bone dealer. The trouble is there isn't another one round here is there? You'll be lucky to get a couple of balloons from the old devil you're going to."

I noticed that my grandmother's valuation of the said items was slightly lower than my mother's but that her view of the likely valuation from the Shoddy Man was slightly higher than Billy's.

"What am I going to do, Billy?" I asked after leaving Grandma Cawson's having decided that we dare delay the inevitable no longer. "My mam's expecting me to go back with one and ninepence."

"I don't know," he replied. "We'll just have to do the best we can."

At that precise moment our eardrums were assaulted by Tony's shout inviting all the residents of Woodhouse that were in hearing range, a distance of about half a mile, to sample one of his ice creams and, as we rounded the corner from the nursery we spied him heading towards the end of Speedwell street.

"Now then lads," he said as we approached his barrow, "Will you be wanting an ice cream then? I don't usually come round in the mornings, but I knew all the kids would be off school today."

Much as we wanted to say yes we couldn't have paid for them anyway.

"No, not today Tony," I said. "My mam's sent me to see the Shoddy Man with these rags and Billy said he'd come with me."

"Safety in numbers then, eh? Well I don't think I'd fancy going round there. His yard's in a disgusting state as far as I've been able to tell. My eyesight's not as good as it was, you understand, and yet I've always managed to keep mine clean and tidy. Still, if you hold those rags a bit closer I'll give you some idea as to how much you should be getting for 'em."

I held them out for him to scrutinise.

"Now, let me see. There's some fairly decent stuff there, but you mustn't let him cheat you do you understand. I reckon they're worth about one and threepence to any rag and bone man worth his salt. But knowing the fellow you're taking 'em to I reckon you'll be lucky to come away with a handful of balloons."

As we watched Tony began his long haul up Speedwell Street I stared down at the bundle of rags.

"We'd better get to the yard quickly," I said. "If we bump into anybody else they're only going to be worth a shilling."

Our nostrils detected the existence of the rag and bone yard before our eyes did and after a slight hesitation we bowed to the inevitable and stepped through the gate. Piles of rags in what appeared to be no specific kind of order almost covered the filthy floor of the yard. They must have been subjected to the elements on countless occasions which would make anyone wonder of what possible use they could be to their latest owner. There was a small undercover area which did appear to contain some better quality stuff, but even there everything was laid out in a haphazard fashion.

"I can't see any bones," observed Billy. "Why do they call it a rag and bone yard then?"

Billy's statement seemed quite a reasonable one.

"I've no idea," I replied. "I can't see a few bones being any use to anyone anyway unless they have a dog."

A huge black cloud chose that moment to block out the sun and as it did so the Shoddy Man emerged into the yard through a side door. I would not have been surprised if his arrival had been accompanied by a peal of thunder or a flash of lightning but everything remained silent, though the air was oppressively heavy.

"Crikey," whispered Billy, as we stared at him open-mouthed, "He's worse than that man from the caravan who chased us at Woodhouse Feast."

The object of Billy's observation glared down at us.

"Right then you two, let's see what you've brought then," he snarled.

I handed over the bundle of rags. "My mam wants one and ninepence for them," I managed to say, though without much conviction.

The Shoddy Man laughed. It was a loud, hard, raucous laugh. "There's nothing here that I can use. I've never seen such a pathetic, moth-eaten bundle in my life."

"We'd better take them back then," said Billy. It was at that moment that I realised how glad I was that he'd agreed to accompany me.

"Now hang on just a minute. You've brought them in here, so here they'll stay. I'm buggered if any of 'em are the slightest use to me but never let it be said that Honest Sid ever turned anybody away. We've got to negotiate that's all. You know what negotiating is all about, don't you? It's about coming to some agreement that suits me. That's the be all and end all of it."

I wasn't sure that his definition was correct but I desperately wanted to be out of the place. At the same time, though, I didn't want to return home without the amount that my mother expected to receive.

"Now then," he continued. "I've got some nice balloons here, but don't be expecting half a dozen each mind."

"No, I have to take one and ninepence back," I persisted.

"Oh, I'm afraid not lads. Can't give you cash for 'em. Not worth anything to me, you see."

Just then a new arrival appeared in the yard. "By heck, Sidney Gudgeon, I reckon I've heard everything now. Taken to robbing bairns have you? I've known your mother for many a year and I don't make any wonder that you're terrified of her. After what I've just witnessed I make no wonder at all."

The object of her wrath was rendered momentarily speechless, but Mrs I-Make-No-Wonder hadn't finished her verbal assault.

"You'll clear at least three shillings on that little lot I wouldn't wonder," She went on after casting a glance at the bundle of rags, "And you're trying to fob off these two young lads with a few balloons. I'll tell you something. I've known your mother for many years and she's a very hard woman but she's always dealt fair with me. Why she allows you to conduct the business of this yard God only knows. No, that's one thing I'll never be able to make any wonder over."

Before he had time to answer the accusation that was being hurled at him the very person in question decided to make an entrance. She was indeed a fearsome looking woman. It was the first time that Billy or I had ever laid eyes on her, but she seemed altogether a fitting companion for her son. She was probably about fifty years of age but looked much older. Her straggly hair, going grey in parts hung below her shoulders.

"I suppose we'll have to start calling her the Shoddy Woman now," whispered Billy.

"Oh my God, I don't believe it," she said after struggling to identify the intruder. "It's Annie Chapman. I wondered what all the commotion was in the yard but I never dreamt you'd decided to pay me a visit. It's been a year or two since we had a drink together at the Primmy. What's made you turn up now all of a sudden?"

"I was just passing Connie, just passing, but you won't make any wonder why I called in when I tell you that I overheard that worthless lad of yours trying to cheat these two bairns. Now, that was never your way Connie. Whether anyone else makes any wonder at it or not, it was never your way. You always dealt fair."

"You skinny bugger," yelled Mrs Gudgeon as she clouted her son on the back of the head. "How many times have I told you to treat customers decent? The way you go about it we soon won't have any left, and didn't I tell you to get these rags sorted out instead of leaving 'em out here to rot. You're a great big useless dollop Sidney Gudgeon."

The Shoddy Man, for all his size and bulk, was like a child when faced with his mother's wrath.

"No, don't say that ma, I'm just trying to get the best price I can for 'em that's all. It's just good business sense," he attempted to explain.

"Don't talk to me about sense," she said, landing him another clout, "Because you haven't got even an ounce of it you big lump. Get yourself inside and try to find something useful to do while I deal with these two lads."

He had no option but to do as he was bidden but we both noticed the grimace he directed towards us as he did so. I decided there and then that I would much prefer it if I didn't encounter him again.

"By heck Annie," his mother went on, "I'll swear to God he gets worse every day. I don't know where I went wrong. If his father hadn't died when he was a nipper I'd say he got it from him because you couldn't fit a pin between 'em."

"Well I've said my piece Connie," said Mrs I-Make-No-Wonder. "I just couldn't let him get away with it. I mean it's no wonder is it that you're not getting the amount of customers you used to. I mean I can't make any wonder at it anyway."

"Right," said Mrs Gudgeon, staring at Billy and me. "What were you expecting to get for these rags then?"

"My mam wants one and ninepence," I said.

A look of horror came over her face. "How much?" she shouted. "One and ninepence for this little bundle? Oh I don't think I ———"

"You were always fair with me, Connie," reminded Mrs I-Make-No-Wonder.

"Only kidding Annie, only kidding. How much did you say lads? One and threepence wasn't it?"

"No, one and ninepence please," I said, surprising myself with my insistence.

"I like this boy Annie. I really do. He'll go far in business he will I'm sure of it. See lad, here's your one and ninepence and another threepence for your cheek but don't expect me to be so benevolent next time. Now best be off home with you."

Billy and I needed no encouragement whatsoever. With a mumbled thanks and a brief glance at the two remaining figures in the yard who immediately picked up the threads of their earlier conversation we were out of the yard like a shot.

"Two shillings," said Billy in wonderment. "Two whole shillings, I can hardly believe it. It's a pity she didn't give it to you in change. You could have given your mam the one-and-nine pence and kept three pence back for some fireworks."

I'd thought of that possibility but I wanted to see my mother's expression when I handed her the two shillings.

It had started to rain quite heavily when we entered our street and Billy disappeared into his house as I entered mine.

"Look how much I got," I said joyously as I handed over the shining two shilling piece."

"Two shillings," she said. "I don't believe it. I only expected you to get half as much."

"But you told me to make sure I got one and ninepence."

"Yes I know, and they were probably worth it to a proper rag and bone dealer, but I never expected you to get as much as that from the Shoddy Man in Meanwood Road. How on earth did you manage it?"

I had decided on the way home not to mention Mrs I-Make-No-Wonder's involvement in the proceedings and take the credit for myself. However, she didn't give me time to answer.

"You know what this means," she went on. "When I tell everybody how much you managed to get out of him you'll probably end up taking rags down for everybody in the street. I reckon he must have taken a fancy to you."

I knew then that it would be only fair to give credit where credit was due.

"It wasn't really me, mam. He was only going to give me a few balloons until Mrs I-Make——-er, I mean Mrs Chapman came into the yard and started talking to his mother."

I told her the entire story so that she knew with absolute certainty that I played virtually no part whatsoever in her good fortune.

"Well then," she said. "I must certainly thank her when I see her."

The rain continued for the remainder of the day. At tea time I called round at Billy's and, as the following day was the last of the brief holiday from school, we agreed to go chumping then, providing it had stopped raining. My mother was so pleased at receiving twice as much money as she had expected that she gave me a whole shilling which she said I could put towards some fireworks and I immediately gave half to Billy for his part in the afternoon's adventure as I knew he would have done the same. With October having nearly run its course, I found myself looking forward to Bonfire Night followed by the run-up to Christmas. My encounter with the Shoddy Man had turned out much better that I had expected. My feeling of well-being would have been complete if only I knew that I would never have to meet him again.

# CHAPTER THIRTEEN

From my very earliest recollections there had always been a fire in our street on Bonfire Night. It was, however, only one of dozens in the Woodhouse area and, apart from Billy and me, the only other lad from our school who was likely to attend it was Nicky Whitehead. As the day after my dealings with the Shoddy Man turned out to be a surprisingly dry one, the three of us therefore met outside Mrs Ormond's sweet shop to discuss the prospect of the morning's chumping expedition. Billy and Nicky were both staring into the sweet shop window when I arrived.

"Nicky says he bags those Aniseed Balls," announced Billy, but I bags those Liquorice Torpedoes. What do you baggy?"

"What's the point in baggying anything?" I replied. "None of us have any coupons left, have we?"

"I know," said Nicky, "But she might let us owe a two ounce coupon until next week. She does that sometimes."

"No. that's no good," Billy pointed out. "She'll only do it if your mam's with you. Anyway, I'm saving my money for some fireworks, but there's nothing wrong with looking is there?"

I decided to get to the point of our being there. "Right then, where shall we go chumping? Is it Woodhouse Ridge?

"What about Death Valley?" suggested Billy indicating the location on the ridge where we had acted out scenes from 'The Lost World' on our way home from the first rugby practice. "There's always loads of dead wood and stuff there."

"But it'd take us ages to drag it all that way back. It's not as if we had a bogie or anything is it?" I answered.

"Well if we go to this end of the ridge," said Nicky, "I don't think we'll find much, and anyway the Wharfies will probably be out chumping as well. Unless we start chopping trees down all the best stuf will probably have gone. We've started later this year. I mean there's only another week to go."

"What about Sugarwell Hill then?" I offered hopefully, though I didn't really think it was a viable option.

No," said Billy. "We'd probably have to climb right to the top to find anything and then it'd be just as far to drag it back as it would if we'd gone to Death Valley."

"I know," I said, suddenly receiving inspiration from somewhere. "Do you remember when we were fishing on the Dammy in summer and we found that old yard on the way back that looked deserted? There was a lot of wood in there just lying about. I bet it's still there unless someone else has found it first. Why don't we go see if anything's happened to it?"

Billy looked thoughtful.

"Wouldn't that be like stealing though?" suggested Nicky.

No, I don't think so," I said. "You weren't with us that day Nicky but it looked as if it had been lying there for ages. The yard itself was almost hidden because the outside of it was almost totally covered by brambles and weeds and things. I don't think anybody's been there for years. It's probably left over from some factory or something that's been knocked down."

"I say we go have a look," suggested Billy, and Nicky agreed.

The Dammy was just an extension of Meanwood Beck but as it approached the area around Buslingthorpe Lane it miraculously, and for no reason that anyone could remember, acquired a completely new name. From here on, in a southerly direction, it lost its muddy banks and gained a concrete footpath on each side as it left any remaining traces of countryside behind and meandered its way adjacent to, or under, the streets of Buslingthorpe and Sheepscar before joining the river Aire in the centre of Leeds. Billy and I, on one occasion, had followed it as far as we dared before turning back, not wishing to make the return journey in the chilling surroundings that darkness would bring. As we now crossed over it by virtue of the bridge close to St Michael's church we headed in the opposite direction to the one just described following the muddy track for a short while before encountering some stone cobbles which ascended the hill to our right.

With the vegetation, despite the lateness of the year, crowding around us we climbed the cobbled road. It was a road which had probably been used during the previous century to transport stones down from the old quarry which had long ago been filled in. It was altogether an eerie place and the dull, cloudy weather did nothing at all to brighten our spirits.

"Maybe we should go on to the ridge after all," said Nicky. "I bet you can't even find this place."

At that moment the prospect of a possible encounter with the Wharfies seemed preferable to remaining in the

God-forsaken place we found ourselves in. I was determined, however, to see the project through and to have my suggestion vindicated.

"We must be nearly there Nicky. It's probably just round this next bend. What do you think Billy?"

"I'm not sure. We were pretending to be in the jungle weren't we, hacking our way through the undergrowth so we must have left the path. It was a nice sunny day though. It wasn't all gloomy like it is now. It's all a bit scary."

We continued for about another fifty yards before Billy's voice broke the eerie silence. "This is it. I'm sure of it," he said excitedly. "I remember that boulder."

"I think you're right Billy," I said looking in the direction he was pointing. "We went through there and look, I think I can see what's left of the walls. The weeds and everything aren't as high as they were in the summer."

It was true. Our way forward did not seem as difficult as it had a few weeks before. The realisation of this, however, was balanced by the fact that the dull and heavy atmosphere and the lateness of the year meant that this particular occasion seemed to hold a lot more menace. It was with more than a little trepidation, therefore, that we left the cobbled road and headed towards our destination. We decided to walk several yards apart in order to improve the chances of achieving our goal. I took the left flank, Billy the centre and Nicky the right.

"I wish I was a few years older," observed Billy, "So that I could wear long trousers. I keep scratching myself on these brambles. I can't seem to get out of the way."

"It's not as bad at this side," I suggested from a few feet away. "There are a lot of nettles though."

"I'm not bothered about that so much," he replied. "You can trample them if you put your feet right. I'll come across to your side

"Hang on a minute," shouted Nicky, who had got a little ahead of us because of fewer painful obstacles in his path. "I think I've found what we've been looking for."

As we joined him I couldn't fail to notice the scratches on Billy's legs. "Don't worry Billy," I said. "It'll be worth it if we get some decent stuff to burn."

The place where we found ourselves was indeed our intended destination. It was obvious that some time in the past it had been a yard of some description. It still had walls on three sides, though the highest was no more than about four feet, but practically nothing remained of the building to which it had once been attached apart from an assortment of bricks and boulders among the undergrowth. What was of more interest, however, was the fact that the various items of wood appeared not to have been disturbed.

"It looks a lot spookier than the last time we were here," remarked Billy.

"Yes," I agreed, "But at least the wood's still here. Let's see what we've got."

"There's loads of it," said Nicky in wonderment. "It looks like it's been here for years."

"It's all rotten though," observed Billy, "Because it's been out in the rain for ages. I bet it'll burn great once it's dried out though. Look, I think there's a lot more buried under all these weeds and grass," and he attempted to prove his point.

We hurried to join him and within minutes we had uncovered quite a sizeable area. It soon became obvious that we would be unable to transport all that was available in one trip, and I pointed this out to my two companions.

"I don't think we need to take all of it anyway," remarked Billy. "Don't forget that we always get old chairs and sideboards and things from other people in the street."

"Yes, but some of it might be going to someone else's bonfire," I reminded him.

"Look," shouted Nicky excitedly, "There's a full door here. It's still got a metal handle on this side. How are we going to carry that home?"

"If it's rotten enough," I suggested, "We might be able to break it into smaller pieces." Just as I finished speaking the sun made an appearance for the first time that day and cast a warm glow over the whole area while lightening our mood in the same instant. It was as if the summer had taken pity on us and decided to go out in one last blaze of glory.

"The sun's come out," said Billy delightedly. "I thought it was going to rain. I feel better already."

I think the spirits of each of us had been given an unexpected lift by this surprising turn of events. All the gloom and foreboding of a few minutes earlier seemed to have disappeared.

"Help me pull this door out," pleaded Nicky.

We went over to assist, dragging it from beneath the vegetation which was spreading over it.

"I've got an idea," he went on. "Why don't we drag it towards that grassy bank over there? It's only a few yards away. We can just about all climb on. I bet it would slide great downhill over all that grass. We could leave it at the bottom and come back up for some of the other stuff."

"Don't be daft Nicky," I said. "That bank's steep. You'd either fall off or end up in the beck at the bottom. Didn't you hear about what happened to Leonard Horsey and Miss Hazlehurst?"

Despite my misgivings, however, the idea of the three of us hurtling down the grassy bank clinging to the door had its undoubted attractions especially as the emergence of the sun had left me with a feeling of euphoria.

"What do you think, Billy?" I asked.

"It should be great," he replied enthusiastically. "We've slid down on pieces of cardboard before but this door's big enough for us all to get on. We can break it up when we get to the bottom and then come back up to see what else we can carry."

As the anticipated excitement of the occasion replaced my feelings of apprehension I helped Billy and Nicky drag the door through what remained of the various assortment of weeds and brambles to the head of the grassy bank a few yards away. However, as I gazed down the hill my earlier misgivings returned. There appeared to be a clear run to the path below and the fast flowing waters of the Dammy just beyond.

"How are we going to stop it going into the beck?" I asked, not a little alarmed at the prospect of a serious ducking.

"The ground levels off a bit near the bottom so I think we'll be able to steer it onto the path," suggested Nicky. "Anyway I can't see it going that fast that we can't stop it."

I remained unconvinced but the adrenalin was already coursing through my veins.

"Somebody's going to have to push it and then jump on," said Billy.

Deciding that that would be my job I waited until my companions had climbed onto the door, each clinging to the handle and pushed as hard as I could, clambering on board as soon as our downhill racer was in motion holding on for dear life to the top of the door. The problem with this was that I was facing uphill and could see nothing at all below me. Despite this the ride would probably have been an exhilarating one had it lasted long enough for me to enjoy it. We cannot have travelled more than a few yards before I found myself losing my grip and reached out desperately to clutch a clump of grass. As I did so the door continued on beneath me leaving me to lie prostrate on the grassy bank. I turned myself around just in time to see the drama unfolding below me. As my intended means of transport neared its destination it struck a boulder causing it to perform an involuntary ninety degree turn causing shrieks of consternation to emanate from its two remaining passengers. In the same instant Billy was thrown clear and continued his journey unaided as he rolled over and over before coming to a halt just before reaching the path. Nicky, though, was even less fortunate. As he remained clinging desperately to the handle the door continued on its journey. It did not slow its descent as it neared the foot of the hill however, as had been hoped, but shot straight across the path and landed in the beck with an almighty splash taking its remaining occupant with it.

I rushed down the slope and ran straight past Billy just as he was he was attempting to stand up. I just had time to notice that he did not seem particularly hurt but was undoubtedly dizzy after his tumble. Nicky, on the other hand, I wasn't too sure about. I knew the Dammy wasn't really deep enough to drown in as we'd all paddled in it on countless occasions, but it was quite a fast flowing stream and he had landed with such force. When I arrived Nicky was sitting in the water motionless his arms around his knees and making no attempt to stand. What surprised me, however, was the fact that he was grinning.

"What a ride," he said. "What a ride. That was fantastic. Did you see it? It was just like flying at the end."

"Are you all right Nicky?" I asked, worriedly, just as Billy arrived to take in the scene.

"I think so," he said. "What a ride though. What a ride."

"You won't be able to travel on it again," I told him as I watched the fragmented pieces of the door disappear round the bend on their journey to the river Aire.

"Are you sure you're all right?" asked Billy. "You're soaking wet."

Nicky stood up and clambered onto the bank. "I've grazed my side a bit that's all, but it's not so bad.

"We've lost the door," I said. "If me and Billy don't go back up to the yard to bring some of the wood back we've wasted our time coming. You'd better go back home so you can dry off."

"Look, I've still got the handle," announced Nicky. "I think I'll keep it as a souvenir."

"It's a wonder you haven't got a few sticklebacks in your pocket as well," laughed Billy.

"Well it was worth getting wet for. I'm glad I didn't fall off like you two. Anyway, I think I'll come back up with you. We'll be able to carry a bit more and it won't take long anyway."

Apart from the soaking he had received Nicky certainly didn't seem any the worse for wear and seemed to regard the whole escapade as a thrilling adventure which was definitely in contrast to his earlier mood. The three of us, therefore, made our way back up the hill and collected as much of the wood as we could possibly carry. With our heavy loads the journey home took much longer than the one we made earlier in the morning and as we knew that Nicky would have to go indoors to dry off and also have a lot of explaining to do we decided not to return for any more that day.

"We haven't got a Guy this year" said Billy as he placed one foot on the open midden in order to hoist himself up onto the lavatory roof which was where we always stored the chumps for Bonfire Night. "Do you think we'll have time to make one?"

"I don't see why not," I said as I began handing him up the fruits of our morning's labour.

"I could make a Guy easily," said a female voice from immediately behind me.

I turned around to see Mary Pearson standing there and I automatically looked down to make sure my buttons were fastened.

"I'll probably be coming to your bonfire anyway," she went on.

It had always been accepted for as long as I could remember that anybody in the street was welcome to attend and nearly everyone contributed something. If it wasn't something to burn it would be a tray of home-made treacle toffee or pieces of parkin or horse chestnuts to roast or various assortments of drink. There was no way, therefore, that we could prevent her from coming.

"Girls can't make Guys properly," sneered Billy. They always end up too floppy and keep falling over."

"Anyway I've seen your willy," she said in answer to Billy's rebuke, "And that's all floppy. I've seen both your willies."

"Well at least we've got one," said Billy. "You haven't."

"Well if I did I bet it would be bigger than yours," she added before turning on her heel and walking away.

"I bet she's got a willy-spotting book," he said, "And writes down the names of all the lads she's copped."

We continued the task of laying out the wood on top of the lavatory roof and were later joined by a dried-out Nicky. Before long everything was in place.

"It doesn't look much when it's all spread out like that," he said.

"We've still got a bit of time to get some more yet," suggested Billy, "And don't forget there'll be plenty of stuff coming from the houses."

The expedition had not been quite as fruitful as we had hoped, but there was no doubt that it had been an interesting one. The main thing, however, was that Bonfire Night was now looming large on the horizon and we were all looking forward to it immensely.

I've just thought of something," said Billy as we made our way along the street. "If Mary Pearson does manage to make a Guy it wouldn't surprise me if she puts a willy on it."

Now that was an interesting thought. I wondered what everybody's reaction would be if she did.

# CHAPTER FOURTEEN

"This conker's a hundred and six", said Billy defiantly, suspecting that his assertion was about to be challenged and holding the said object in the palm of his hand for me to scrutinise.

"How do you make that out?" I asked, incredulously, as we continued to walk home from school on the Friday before Bonfire Night. "You told me you'd only won four times with it."

"Yes, I know, but three of the lads I beat had conkers that added up to twenty-two. Then I played Ken Stacey. He said that his conker was eighty-four, so I was keen to win that one. With him being so tall I held the string as low as I could so that he had to bend down to try to hit it. He kept missing and I beat him easily. So, after all those four matches, it means that this conker is now a hundred and six."

I was never entirely happy with Billy's method of calculating the combat age of a conker, but decided not to press the point as we'd had this disagreement many times before and it had never been satisfactorily resolved. I was more concerned with what we were likely to be doing that same evening.

"You know the fifth of November's on Sunday this year," I reminded him, "And we won't be allowed to have a bonfire on that day. We'll have to have it tomorrow."

"Well, what difference does it make so long as we have one?"

"If we're having the fire tomorrow, that means that today has to be Mischievous Night, the day that we usually go to the pictures. So what do you want to do?"

Billy thought for a few seconds before answering. "I'd forgotten about that. I think I'd rather go mischieving. It looks like a boring film and anyway it's an 'A' so we'd have to get somebody to take us in. We can miss an episode of 'Nyoka' and catch up on it next week."

I agreed with what he said. I hadn't fancied the picture anyway and thought we'd have a lot more fun by staying at home.

"Let's see if we can think of something good," Billy suggested. "We've usually just gone around knocking on doors or spreading treacle onto somebody's door handle."

"Well, what do you suggest?"

"I don't know. I haven't had time to think of anything yet."

"Well then, let's see if we can think of something different for this year," I decided, "And I'll call round for you after tea."

When I entered the house I was greeted by Grandad Miller who must have called in after finishing his round. "Now then lad," he said, "Your mother's at the shop and your father's still at work so there's only the two of us for now."

From her position on the clip rug in front of the fire Nell gazed up at him with a disapproving look as if to say "What about me then?" I'm a member of this family you know." I was well aware that the Guy Fawkes season wasn't her favourite time of year. I think she would have been far happier if he had succeeded in his attempt to blow up the Houses of Parliament then there would have been no need for the entire canine world to be scared senseless by the incessant noise that accompanied the celebration of his failed attempt.

"Now why do I suspect that you won't be going to the pictures tonight then?" asked my grandfather already knowing the answer. "I suppose you and that friend of yours along the street will be getting up to all sorts of mischief, making life miserable for the rest of us. Mind you, it was no different when I was a lad."

"What sort of things did you do grandad?" I asked, hoping to get some ideas that we might not have thought of.

"Oh, me and Harry Crabtree used to be called the tearaway twins round Hunslet way where we used to live just after the turn of the century. We never did anything really malicious mind. We created plenty of mischief all right, but it was just good clean fun, although I don't think old Ma Tubshaw would have agreed with me."

"Who was she?" I inquired, my interest immediately excited.

"Old Ma Tubshaw was the meanest woman that ever drew breath. At least that's what me and Harry used to think. Your judgement tends to be a little cloudy however when you're just a nipper, and I did hear some time later how she'd led a very hard life, but to the two of us she was fair game for whatever escapade we could think up. About half a mile from our house there was an old pond that must have been there for centuries, but it must have been drained quite some years ago because the last time I was in the area a factory had been built on the site. Anyway, this pond had more weird and wonderful creatures in it than I bet Nomad ever came across in all his nature rambles for that wireless programme he does. One thing it seemed to have in abundance was a varied selection of frogs and what a racket they made when they were all croaking at once. Now, one year Harry came up with this idea and it was an absolute corker for Mischievous Night. He suggested that we collect as many frogs as we could and shove them through Old Ma Tubshaw's letterbox. He was an expert at catching frogs was Harry though he'd always let them go again once he'd demonstrated his expertise. On this occasion, however, he managed to catch half a dozen which he thought to be just about the right amount. We'd brought along a couple of paper bags to carry them in but it wasn't easy I might tell you what with them jumping about so much. Anyway, we were so keen on this particular jape that we waited for the best part of an hour before our intended victim stepped outside and made her way to the lavatory yard. As soon as the coast was clear we walked over to her door and pushed them, one by one, through her letterbox. We hid round the corner again until she returned and opened the door. No sound came from inside for several minutes which left us wondering what had gone wrong when suddenly we heard an almighty shriek emanating from the house. We congratulated ourselves on what had been the best Mischievous Night ever. It didn't stop there, however, as I could swear I heard the sound of croaking when I walked past two days later."

I was fascinated by Grandad Miller's story and it seemed just the sort of escapade that Billy and I were looking for to brighten up our Mischievous Night adventure. One thing bothered me though.

"Didn't you get into trouble at home when your mam and dad found out?" I asked him.

"Well, let's put it this way. We would have got clean away with it if it wasn't for Harry. He just couldn't help bragging about it. He insisted on telling people about how original we'd been and of course it wasn't long before my mother heard about it, and that of course meant my father too. There were certain things I could always get away with on Mischievous Night but if I went beyond what they considered to be the boundary line then I was in serious trouble. This was one of those occasions and I got a real towelling over it. I suppose if Harry hadn't been so forthcoming with the details of our exploits and if we'd selected someone who lived away from our immediate vicinity then we might have been in the clear. I often wondered though whether perhaps both my parents might have taken a different view and appreciated the funny side of it all when they were alone together. After all Old Ma Tubshaw wasn't anybody's particular favourite."

A thoughtful look came over his face before he continued.

"Now then, I haven't told you any of this so that you can go out tonight and do something similar mind. I don't want to be getting into bother with your mother next time I come down. Anyway I'm sure you're much too sensible."

Did I detect a sly grin on his face after he'd finished speaking? To be honest I wasn't quite sure.

I could hardly wait to contact Billy as an idea was already forming in my mind. After my parents had arrived and we were seated at the table for our evening meal I was determined to rush through it as quickly as I could. My mother was fully aware of the reasons for my eagerness to finish it.

"If you and Billy are going mischieving tonight I don't want to be hearing that you've done anything really unpleasant. I never saw the point of Mischievous Night anyway, youngsters running around in the dark and scaring people out of their senses. It seems to me that they could find a lot more meaningful things to do with their time, and don't be letting off any fireworks before tomorrow."

Nell got up from the clip rug and sat by her side, her eyes conveying full agreement with the statement just made.

"Aw, leave the lad alone," said my father. "I'm sure he's sensible enough to know not to go too far, especially when he knows what will happen if he does."

I gulped.

"Ah, Well," added Grandad Miller, "I reckon it's not much different to when I was a lad," And when my mother wasn't looking he winked.

"I've got a great idea," I said as Billy joined me in the street after I'd called round for him, and I immediately related the story I'd heard from my grandfather.

I could see he was very interested but he looked a little puzzled.

"I think it's a super idea," he said. "But we're hardly likely to get hold of any frogs around here, are we?"

"I've already thought of that. It doesn't have to be frogs though does it? I mean won't spiders do just as well? There must be hundreds of them in the lavatory yard," and I showed him the jam jar containing seven of the creatures which I had caught in the cellar and managed to smuggle out without any of the occupants of our house paying undue attention. "Try to get some as big as possible though."

Billy thought for a minute. Well we'd certainly need more than half a dozen for it to work, wouldn't we? Let's see if we can get any from our cellar. My mam will be too busy to know what we're doing."

After an investigation of Billy's basement and a diligent search in the afore-mentioned yard we re-examined the contents of the jar. It was almost impossible to count its temporary residents as they kept moving about. However, we estimated that we had acquired somewhere in the region of twenty which we decided was just about the right amount.

"This jam jar isn't going to fit through anybody's letterbox," observed Billy. "We'll have to transfer them into an envelope or something."

"Listen," I told him. I was going to call at Mrs Ormond's for some spice. My mam says she'll let me use a two-ounce coupon. If you can get some as well we can eat a few and then transfer them into one bag and use the other one to put the spiders in. What do you think?"

Billy was always better than I at persuading his mother to release sweet coupons. In fact she was probably impressed by the fact that he was only asking for a two-ounce one, and a few minutes later found us gazing into the sweet shop window.

"I was going to get Liquorice Allsorts," I said, "But you only get a few for two ounces and they don't last long so I'll get some Midget Gems instead."

"Why do they call them Midget Gems?" pondered Billy. "It's not as though you can get any ordinary-sized gems is it?"

That was a question I couldn't answer. "Anyway, what are you having? I asked.

"Liquorice Torpedoes I think. I haven't had any for ages."

As we entered the small shop taking great care to keep the jar and its contents hidden, Mrs Ormond greeted us with the same warm smile that she gave everyone. "I suppose you two lads will be going mischieving then," she suggested. "I hope you'll be leaving me alone tonight."

"Yes Mrs Ormond," we said, almost in unison. We had never considered her as a legitimate target anyway. She was always too pleasant.

"Well, that's good to know," she said. "I can't say as how I hold with Mischievous Night mind. No, I never did. My mother never held with it either and my younger brother was always too frightened of the repercussions if he ever got involved. Now, there are your sweets, and make sure you don't do anything that's likely to get you into any bother when you get home."

As we were leaving the shop I suddenly realised that I wasn't too sure about the possible consequences of what we were intending to do. However, I recalled my grandfather's earlier statement that he and his friend Harry Crabtree might have got away with it if they hadn't targeted someone in their immediate locality.

"I've been thinking," I said to Billy as he shoved about half a dozen Liquorice Torpedoes into his mouth and began munching away. "Why don't we go up towards the ridge and find a house in that area?" I explained my reasoning.

"It won't be much fun unless it's someone we know though," he spluttered, bits of the afore-mentioned delicacy dislodging themselves from his mouth to dribble down his chin before falling to the floor.

"You don't need to eat them that quickly," I scolded. "I'm still sucking the same Midget Gem."

"Well I've nearly finished them now, anyway," he replied. "I'll shove what's left into my pocket. Then we can transfer the spiders from the jam jar into the bag."

I wasn't sure what else he might have had in his pocket and I wasn't going to ask. I had always found Billy's pockets to be a source of wonder. I was never sure what he was going to pull out of there. One thing I knew for sure was that they were never empty.

Transferring twenty or so moving creatures from a large container into a smaller one was not an easy task but we managed it without losing any.

"What do you think about what I said?" I asked him.

"What! Do you mean about eating too many Liquorice Torpedoes at the same time?"

"No," I said with exasperation. "I mean about choosing a house up near the ridge instead of one near here."

"Well, like I said it really needs to be someone we know, doesn't it? What about that woman who lives near the top of the hill who stood in the doorway and shouted at us for making a noise?"

I remembered the occasion. She was an elderly lady and we had indeed been making quite a bit of noise but I couldn't think of anyone else up there that we knew.

"Can you remember which house it was?" I asked him.

"Yes, I think it was the second house from the far end of that row."

We made our way up the hill. It was already dark. I was beginning to wonder whether all the preparation needed for this one exploit was really worth all the hassle. However, as we arrived at the house in question both Billy and I agreed that it was definitely the correct one. We noted the house number, which was twenty-six, and moved further along the row to confer.

"I don't fancy anyone seeing me do this," I said. "Do you think we're doing the right thing?"

"Well, it was your idea, don't forget," he replied, looking rather uncertain himself.

Despite our misgivings we both decided to go ahead with it. We arranged, however, for one of us to keep watch around the corner while the other pushed the contents of the envelope through the letterbox of number twenty-six.

Billy decided that he would be he one to perform the dastardly deed while I kept look-out. Fortunately, it was dark and there did not seem to be many people about though the occasional firework could be heard in the distance. He seemed to be taking his time though, as if he couldn't quite make up his mind, and I wondered again about our reasons for going through with this. It was unlikely that the occupant of the premises would be aware of her unwelcome lodgers immediately, and we couldn't hang around indefinitely awaiting a reaction. I couldn't see how we were going to get much satisfaction out of it, as bragging about it could lead to the same painful conclusion that Grandad Miller encountered all those years ago.

Eventually, he joined me and, after staying in the area for several minutes without hearing a sound from the house in question, we began walking down the street in the direction of home.

"You seemed to be taking a long time. Are you sure you didn't chicken out?" I asked him.

"Of course I didn't. I was just listening first that's all. As soon as I heard someone in the house I emptied the bag through the letterbox."

The whole adventure seemed rather pointless especially if we were unable to brag about it at school and I was beginning to wish I'd never listened to my grandfather's story. Surely the buzz we got from knocking on doors and hiding round a corner would have been more exciting. I got the impression that Billy was also feeling a little despondent. He had gone very quiet. As we continued to make our way slowly down the hill, Billy suddenly gave me a sharp nudge with his elbow.

"You'll never guess who's walking up the other side," he said with a hint of mischief in his voice.

I looked across to where he was indicating and immediately felt my cheeks start to burn. The one girl in the entire school who could make me tongue-tied was casually walking along the pavement in the opposite direction.

"Hello Susan," said Billy, deciding to call out first, which was just as well for had I been on my own I knew I would probably have been too embarrassed to say anything.

"Hello Billy," she replied in answer to his greeting, "Hello Neil."

Did she really say my name with a little more feeling or was it just wishful thinking on my part?

Billy took up the conversation again. Why couldn't I say anything? Why couldn't I just say: "Susan, I think you're wonderful?" After all I was standing there thinking it.

"We're out mischieving," He was saying.

"I don't like Mischievous Night," she said in reply. "Some boys go around doing really hurtful things."

"Oh, we don't do anything bad," he went on. "We just go around knocking on doors."

A strong feeling of guilt crept over me but I was still unable to utter a sound. I must have looked really sheepish.

Billy was continuing to speak. "You'll never guess what Neil told me the other day," he said.

My cheeks burned more fiercely. Surely he wasn't going to betray my secret. I gave him a startled look.

"What's that?" she asked.

"Oh, it doesn't matter," he replied, mischievously, while giving me a wink, "It was nothing really. It was just something about school. Anyway, where are you going Susan?"

"I'm going to my grandma's house. She lives alone and she's been very poorly lately. She's likely to get frightened on Mischievous Night because her dog died last week and she's very upset because she was devoted to it, so I said I'd go and sit with her for a while."

"Does she live near the top of the hill?" asked Billy.

"Yes, she lives at number twenty-six. Anyway I have to go now, because she's expecting me. I'll see you both at school."

She set off walking again leaving Billy and me staring at each other.

"You've just put twenty spiders through Susan Brown's grandmother's letterbox, "I said horrified.

"Well it was your idea, don't forget."

"Well I didn't know who she was did I? What are we going to do now Billy?"

"We'll be all right she doesn't know it was us does she?"

"No, but how am I going to face her at school after this?"

"Well, you never talk to her anyway. You're always too embarrassed."

Billy was right in that respect but I remained deeply unhappy with the situation. I was dreading Monday morning. I had it in mind to confess it all yet I don't think I would have been able to bear her thinking bad things of me. Earlier in the evening I had visions of returning home in triumph, but as the two of us trudged our weary way there was one thing that I felt reasonably certain of. It would probably be the last time that I ever celebrated Mischievous Night.

# CHAPTER FIFTEEN

When I awoke after a disturbed sleep I made a determined effort to forget for a while the happenings of the previous day which I knew had been dominating my subconscious mind. I found it very hard to erase the fact that on Monday I would either have to admit to Susan my part in the shameful actions of Mischievous Night and face her revulsion or say nothing at all but be aware that an impregnable barrier had fallen between us. I tried really hard to concentrate on the evening's bonfire and, to a certain extent I succeeded right up to the midday meal. It was then, when I realised that I had arranged to sort out the chumps with Billy immediately afterwards, that my despondency returned. For a very different reason to my own, it was obvious that Nell was in a similar mood, which was not surprising on this particular day. She had shown very little interest in food, preferring instead to remain on the clip rug in front of the fire and direct accusing looks to anyone who glanced in her direction.

I had barely finished eating when Billy knocked on the door and announced his presence. "Are we sorting the chumps out then?" he asked excitedly.

"I suppose so, "I said, and when we were safely outside the door added, "I can't get interested much after what happened last night. It's spoilt it all."

Billy gave me a disapproving look. "Oh come on, Neil. You're not still worried about that are you?"

As we walked the short distance towards the lavatory yard I explained to him again my dilemma.

"If you're bothered about Susan Brown, you've no need to say anything have you? I mean it's not as if she knows it was us is it?"

We began climbing onto the lavatory roof via the usual route which was the midden at the end of the yard.

"I can't just not tell her," I said. "I'll feel so guilty."

"You can't talk to her anyway. You always go red and start spluttering."

"Shut up, Billy" I said angrily. "I don't want to talk about it any more."

Billy realised the mood I was in and said nothing more on the subject and we began to hurl all the assorted pieces of wood that we had collected into the yard below paying no regard whatsoever to the needs of anyone who might be taken short and want to use one of the cubicles. It was no surprise, therefore, when Mrs Wormley, who lived a few doors away from Mrs. Ormond's sweet shop, decided to make an appearance and, as she stared at the barrier which was preventing her considerable bulk from reaching its intended destination, allowed an angry scowl to appear on her face.

"I'm not having this," she spluttered, her blood pressure starting to rise. "I'm not having this. What am I supposed to do, stand here with my legs crossed while somebody orders a crane? It'll take ages to move all that lot."

"We're very sorry," said Billy, apologetically. "We have to get it all ready for the fire tonight."

Our antagonist stared defiantly at us. "If you don't manage to get it all shifted in about three minutes there'll probably be enough water in the street to put it out," she announced, "Because I can't wait any longer than that."

Fortunately, Nicky Whitehead chose that moment to make an appearance, and immediately sized up the situation. Billy and I climbed down and the three of us set to work to clear as many of the offending articles as we could. Not wishing to witness the possible consequences of our failing to do so, we managed to clear sufficient space for Mrs Wormley to squeeze through in order for her to reach the far end of the yard in the allotted three minutes. After she had returned to her house, no doubt very much relieved, we made rapid progress in transferring all the various pieces of wood to the designated site for the bonfire which was immediately outside my parents' house and my Auntie Molly's next door. It would all be assembled later in the afternoon. That was traditionally the task of my Cousin Raymond. By that time various articles of furniture would have appeared alongside provided by many of the adults who lived in the area and who, if they cared to admit it, probably enjoyed the occasion as much as the younger element.

As the afternoon wore on, most of the houses in the street were a hive of activity as treacle toffee was being made, pieces of parkin were being carefully laid out on trays and potatoes were being carefully sized, pricked and prepared for roasting in the bonfire. In our house the fireworks we had bought were carefully unwrapped and sorted. When they were put together with all the other fireworks provided by the other participants of the evening's festivities they would include Little Demons,

Cannons, Rockets, Squibs, Snowstorms, Catherine
Wheels, Volcanoes and many others, including Jumping
Crackers which were my favourites. Tea for everyone in
the street would be a rather hurried affair and even my
father seemed to be anxious for the meal to be over.
My mood, however, had not changed and I could find
very little enthusiasm for the forthcoming entertainment.

Six-thirty was the agreed time for the bonfire to be lit
and I emerged from the house with half an hour still to
go. Both Billy and Nicky were already there and, along
with several other eager youngsters, were helping
Raymond to get everything prepared.

"Have you seen this?" asked Billy pointing in the
direction of an old moth-eaten sofa standing on the
pavement outside Mr Senior's house. I could see
immediately that the object of his excitement was the
magnificent image of Guy Fawkes seated on it.

"Crikey!" I exclaimed, temporarily betraying an
interest in the proceedings. "That's great. Who made it?"

"I think Mary Pearson made it," suggested Raymond.
"Yes, I'm pretty sure it was her."

Billy and I immediately examined the effigy but could
find no embarrassing extensions and we had to admit
that she had really excelled herself.

"I hope you're going to be in a better mood than you
were earlier," announced Billy.

"Why what's up with him?" asked Nicky.

"He's moping over Susan Brown," he replied.

I could feel my cheeks starting to burn again. "Why
don't you tell him what happened, Billy?" I suggested,
rather strongly.

Billy informed him of the events of the previous
evening.

"Well, I don't see much of a problem," said Nicky. "She's no idea who it was, has she? All we have to do is make a solemn pact not to mention it to anyone. No one else knows anything about it, do they?"

"That's not the point though is it?" I said exasperatedly. "I know I was involved and if I don't tell her the guilt I would feel would make it impossible to speak to her again. It's like a barrier."

"But you can't talk to her anyway," said Nicky, taking Billy's earlier line. "You never seem to be able to get your words out."

"Well it's ruined tonight for me," I said, rather petulantly.

Billy looked thoughtful. "Are you telling us that you're going to be miserable all through Bonfire Night because of what happened yesterday?" he asked, "Because it'll be a whole year before we get another one."

"Yes," I said rather forcefully.

Billy rubbed his chin and looked thoughtful. "Supposing I told you it never happened, what then eh?"

"What do you mean?" I said, puzzled.

"Like I say, I never put any spiders through the letterbox."

"Yes you did. I saw you."

"No you didn't. You were keeping a look-out. You were too far away to see properly. I waited until I thought I could hear someone moving about, and I was about to empty the contents of the bag into the house when the lady inside started having a coughing fit. It sounded absolutely terrible and it made me realise that I couldn't go through with it, so I let all the spiders fall to the floor and watched them scamper away in all directions. I couldn't tell you that I'd chickened out could I? I would never have heard the end of it and it would have been all round the schoolyard in no time. So you can forget about having to confess all to your lady-love, who you can't even talk to, and get yourself in the mood for the Bonfire."

"Crikey," said Nicky. "Did you really chicken out?"

"Yes," replied Billy, "And I don't want to talk about it anymore, and you'd better keep your mouth shut, Nicky."

I listened hesitantly to what he was saying. "How do I know that you haven't just made that story up? Swear on your mother's life that it's true and cross your heart."

"I swear on my mother's life that what I've just told you is true," he replied, crossing his heart as he finished.

I wanted to believe it, but I had to be absolutely sure.

"You didn't spit on your hands," I reminded him.

I made him go through the whole ritual again before I became convinced that he was telling the truth. I felt as though a huge weight had been removed from my shoulders.

"I should have known you'd chicken out," I scolded, mischievously, while remaining very relieved that he had.

"You'd have done exactly the same if you'd heard all that coughing," he said, beginning to look angry. "I felt sorry for her that's all, and I couldn't go through with it. Anyway, you've no need to worry about your girlfriend now have you?"

I knew Billy was right. I wouldn't have done it either in those circumstances, and what Susan had told me about her grandmother made me feel ashamed.

My thoughts on that subject, however, were soon interrupted by a voice immediately behind us.

"I told you I knew how to make a Guy properly," announced Mary Pearson.

All three of us took the precaution of looking down and checking our buttons before turning around.

"Crikey, you don't half creep up on people," I said.

"I think you might have left a bit off," added Billy.

"I'm sure I don't now what you mean," she said, grinning.

We left her and walked over to where Raymond was surveying the fireworks laid out across an old table.

"What time are we going to light the fire?" I asked him eagerly.

"Anytime now," he replied. "There's plenty of stuff to burn. It's Sunday tomorrow and I don't have to go to work so we should be able to keep it going for ages. You don't have to go to school either so you'll probably be able to stay up longer. It could be the best Bonfire Night ever."

"Right," he said. "You can give me a hand to place Guy Fawkes in his accustomed position."

The inhabitants of Cross Speedwell Street were beginning to settle onto the various chairs and sofas which had been placed in various locations but all of which were close to the construction which was to provide the main entertainment of the evening. Some of the furniture was waiting to be burned, though there were a few items which were there for the sole purpose of providing seating accommodation and I knew that these would be anxiously watched by their owners as the night progressed to make sure they didn't mysteriously find their way onto the bonfire.

After the Guy was set in place, we all gathered round while Raymond lit the bundles of newspaper under the dry twigs which formed the base of the bonfire. Within minutes it was fully alight and flames were already dancing around the magnificent figure perched on top.

"Did you know," said my cousin, quietly, "That there's a certain school in York whose pupils aren't allowed to burn am effigy of Guy Fawkes?"

Raymond always seemed to know a lot about everything.

"Why not?" Billy and I asked together.

"Well, it's because he attended the same school as them and that's well over three hundred years ago."

"I didn't know there'd been schools as long ago as that," said Nicky.

"Me neither," I added.

Raymond was right. It turned out to be the best and most memorable Bonfire Night ever. I don't know whether it was because of the sheer relief that I felt knowing that I would not have to try to justify my actions of the previous evening to Susan, or whether it was because I did not have to go to school on the following day. I suppose it must have been a combination of the two, but everything seemed to go just right, at least as far as Billy, Nicky and I were concerned. Mary Pearson thought it was a pity that the Guy was burnt so early and that it would have been much better if it had been saved to near the end. As my Auntie Molly and Mrs Wormley both produced a tray of treacle toffee at approximately the same time, a heated altercation broke out. Mrs Wormley firmly declared that she just wasn't having it, and that she was always the one who made this particular delicacy, quite simply because it tasted better than anyone else's. She insisted that my Auntie Molly should stick to making parkin in future. Billy, Nicky and

I sampled both and though we could hardly tell the difference felt it much safer to declare Mrs Wormley the winner in the dispute. The potatoes we had joyfully prodded into the base of the fire were burnt to a crisp by the time we managed to get them out again, just as they were every year. Even now I don't know why we ever bothered. Mr Senior was delighted when, just as we were about to place the old arm chair he had provided onto the bonfire, we discovered under the seat an old holiday postcard depicting a scene at Scarborough with a faded message on the back stating it was from his Auntie Clara and asking him and his wife to pay her a visit when she moved to Dewsbury. Billy, Nicky and I stayed up longer than we'd ever done before on Bonfire Night and I retired to bed with a warm contented feeling, knowing that I would undoubtedly be up very early on the following morning just to poke the remaining embers in a vain attempt to bring the fire back to life.

# CHAPTER SIXTEEN

"I don't see how we can keep on playing," suggested Ken Stacey. "I can only see three other people on the entire pitch."

The fog had certainly got thicker. When the game had started I could see both goal posts from the centre of the field. Now, visibility seemed to be down to about twenty yards. Despite the fact that the game had been in progress for about ten minutes nobody had the faintest idea of the score. The noise emanating from different parts of the ground was the only evidence I had that the remainder of the players hadn't packed up and gone home. My thoughts were suddenly interrupted by the sight of Tucker Lane, charging out of the mist like a raging bull with the ball tucked securely under his arm

"He's running the wrong way isn't he?" I asked Ken.

"It looks like it to me. I'm sure we were playing in the opposite direction."

At that moment, as Tucker disappeared into the gloom at the other end, our ears fell victim to three sharp blasts on a whistle. This had usually signalled the end of a game. On this occasion I assumed that the match was being abandoned. It occurred to me that Tucker, if he failed to hear it and was unable to find the try line, would carry on running until his legs gave out.

With great difficulty I managed to find my way to the hut where our clothes were stored and one by one all those who had been on the pitch found their way back, Tucker being the very last. He did not seem at all pleased with the situation though. I immediately sought out Billy and joined him just as he was about to step into the hut

"I'm freezing," he said, blowing on his hands and jumping up and down.

"So am I," I replied. "I feel as though I've been standing under a waterfall for half an hour. I don't know why we bothered starting the game in the first place."

As we changed into our street clothes Mr Barnes entered the hut and apologised to everyone for the fact that the game had ended in this way. "There was absolutely no way we could have carried on," he said. "In fact, if it was up to me I would not even have bothered to ask you to get changed. It was fairly obvious that the fog would get worse. Anyway, I would like to thank you for your efforts and be very careful when you're walking back home."

We had been playing at Bedford's Field, so the obvious way back home would be straight down Woodhouse Street but Billy had other ideas.

"We sometimes go home via the ridge," he suggested.

"Well we can't do it this time," I said, "Not in this fog anyway."

"It would be interesting though, to see whether we could find our way back. We could pretend that we'd survived a plane crash and that everybody had been killed except us. Don't forget we're not expected back until dinner time and with the game finishing early I bet it isn't even ten o'clock yet."

Mr Barnes and the other members of the team were beginning to walk off towards Woodhouse Street while Billy was pointing out the dubious merits of getting lost in the fog on Woodhouse Ridge. I had to admit that I didn't find it in the least amusing.

"It sounds like a great idea to me," said a voice behind me. I turned around to see Tucker Lane emerging out of the fog, walking with the usual swagger that always emphasized his arrival.

"Hang on a minute lads," he shouted. "Some of us are going home via the ridge."

I silently cursed Billy for his rash statement. I knew that my main reason for not attempting to return home that way, namely the prospect of getting lost, would only be seen by Tucker as a weakness. I felt that we had no option now but to go through with it. At least in the unlikely event that the Wharfies might be roaming the ridge in the fog we had the most aggressive person in the entire school with us.

Either only two boys heard his shout or, like me, they didn't relish the prospect. However, Alan Bartle and Johnny Jackson made an appearance and agreed to accompany us on the adventure.

"Right, I'll be the leader," declared Tucker, "And what I say goes. Otherwise we're likely to get lost. If anybody disagrees you'd better say so now. I haven't had a proper scrap for quite a few days."

No one was prepared to argue the point. The fog was indeed very thick and I had to admit that what lay before us could be an exciting experience but equally so it could prove to be a frightening one. Nevertheless, I wished Billy had never suggested it, especially now that Tucker had got himself involved.

We left the field in a close group, none of us wanting to stray too far from the other four, and stepped through a gate onto the topmost path of the Ridge.

"Don't you think we'd better stay on this path, Tucker?" I suggested hopefully. It's made of concrete so it won't be as easy to get lost."

"No way!" he replied. "That'll make things much too easy. I think it would be a lot more adventurous if we got lost on purpose and then found our way out. Don't you?"

A feeling of impending doom crept over me and I realised that I wasn't relishing this at all. What had seemed a difficult assignment when only Billy and I were involved had suddenly become much more hazardous now that Tucker had decided to take charge.

"I wish I'd never suggested this," Billy whispered in my ear as the five of us set off in what I hoped was the correct direction. After we had travelled for what could have been no more than about a hundred yards we came across a path on the left of the main thoroughfare which descended in a gentle slope but appeared to be going in the general direction that we were heading.

"I think we'll go down here," decided our leader. "This is going to be great," he added. "It'll be like being in a maze."

"I'm not too sure about going down there," suggested Johnny Jackson.

"The ground's a bit soft underfoot. It'll be difficult just to stay on the path," added Billy.

"Don't be such chickens," chided Tucker. If we make it that simple there'll be no point in doing it."

"I think we might as well go along with it," said Alan Bartle. "It might prove interesting and anyway, if we get lost all we have to do is go uphill and we're bound to find the concrete path at the top again."

"We'd better stay close together then," I suggested. "We don't want anyone to go wandering off by themselves."

I had to admit to myself that I wasn't enjoying this one bit. If we kept going downhill for too long we would be bound to find ourselves in the area near the beck and I had vivid recollections of the day that Leonard Horsey was stuck in the bog and realised that wandering around the area in thick fog could have even worse consequences.

The path we were on suddenly became much steeper and began to twist and turn so that it was becoming impossible to detect which way we were facing.

Tucker called a halt as the path suddenly swung to the left and seemed to level off at the same time. I listened to see if I could hear the sound of running water from the beck, but everything was silent, eerie and oppressive, though thankfully the ground remained fairly solid underfoot.

"Right," he announced. "I think we've been on this path long enough. We'll leave it and start walking on the grass in this direction." He pointed to his right.

This was the first time I had been on the ridge since Miss Hazlehirst's autumn ramble but what was immediately apparent as we left the comparative safety of the path was the fact that the gnarled appearance of the trees which seemed to leap out at us from the fog as we carefully made our way were particularly alarming. The five of us stayed close together led by our intrepid leader who strode on undeterred.

"My feet are freezing," whispered Billy. "The grass is soaking wet. Why couldn't we have stayed on the path?"

Suddenly there was a loud shout of alarm as Johnny Jackson walked directly into a tree. Everyone paused.

"I don't think this is going to work," offered Alan Bartle as the bedraggled procession came to a halt. I think the fog's thicker down here because we must be nearer the beck. I think we ought to move up the hill a way."

"I was just going to suggest that," decided Tucker. "I'm sure we're sufficiently lost. Now, this is where my leadership qualities come in, because I'm going to show you all how to get home without any fuss," and he immediately started to climb higher up the ridge while we all obediently followed.

We had climbed no more than a few yards when Billy suddenly stopped and grabbed my arm. "I've left my rugby kit," he said. "When I told you my feet were freezing I put my duffle bag down while I tied my shoe lace. I'll have to go back for it or my mam'll kill me."

Our three companions were no longer in view. "Hang on a bit," I shouted, as loud as I could. "Billy has to go back down for his duffle bag."

There was no answer and the muffled voices we heard were either further away than they should have been or were muffled by the fog. We both shouted this time but with the same result. The two of us stared into the gloom.

"This is great," I said with some petulance. "First you suggest that we lose ourselves in the fog instead of going home the sensible way. Then you say it loud enough for Tucker to get involved and now, on top of all that, we have to go back to look for your rugby kit. Now we really are on our own."

We made our way back down the hill but neither of us could be sure how many yards we'd climbed or whether we had been going in a straight line. It must have taken us a good five minutes to locate the duffle bag propped up against a tree. Visibility had not improved and there seemed little hope of being reunited with our companions. Even if we could have worked out in which direction they had gone they would surely have been too far ahead of us.

"What do we do now, Billy?" I asked. "I haven't a clue where we are and I'm starting to feel really cold. I bet I get frostbite in my toes like in that film 'Scott of the Antarctic' and have to have to them cut off."

"It's not as bad as that," he replied. "If we keep climbing up the hill we're bound to reach the top path eventually."

"Well make sure you don't leave your bag behind again," I chided, as we began to move upwards.

We had progressed no more than a few yards when Billy stopped suddenly and I walked straight into him.

What's the matter?" I asked. "What did you stop for?"

"Shush" he said. "Can't you hear anything?"

I listened, but everything seemed deathly quiet. At that moment I would have gladly welcomed any sound to disturb that awful and sinister silence.

"There," said Billy again. "Did you hear that? It sounded like someone crying."

This time I heard it. "It sounds more like some animal," I suggested.

We both heard it again and tried to pinpoint the location.

"I think it came from over there said Billy pointing to the left but slightly downhill."

"I think you're right," I said. I suppose we'd better investigate but it's taking us back down towards the beck again."

We tried to follow the sound as best we could and, though it was definitely getting louder, visibility on this part of the ridge was so bad that we were having difficulty pinpointing the source of the noise. The fact that we were not walking on a recognised path did not help. At least the animal, whatever it was, did not appear to be moving.

With perseverance and not a little luck we eventually encountered our quarry.

It's a border collie," I said immediately recognizing the breed, "And it doesn't look more than a few months old."

As we approached it was easy to see why it was whimpering so pitifully. It was shivering profusely, both from fear and cold I imagined.

"The poor thing's terrified," declared Billy. "It's obviously lost and I bet it's never even encountered fog before."

As we drew nearer it shrank away at first, but started to wag its tail when it realised we meant it no harm.

"What shall we do with it?" I asked as I picked it up and let it lick my face. "We can't just leave it here."

"We don't know who it belongs to," he replied. "Look, it's got a collar on. There might be an address on it."

There was indeed some printing on it but it wasn't easy to decipher it in the murky surroundings. However, with a little effort we eventually agreed that the dog's name was Bess and that it lived at number fourteen Delph Avenue.

"It won't do us much good though," I said, "Unless we can find our way back to the top path."

I was reluctant to put the dog down again in case it ran off, but it did seem to have more confidence in us than it had originally, and anyway climbing the hill even without an added burden was not an easy task as the grass was so slippery. I decided to risk it and set the dog down. It stayed where it was and did not seem to be shivering quite so much.

"We need to find the path quickly Billy. I'm freezing. I think it might follow us now."

We started to make our way up the hill. "Come on Bess," I shouted and, much to our relief it came up alongside us.

Thoughts of trying to rejoin the rest of our group were now abandoned as we put all our efforts into reaching the concrete path at the top of the ridge. Fortunately the young collie seemed eager to keep up with us and, despite the poor visibility, we managed to keep it in view. We knew that by continuing to move upwards we would eventually reach our destination and were delighted when, a few minutes later, our feet came into contact with a firm surface. All we had to do now was decide whether to turn left or right.

"What do you think, Billy?" I asked. "Do we go left in the direction of home, leave the ridge and go back up the road to find Delph Avenue or do we go back the other way and look for the exit that takes us into that area."

"I'd rather head towards home," he replied. "Once we're onto a proper road it'll be a lot quicker, even if we have to walk all the way up the hill."

Knowing that provided we didn't stray from the path this time we would be unlikely to come across any more obstacles we managed to make more rapid progress. Bess was now walking almost jauntily alongside secure at least in the knowledge that her situation was at least an improvement on a few moments before. We were still surprised, however, when we encountered the exit from the ridge that we had been looking for much quicker than we expected. Though the density of the fog had hardly changed from the time when we began this foolhardy journey it was a great relief when we stepped out onto the street. If we turned left and walked down the hill we could have been home in five minutes but we knew that the address shown on the collar of our companion had to lie in the opposite direction.

"Delph Avenue must be one of the streets running off Delph Lane," observed Billy, "Or at least it must be very near there."

Leaving the dog to find its own way back while we travelled towards the long anticipated warmth of our own houses was never really an option for either of us and she would probably have followed us anyway. So we set off back in the direction from which we had come, though this time with the comfort of the pavement beneath our feet.

When we eventually located the street named Delph Avenue neither of us had expected the houses it contained to be quite so grand. We were both used to the traditional terrace houses or back to backs which dominated the area where we lived. It was obvious, however, that our canine companion did not share our sense of awe. She just knew she was back home. We didn't even have to look for number fourteen as Bess headed straight for it with an excited yelping sound. She stopped at the gate and allowed me to pick her up as Billy opened it. Before we had time to knock, the door was opened by a small girl who appeared to be about four years old, closely followed by a lady who we assumed to be her mother.

"Bess has come home, mummy." She cried delightedly, trying to pick up the excited collie and allowing it to lick her face. "Look, Bess has come home."

Seeing the two re-united was to Billy and me worth everything that we had endured during the morning.

"That's funny," he said, "I don't feel cold anymore" I knew exactly what he meant and I felt exactly the same way.

The little girl's parents, Mr and Mrs Tompkinson immediately took us inside and they couldn't have made any more fuss if it was King George the Sixth who had walked through the door. They told us that their child's name was Julie and that they had been in absolute despair as she was absolutely devoted to the dog. Indeed, we could see the evidence with our own eyes. Apparently it had managed to slip its lead the day before and the fog had severely restricted their ability to search. We were told to sit down and were immediately served cake and lemonade as they asked us to relate the story of how we stumbled across the little girl's pet. When, around mid-day they finally decided to let us go we each had in our pocket a shiny half crown. What had promised to be a morning's fiasco had turned out to be very profitable, and as we made our way home we each had a satisfied smile on our face. The fog was still around but it was much easier finding our way via the street. As we passed the exit from the ridge we were fortunate to find Johnny Jackson and Alan Bartle just emerging, and therefore providing us with an opportunity to tell them of the fortunate outcome of our adventure. There was no sign of Tucker, and when we asked they pointed out that they had grown tired of wandering around in the murk and decided to drop back and find there own way home. They had no idea what had happened to him. When I went to bed that night I had a very pleasing vision of him still soldiering on in an attempt to lead his non-existent troops to safety.

# CHAPTER SEVENTEEN

"Oh no," said Billy as we paused outside the Electra on our way home from school, "It's an 'A'. That means we'll have to try to get somebody to take us in."

As it was a Friday we were looking forward to our usual visit to the pictures. Every so often the film that was showing was deemed unsuitable for children under sixteen unless accompanied by an adult. On these occasions, if we weren't with our parents, we had to rely on someone in the queue taking pity on us. We scrutinised the poster.

"Humphrey Bogart in 'The Big Sleep'," he announced. "It looks like a gangster picture. What do you think?"

"My Cousin Raymond thinks it's about a detective. He says it's from a book he read that's been turned into a film. He reads a lot of books does Raymond. I didn't know it was going to be an 'A' though."

"It should be good then. I'll ask my mam if it's all right for us to ask someone to take us in."

"Me too, she was okay about it last time."

My mother was never very happy with the situation but she always allowed it with one proviso. "Make sure it's a nice couple that you ask and don't make a nuisance of yourself when you're there, and if they don't want you to sit with them then you'll have to go and sit by yourself somewhere."

I called round for Billy immediately after tea. I didn't expect him to be refused permission and I was right. I envied him sometimes. If ever he asked for something within reason, he didn't always get the conditions attached that I did.

The film started at seven o'clock on a Friday as the only day when they had two houses was on a Saturday. We had to wait until there was a sizeable queue in order to look for suitable candidates. We were aware, however, that we wouldn't be the only kids on the night searching for adopted parents for a couple of hours. Fortunately, Billy was in a talkative mood so I knew the waiting time would pass fairly quickly.

"It looks a bit cloudy outside," he said. "I hope it doesn't rain because there won't be as many people queuing up. They'll all arrive at the last minute."

"My dad says Humphrey Bogart is one of the most popular film stars these days, especially with adults," I told him. "My mam likes Alan Ladd best though, but I think he's only been in a few pictures. He's usually with a woman called Veronica Lake."

"I hope The Three stooges are on though or Tom and Jerry in case it's a boring film. Otherwise all we've got is 'Nyoka, The Jungle Girl' to look forward to.

"I think we'll enjoy it Billy, even if it is in black and white. My Cousin Raymond says it's good anyway."

"How is it that your Cousin Raymond knows so much? You're always coming out with something he's said. He's only seventeen isn't he?"

"I don't know, but he went to Leeds Central High School in town. Maybe he learnt a lot there."

The conversation continued for the best part of half an hour before we noticed that a queue had started to form outside the cinema and the threatened rain had not yet made an appearance. It was time to start sizing people up before making a choice.

There were about fifty people in the queue and the ticket office would be opening in about five minutes. We began searching for suitable couples.

"We'd better start asking," said Billy. "There'll probably be some other kids coming soon."

We went to the first likely candidates and received a prompt refusal. We also received the same result with the second couple. By now people further along the line were becoming aware of what was happening and were attempting to look the other way in the hope that they wouldn't be bothered. We seemed to be getting nowhere and the queue had begun to move. Soon it would be a matter of camping on the doorstep and asking people as they entered.

"Do you know what I wish Billy?" I said, exasperated at our lack of success.

"What?"

"I wish Susan Brown and her parents would come round the corner right now and agree to take us in."

"You wouldn't be bothered if I was with you or not then, would you? You'd just want to be sitting with your girl friend holding hands."

"That's not true," I said, wishing I'd never suggested it and feeling my face burning again. The more I thought about it though, the more I realised he might be right. I decided to change the subject.

"I don't think we're going to get in. Shall we not bother and go listen to the wireless? 'Up The Pole's' on tonight, with Jimmy Jewell and Ben Warris."

It's not as good as going to the pictures though is it?" declared Billy.

As it happened we didn't have to make that decision. A couple of minutes later we spied a familiar face walking towards the cinema, though regrettably, from my point of view, it wasn't Susan.

"Are you trying to get in?" asked Ken Stacy.

"Yes," replied Billy," But it's an 'A' film."

"Can they come in with us dad?" he asked, turning to the only person who accompanied him.

"Aye, I suppose so, but you'd better keep quiet. I've enough hassle with our Kenneth, especially with people saying they can't see anything if they sit behind him."

"He was hoping somebody else might turn up," said Billy turning towards Ken and making me feel uncomfortable again.

"Who's that then?" he asked.

"I think he likes Sophie Morton."

Ken started laughing. "Now I know you're kidding. Nobody likes Sophie Morton."

"I wish you'd both shut up," I said, not enjoying being the subject of the joke.

"Now if you're going to argue all the time," declared Mr Stacey, "Then I might change my mind about taking you in. I'm sure this Sophie Morton you're talking about is a very nice girl anyway."

None of us said anything as we handed him the money for our ticket.

There was no 'Three Stooges' and no 'Tom and Jerry' yet we both had to admit that the picture was well worth everything we'd had to endure in order to get in. It occurred to me that even if I had been sitting next to Susan Brown I would probably have been too engrossed in it to notice, though on the other hand perhaps not. Anyway it seemed very unlikely with the way things were going that I would ever find out.

When Billy and I left the cinema and said farewell to Ken Stacey and his father, we hung back a while in the doorway watching other people depart as we took the opportunity to discuss the picture before heading back to our respective houses.

"I don't know why they made it an 'A' film," I said. "It's not as if there was anything scary in it?"

"Me neither. Sometimes they make them an 'A' because they have girls walking around in their underwear, but there was nothing like that was there?" Billy sounded disappointed.

"I like the way Humphrey Bogart talks," I told him. "He makes that Phillip Marlowe sound really tough."

We both spent a couple of minutes trying to imitate the sound while attempting at the same time to portray a face that looked really menacing. I don't think either of us succeeded very well.

"Look," I suggested, having a sudden brainwave, "Why don't we start our own detective agency. There must be a lot of people round here with problems that need solving. All we need to do is to let people know. We needn't charge them or anything like that, and it's Saturday tomorrow so we could start straightaway."

"Yes," replied Billy, visibly warming to the idea. I think it would be great. "We could call it The Speedwell Detective Agency and have an office in my cellar."

"Why not my cellar?" I asked him.

"Because I thought of it first, that's why."

"No you didn't. It was me who thought about starting a detective agency, not you."

"Yes, but it was me who suggested having an office in the cellar."

Instead of allowing the dispute to continue indefinitely we decided to alternate between the two cellars.

"I can't wait to tell my mam," I said, as we made our way home, agreeing to meet on the following morning to discuss our plans. Billy attempted one more Humphrey Bogart impression before entering his house.

"Mam, me and Billy are forming a detective agency," I announced as I walked through the door.

"Yes, well you'd better get into the bath first," she said, displaying a complete lack of interest. "It is Friday night you know."

When I lay in bed that night I wondered if Susan would be impressed if she heard of our latest venture. I turned the light out, closed my eyes and dreamed of the Speedwell Detective Agency

*I left my desk and walked over to the window. Outside the weather was as miserable as I felt. From further down the street I could hear the mournful sound emanating from a lone saxophone player. He was there most days. I guess the poor guy was just trying to earn enough money to get some food on the table. This morning though, the tune he was playing matched my mood perfectly. What was I doing here day after day? Was the job ever going to pay enough to enable me to move out of this dump? My partner, Bill Maddocks was at that moment engaged on the only case we'd had for weeks. It wasn't the sort of case that could give you any sense of satisfaction, nothing that you could really get your teeth into. It was just the usual sort of thing; some dame wanting to keep tabs on her errant husband. We couldn't be too particular these days though. Circumstances were such that we had to accept just about anything that was thrown our way. I thought again about the saxophone player. Was his situation any worse than mine? I immediately dismissed the thought. Start thinking that way and it could send a guy crazy. I thought about packing up for the day. The trouble was my dinghy apartment was probably in a worse state than the office, and it was just as lonely an existence there. I realised I was lacking some female company. Unfortunately, the sort of dame I usually attracted never seemed to be interested in a lengthy relationship. It suited me that way when I first started out in this business, but lately I had begun to realise that there must be a lot more to life. Bill never had that problem with women. I suppose he treated them better.*

*My thoughts were suddenly interrupted when my secretary entered from the adjoining room. No, we couldn't really afford one and she wasn't particularly good at the job? So why did we hire her? It was for the simple reason that her old man was loaded. He was the owner of Gilly's Paper Box Factory downtown and we never knew when we might need a few extra bucks, like right now for instance. His daughter Laura had another failing. Once she started talking, which was often, she never wanted to shut up and never seemed to get to the point. So it was one of those unfortunate situations we were stuck with.*

*I decided to get in first. "What is it Laura? Is the water dispenser on the blink again?*

*"No Mr. Cawson. Well, when I say no, what I mean is that it was working fine an hour ago. Well, not fine*

*exactly but better than it was working yesterday.
I suppose it could have gone off again since. I mean,
I could check for you if you like, but then I'd have to go
away without telling you what I came in for. Now what
did I come in for?"*

I regretted mentioning the water dispenser. I waited
for Laura to gather her thoughts being reluctant
to speak in case it started her off on the wrong track
again.

"Oh, yes I know what it was. A woman rang and
asked to make an appointment. It's funny really with
the phone only just having been re-connected. Anyway,
like I was saying she asked for an appointment and she
said her name was, oh dear I seem to have forgotten it,
but I'm sure I must have written it down. Yes, I did for
I remember the pencil broke halfway through and
I had to ask her to wait until I'd sharpened it."

"Never mind the name Laura" I interrupted. "When
did you make the appointment for?"

"Now let me see. Yes, I remember it was for a quarter
before two this afternoon, or was it a quarter past? Just
a minute I'll go check. I know I wrote that down."

She came back a few seconds later proudly displaying
a piece of paper. "The lady's name is Miss Susan
Brownlow and the appointment is for a quarter past two
this afternoon."

I looked at my watch. There were nearly three hours
to go. I had no idea what this dame was like, or to what
sort of social status she belonged. I decided it wouldn't
go amiss if I made an attempt to smarten myself up
a little.

"I'm going home for a couple of hours Laura,"
I shouted, as I rose from my desk and reached for my

trench coat. "If Bill rings tell him I'll be back in the office by two o'clock."

I was back by one thirty, hoping I had succeeded in making myself look a little more presentable. I'd even taken the time to have my fist shave for nearly a week.

As things turned out I was glad to have gone to the trouble, and I have to say I was totally taken aback by the vision that was ushered into the office at the appointed time. To say she was tops in the looks department would be an understatement. I could see immediately, however, that the kid was in some kind of trouble. When you've been in this business for as long as I have you can always tell from a girl's face whether she's been crying or not, and I have always been an absolute sucker for any dame with tears in her eyes. I suppose I must have been born with some kind of protective instinct.

"Please take a seat." I said.

She thanked me and did just that, but instead of sitting in the chair opposite she decided to perch on the edge of Bill's desk adjacent to mine. I didn't mind that as it allowed her slender legs to dangle free, and I wondered why I never seemed to attract this kind of dame. She took off the cute beret which she had worn tilted to one side and gave her hair a shake. I realised then that I desperately wanted to take the case whatever it was.

"What can I do for you Miss Brownlow?" I asked, trying to take my eyes off her dangling legs and concentrate on her exquisite face.

"Can you be discreet?" She asked. "I'm afraid I must insist on absolute discretion."

The voice perfectly matched the looks and I was totally in her hands.

"*You've absolutely no need to worry on that score. Unless you've committed some heinous crime, which I'm sure you haven't, I can promise you total secrecy. Whatever is said in this office stays with me. If I need the assistance of my partner, Bill Maddocks, I'll check with you first. Is that satisfactory?*"

"*Perfectly, Mr Cawson. In that case I'd better tell you why I'm here.*"

# CHAPTER EIGHTEEN

When I awoke on the following morning the only thought on my mind was The Speedwell Detective Agency and I wondered if it was the same with Billy. I did not have long to wait to find out having barely finished my breakfast when the door swung open and Billy announced his presence.

"Are you coming Neil? I've got a couple of chairs ready in the cellar."

There was certainly no doubting his enthusiasm. However, as we occupied them about fifteen minutes later, we both realised that Billy Mathieson's cellar in no way resembled Phillip Marlowe's office.

"We need to find something to investigate Billy or it's all a waste of time," I said. Nobody's just going to walk in and give us a problem to solve are they? I mean nobody knows we're here and we can't just sit around all day trying to do Humphrey Bogart impressions can we?"

"I don't think this is going to work anyway," declared Billy despondently. "I just can't think of anybody that's going to give us anything to investigate. Can you? I mean everybody knew that Phillip Marlowe was a detective, and even if they didn't there was a big sign outside his office saying so."

The longer we remained seated without coming up with any useful ideas, the more the Speedwell Detective Agency looked like folding on its first day.

"I'm going back home now Billy," I said eventually, giving way to my own feelings of anti-climax. "Grandad Miller's coming this morning and I'll probably have to go to the fish and chip shop. I'll call round again after dinner."

"So you and your friend are going to be detectives," said my grandfather after I had barely given him time to remove his postman's jacket and lay his empty sack on the floor. "Well then, whatever next? That's quite an ambitious project to be engaged in I should think."

"Well, me and Billy saw this picture at the Electra last night and it was all about this detective called Phillip Marlowe and he was really tough. So we decided it would be great if we could be just like him."

"So that's it, is it? And what does your mother think of this idea?"

"I told her about it but she didn't seem really interested in it."

"Well. I suppose she would be much too busy to concern herself with it. Mothers are like that sometimes."

So how many cases have you got to solve so far?"

"We haven't got any at the moment grandad. We only started this morning."

"I see. So what are you going to do about it then? I suppose while waiting for a client to turn up you'll probably start by learning how to follow a suspect without being detected. Is that what you had in mind?"

My interest was immediately aroused. "How do you go about doing that?" I asked him.

"Well I'll tell you. Did I ever mention a school friend of mine called Harry Crabtree?"

"Yes, grandad," I said, recalling how Billy and I nearly got into a lot of bother trying to emulate their escapades on Mischievous Night. I wondered what story he was about to tell me now.

"Well one day me and Harry were on the tram travelling from Hunslet into Leeds town centre. We used to do that quite a lot on a Saturday morning and it only cost us a penny. The trouble was we never really knew what to do when we got there and spent most of the time hanging around the market. It was full of wonderful characters in those days you understand and we used to listen to all the different stallholders all shouting and advertising there wares at the same time. Occasionally, although I feel ashamed to admit it now, we'd nick the odd apple or pear if we thought we could get away with it. It's probably from the time I used to spend with Harry that I'm struggling now to get myself enough points to get accepted when I finally get called upstairs. Anyway, on the tram we noticed a very suspicious looking individual. I suppose what made him so noticeable was his long bushy beard and his dark glasses. Now this was winter you understand. I mean who would wear sunglasses in the middle of January? It wasn't as if there was any snow about to give off a bright glare. We knew he wasn't blind because he had no problem at all in finding a seat."

As usual I was finding one of Grandad Miller's stories intriguing. "Maybe he was in disguise," I suggested when he made a brief pause in his narrative.

"Well, that's precisely what me and Harry wondered. So we thought it would be a great idea to follow him. When he got off the tram at Dyson's clock just after Leeds Bridge we hung back for a while to let him get some way in front so he didn't suspect anything, and to make it less obvious we decided that Harry would walk about thirty yards behind him and I would walk a further thirty yards behind Harry. We agreed to change places every so often so that he wouldn't get suspicious. If he went into a shop we would wait across the road until he came out again."

"And did you find out whether he was in disguise or not?" I asked eagerly.

"No, he went into a dress shop in Boar Lane in the first few minutes and, though we waited across the road for nearly an hour he never came out again. I suppose it's possible he just worked there. Neither me nor Harry would be seen dead entering a shop that sold women's clothing no matter what the circumstances were. So we never found out. It just goes to show I suppose that you can never really judge by appearances."

I was disappointed with the end of Grandad Miller's story, but at least it provided me with an idea of how to spend the afternoon, and I called on Billy immediately after dinner.

"I've got a great idea," I told him and related the whole of my grandfather's story. When I got to the end I could see his eyes light up with excitement.

"Why don't we get used to following people while we're waiting for a proper case to solve?" I added.

"Yes I think you're right but it can't be anybody we know can it? I mean if they spotted us we'd have to explain what we were doing it for."

"Well, why don't we go to the end of Melville Road and find someone walking along Woodhouse Street?"

A few minutes later found us standing outside the shop window at the end of the street contemplating what we were about to do.

"Instead of both of us following the suspect," I said, "You walk about thirty yards behind and I'll walk about the same distance behind you. Then we'll change places after a while to avoid the one doing the following being noticed."

It wasn't long before we spotted our first 'suspect', a man of about forty walking up the street. We decided that Billy would be the lead follower and that we would change places if the man stopped anywhere. We might as well have not bothered, however, as he immediately turned into Institution Street, walked a few yards further and then entered what we assumed was his own house. The results from the next three individuals that we chose to follow were equally unrewarding and we were beginning to think that we were simply wasting our time. Then suddenly it got more interesting. A very well-dressed man, probably in his thirties and carrying a briefcase walked briskly past us and headed up Woodhouse Street.

"He looks like he might be an insurance man," I whispered to Billy.

"I don't think so Neil. None of the insurance men I've seen have been dressed as smartly as that. Let's follow him. This one looks more interesting."

Billy took the lead while I hung back. He continued to walk at a brisk pace up the hill and I could see that Billy was almost having to run to keep him in sight. Just before he reached the moor he seemed, from my vantage point, to disappear.

"He's gone into that newsagent's shop," whispered Billy when I caught him up. "You follow behind him when he comes out and I'll hang back."

He emerged a couple of minutes later clutching a newspaper but instead of immediately setting off again he produced a pair of spectacles from his breast pocket, opened the paper hurriedly, flipped over a few pages, found what he was looking for and spent a further minute scrutinising its contents.

"Well, well, well," he mumbled to himself but just loud enough for us to hear. "That can't be right. I can hardly believe it."

He tucked the paper under his arm and continued walking in the same direction. When I took up my position about thirty yards behind I was just in time to see him cross the street and turn left into Rampart Road. He turned again shortly afterwards and walked past the Mechanics Institute. He seemed to be in even more of a hurry. I looked back to make sure that Billy was keeping up. Within a few seconds I saw him turn the corner. My quarry by this time had started to walk across the spare ground heading towards Woodhouse Lane. It looked like he was heading for either the moor or the library. As he arrived at the busy main road he waited for a tram to pass then rushed across. I managed to get across just behind him, secure in the realisation that he had never once looked back since we had started following him. He stepped onto the moor and began walking along the concrete path. As he approached the old bandstand I saw something that made me stop dead in my tracks.

Billy came rushing up behind me as I stared open-mouthed.

"What did you stop for?" He asked. "Where did he go?"

I could only stand there looking shocked.

"What's the matter with you?" Billy persisted. "What happened?"

"I've just seen Susan Brown," I managed to stumble out.

"What's wrong with that? She must have been on the moor dozens of times."

"She's got a boy friend Billy. They were holding hands while walking down the path."

Billy didn't seem in the least sympathetic to my feeling of despair.

"She's got a boy friend," I could only repeat, rather sheepishly.

"Never mind that, where did our suspect go? He was getting interesting. I bet he's a spy or something. Maybe he's an absent-minded professor working on a secret invention and you let him get away."

"But she was holding his hand," was the only thing I could say.

"I'm getting fed up about you going on about Susan Brown all the time," he said angrily. "We're supposed to be running a detective agency and learning how to follow people without being seen and you've lost the only person worth following all day. We might as well go home now."

The truth of the matter was I had lost all interest in what we had been doing. All I could see was the image of Susan walking hand in hand with a boy I had never seen before, but who looked a year or two older.

Billy, seeing how disturbed I was, started to relent a little.

"Look," He said. "Why don't we make this our first case? Let's see if we can find out who he is."

Despite Billy's suggestion I now had little enthusiasm for anything connected with the Speedwell Detective agency.

"Let's go home, Billy," I suggested. "I don't think I'm bothered any more."

When I went to bed that night my mood had not altered despite all Billy's efforts to change it. All I could see as I lay there was the picture of Susan walking hand in hand with an unknown boy. Sleep was a long time in coming.

*"I'm being blackmailed Mr Cawson." If she had noticed my eyes drifting towards her legs as she spoke then she chose to ignore it. She took out a crumpled piece of paper from her handbag and handed it over.*

*It was a brief note and straight to the point. "A certain document has come into my possession Miss Brownlow, the contents of which I will keep secret for the time being. I suggest, however, that it would be in your best interests to pay me the sum of five hundred dollars before I hand it over to you. If you agree, then I suggest you meet me at the old bandstand in the park. Be there at four in the afternoon on Thursday the 23rd and make sure you come alone." The note was unsigned.*

*"The 23rd is today," I announced after handing back the note.*

*"I know. I'm going there after I leave your office."*

*"And you've been able to raise the dough?" I enquired.*

*"My family isn't poor, Mr Cawson, and I have my own account."*

*I should have known she was too classy a dame not to have funds of her own.*

*"Do you know which park he's referring to?"*

*"Yes, I think so. I assume it's the one a few blocks from where I live."*

"My advice Miss Brownlow is not to pay this money."

"I don't intend to yet, but I need to know what this document contains."

"Have you no inkling at all of what this is all about?"

"None whatsoever, Mr. Cawson."

I would have liked to have pried further but I desperately wanted to accept what could prove to be the only decent case we'd had in weeks. I decided to accept, based only on what I had heard so far.

"You mustn't follow me you know," she continued.

It was as if she could read my thoughts.

"Are you sure you want to go alone? I mean you don't really know what you're getting yourself into."

"I feel I must, but I'll make sure I report back to you tomorrow. That's if you agree to take the case.

My eyes strayed to her legs again. I'd noticed that she appeared to have an embarrassing itch that she was dying to relieve.

"Go ahead and scratch," I said. "If we're going to be working together I don't see any need for protocol."

She raised the hem of her skirt slightly and gave the offending area a brisk rub, then lowered herself from the table and replaced the beret on her head.

"I'll see you tomorrow then, Miss Brownlow," I said, offering her my hand. She took it then walked towards the door. I opened it for her and called for my secretary.

"Laura, please show Miss Brownlow out."

"Certainly, Mr Cawson, I hope everything works out for you Miss Brownlow. I mean whatever it is, not that I want to know anything about it. Oh no, I wouldn't presume to ask questions about it. I mean it's between you and Mr Cawson isn't it? What I meant to say was that if you're in any kind of trouble that you manage to get out of it fairly quickly. I don't necessarily mean to infer that you are in some kind of trouble because I don't know, do I? Oh dear, I'm getting everything confused again aren't I?"

"It's all right, Laura. I'll see myself out," said my client.

I wondered if I really needed a secretary after all.

As Susan Brownlow walked out of the door I knew I wouldn't be waiting until the following day before seeing her again. There was no way I was going to allow her to walk into a potentially dangerous situation without being on hand to offer assistance if it was needed. It was time to give the disguise another outing.

She was an easy target to follow, but wearing the beard always made me itch. The dark glasses seemed totally out of place in the gloomy atmosphere and I felt decidedly uncomfortable. I passed the saxophone player who was still churning out the same mournful melody and threw him a quarter. What the Hell, the poor guy probably needed it more than I did.

When she reached the park I knew it would not be as easy to avoid being seen if she turned around. The park due to the inclement weather was almost deserted. As she approached the old bandstand I hid behind a bush and waited. I did not have to wait long. The guy that approached her looked nothing like I expected. There was certainly nothing sinister-looking in his appearance. I heard my client say "That can't be right. I can hardly believe it," and then the two of them were locked together in an embrace.

# CHAPTER NINETEEN

Waking up on a Sunday morning, with a full day ahead of me and no school to attend, had always been a source of delight to me yet on this occasion the discovery I had made on the preceding day prevented me from experiencing that familiar feeling. Immediately after breakfast I went straight round to Billy's.

"What do you want to do Neil?" He asked. "Shall we see if we can find out who Susan's boyfriend is?"

"I don't see how we can do that and I don't think I'm bothered any more." I knew that wasn't true but I just felt like saying it. "I even used to dream about her sometimes."

"Well, can't you dream about somebody else now?"

"One night last week I dreamt about Nyoka the Jungle Girl, but before the end of the dream she changed into Susan Brown."

"Well, what about the Speedwell Detective Agency? Are we carrying on with it? We haven't investigated anything yet."

"I suppose so," I replied rather unconvincingly.

Billy stared at me with a disapproving look. "I wish you'd never met Susan Brown," he said. "Every time she's involved you lose interest in everything else."

"You just don't understand that's all."

I thought about his comments for a while and realised, that at least from his point of view, he was right.

"Yes," I said, in answer to his earlier question attempting to assume a better mood, "Let's keep going with it."

Realising that no one was going to call round to ask us to solve a problem for them we decided to ask around ourselves. With this in mind we decided to start in our own street.

The end house, next to the lavatory yard, was where Mary Pearson lived. We both decided to give that one a miss. Up to the point where we knocked on Mr Senior's door no one had taken us seriously.

"Now then lads, what can I be doing for you?" he asked, peering at us over the top of his spectacles.

"Me and Neil have formed a detective agency," said Billy, "And we wondered if you might have a problem that needs solving."

"A detective agency eh, well, well, well. Now who thought that one up?"

"Both of us really," I said.

"We thought about it after watching that picture at the Electra," added Billy. "You know, the one that Humphrey Bogart was in."

"And how many cases have you solved so far then?"

"Well we haven't actually had any yet because we only started yesterday," I told him.

"Well, as a matter of fact, there is one thing that's been puzzling me."

We both leaned forward eagerly.

"You've noticed I dare say how I like to smoke a pipe most days. It started when I first joined the merchant navy, do you see, and I've continued it ever since."

It was in fact very unusual to see him without one in his mouth, but we couldn't fail to notice that this was one of those rare occasions.

"Anyhow," he went on after a slight pause, "Yesterday morning I realised that I'd run out of baccy. So I walked over to Doughty's first thing and got myself a new packet. The only trouble now is I can't find my pipe. I always keep it in my top pocket, do you see, and I've looked everywhere I can think of."

"When did you see it last?" I asked him.

"Well I certainly haven't seen it today and I don't remember seeing it yesterday afternoon either."

"Did you have it with you when you went to the shop?" asked Billy.

"I'd already thought of that possibility, so I went round there to find out, do you see, but Mrs Doughty was adamant that it hadn't been left there. I'm blowed if I know where it is I've turned the house nearly upside-down. I reckon I'll have to buy a new one now. It won't be the same though. I mean I've smoked the same pipe for so long."

"We'll go back to the office and have a think about it Mr Senior. Then we'll call round again if we can work out what's happened to it," I said.

"Oh, so you've already got an office have you?"

"Yes, it's in my cellar today, but tomorrow it'll be in Billy's."

When we arrived there Nell had followed us down the steps.

"Maybe we should have a dog in the agency," suggested my partner. "I know Phillip Marlowe didn't have one but sometimes they can find things that humans can't because of their strong sense of smell."

Our canine companion gazed up at us with an eager look of approval.

"I'm not sure Nell could do that though. It's usually a special sort of dog."

It seemed to me that the object of our conversation had a hurt expression on her face.

"I suppose we could give it a try though," I relented, "But how will we know if she understands what we want her to do?"

As we pondered about this Nell walked over to the pile of coal under the cellar grate, peed on it and then sniffed.

"There you are," said Billy. "It's a sign."

After a brief ceremony, in which Nell was sworn in to accept the principles of the organization, the number of members of the Speedwell Detective Agency was increased to three and we began to think about the case before us.

"If we can find Mr Senior's pipe," said Billy, "People might notice and we might get other cases."

Despite Susan's new boyfriend being uppermost in my mind I couldn't help but retain an interest in what we were hoping to achieve. We decided to pay him another visit and took Nell with us.

"Well I can't really see much point in her sniffing around in here," declared Mr Senior as he stood in his doorway and directed his gaze at our new partner. "I mean I've already searched everywhere myself do you see, and she doesn't look exactly like a police dog does she?"

"Have you been anywhere else," asked Billy, "Apart from Doughty's shop I mean?"

"No. lad, I can't say as how I have."

We left Mr Senior's house with no fresh leads. "Do you think we should give it all up?" I suggested.

Nell chose that moment to bark, but I had no idea whether it indicated that she was in favour or not.

"I don't know," he answered. "We could walk over to Doughty's to see if he dropped it somewhere on the way, but I should think he'll have already done that."

"Well I'm getting bored with it all now," I said. "I mean you never saw Phillip Marlowe looking for somebody's pipe did you? His cases were always a lot more exciting."

As we walked along the street wondering what to do next I could hear a crunching sound underfoot. As I looked down I could see Nell sniffing at a few cinders. They were there every morning, the remains of the previous night's coal fires. At this time of year every house in the street would have had one. We stared at each other.

"Are you thinking what I'm thinking?" I asked.

"Every housewife in the street takes her ashes and cinders to the midden first thing in the morning before starting her housework," he said by way of reply, "And with Mr Senior living alone he would have had to take them himself."

"Do you remember Billy? He said he always kept his pipe in his top pocket. I bet it fell into the tray as he was clearing out the ashes."

Nell barked her agreement.

"If that's true Neil then it must be in the midden, but look at it, it's the weekend and it's nearly full."

We had climbed in there many times before, much to our parents' dismay, to see if we could find anything interesting, but neither of us fancied climbing in on this occasion. Unfortunately, it wasn't only ashes and cinders that were in there.

"It stinks," said Billy holding his nose.

"We could put Nell in," I suggested. "She might be able to sniff it out."

The newest recruit of the Speedwell Detective Agency chose that moment to resign and ran back along the street.

"I don't think she'd have found it anyway," said Billy. "There's too many other smells in there."

We stood there a while pondering the situation. Unfortunately, now that there seemed a strong possibility that we might have discovered the location of what we were seeking neither of us wanted to give up.

"Can't we just tell him where it might be?" I asked.

"I don't think he's likely to get it out himself is he? Anyway, I want to see his face when we take it back to him."

Eventually we decided to both climb in as it seemed the only solution.

"We'll just look near the top," said Billy. "If it was in yesterday's ashes it can't be that far down can it?"

Holding our breath as best we could we climbed in and stood on top of the whole of Cross Speedwell Street's weekly waste products. Concentrating on the cinders and ashes near the surface we prodded and poked until Billy eventually shouted in delight.

"We were right. Look I think I've found it."

As Billy pulled the object out and held it for me to see, I blew away the ashes and it became clear that our first case had reached a successful conclusion. We began to jump up and down on the accumulated rubbish in our excitement, totally oblivious now to the various obnoxious aromas that had so disgusted us only a few moments before.

"It's got to be his," I said. It looks just like the one he used to smoke."

Because of our feeling of euphoria as we triumphantly emerged from the midden and made our way along the street neither of us paid any attention to the sorry state we were in. Foremost in our minds was the overwhelming desire to present Mr Senior with his lost pipe and to witness the look of joy that would surely appear on his face. When he opened the door, however, he presented a different look entirely.

"Good heavens," he said, aghast, "What on earth have you two been doing to get yourselves in that state?"

It was at that moment that I realised what the possible consequences of our actions might be when I got home.

"We've found your pipe though, Mr Senior," said Billy after we had told him of our adventure and offered it to him.

"Well, who'd have thought it? I can see how it happened now. Mind you, you must know I can't use it any more. I mean I'll clean it up and keep it as a souvenir do you see, what with having had it for so long, but I don't know as how I could get myself to put it in my mouth again, not when I know where it's been. No, I reckon I'll have to get myself a new one."

'The Case of the Missing Pipe' turned out to be the first and last in the annals of The Speedwell Detective Agency. My mother was very forceful in her condemnation of its activities. The fact that we had succeeded in finding what we had been searching for was, to her, of no consequence, considering what we had had to do to find it. "Look at Nell," she had said. "Look how clean she is and she's a dog who you might expect to attract a bit of dirt occasionally. Compared to the state of you she's a veritable angel." It had made it much worse when the object of her praise walked over to me, took a sniff and walked away with her head held high as if to indicate her disgust. Still, as I lay in bed that night after what was probably the longest bath I ever had I realised that, despite the demise of the short-lived agency, I would always know that it had closed with a 100% success rate.

*When I checked in at the office on the morning after witnessing Miss Brownlow's indiscretion I did not have time to reflect on what I had seen, for my attention was immediately focussed elsewhere.*

*"What on earth is that ghastly smell?" I asked my secretary. "It's coming from the John, isn't it?"*

*"There's something wrong with the plumbing, Mr Cawson. Well, I mean it must be the plumbing mustn't it? Anyway, I've been trying to locate a plumber for the last half-hour, well, a bit longer really because I arrived ten minutes early today. That doesn't mean that I'm sometimes late, it's just that I was earlier than usual today. I think the driver of the streetcar must have been in an almighty hurry for some reason. Anyway, I noticed the smell before I'd even taken off my coat, and checked to see where it was coming from. As soon as I found out I started looking through the phone book for someone suitable. Well, that's not strictly true because I hung my coat up first and then started to look."*

*Just sort it, Laura," I said, wearily. "I'll be in my office."*

*Yes, Mr Cawson."*

*I puzzled over the previous day's unexpected turn of events, and tried not to notice the awful stench that dominated the office. It wasn't long before I realised* that my thought processes were not leading me to any conclusions. I tried to blame the plumbing situation but I knew that had nothing to do with it. The truth was that what I had witnessed had reinforced my feeling of disillusionment with the job. When I saw the two of them in that embrace something inside of me died a little. I was growing weary of the tedium of routine cases and now that I had finally found one that had promised to be more rewarding it looked like it was about to blow up in my face. I was still in the same frame of mind, and therefore a little taken aback, when the very person I was thinking of was ushered into the room. My immediate concern, however, was to protect her in some way from the putrid aroma that seemed to permeate every crevice.

"I must apologise for the plumbing Miss Brownlow," I got in hastily before she had time to respond to the assault on her nostrils. "Rather than attempt a conversation here I hope you will allow me to buy you a coffee in the bar down the street. The proprietor's a close friend of mine and I know he'll be able to provide us with a booth where we can discuss things in private. I've taken many of my clients there in the past."

"Thank you, Mr Cawson. I think it might be better in view of what I have to say."

As we stepped out into the street leaving, my loyal secretary to take care of the plumbing, the swirling fog was more like a breath of spring air. The establishment in question was only a few doors away and as we entered I could see, much to my relief, that the place was half empty. Charlie, the proprietor, gave me a knowing look as he directed us to an empty booth in the corner. I knew what he was thinking. Yes, he'd seen me bringing dames in before, not all of which were clients, but none as classy as this one. All heads had turned as soon as she had walked through the door.

"So, what have you got to tell me, Miss Brownlow?" I asked as soon as she had got settled and two coffees had been ordered. I took out a pack of cigarettes and offered her one. She took it rather eagerly and produced a long holder from her handbag. This meant that I didn't have to lean over quite so far to light her, which was a pity. Within seconds we were both inhaling.

"Well, it's like this, Mr Cawson. I've decided that I don't want you to continue with the investigation."

I presume I was supposed to act with surprise but I had seen it coming.

"Of course I'll pay you for the trouble you've gone to so far," she went on, "And I'd like to offer you a bonus as compensation."

"Would you like to tell me what made you change your mind?"

"Well, I suppose I owe you some explanation, don't I? You see, the letter I showed you was actually from my former fiancé, though I wasn't aware of it until I kept the appointment in the park. A year ago, to the day in fact, just before we were about to be married we had this silly argument about a five hundred dollar inheritance from my grandfather's will. I was due to receive the money on my twenty-first birthday which was in two months time. I wanted us to use the money as a down-payment on a house in one of the better class areas of the city. Steve, however, wanted none of it. He came from a much humbler background and was insistent on making his own way in life without financial assistance from anyone."

*She paused and blew out a long cloud of smoke. I could see that recalling details of the altercation was proving painful for her.*

*"Please go on," I encouraged.*

*She continued. "Because of my obstinacy and his pride the situation got progressively worse and before long we were hurling insults at each other. I said some really hurtful things to him Mr Cawson of which I feel bitterly ashamed. Things got so bad that within a few days we had called off the wedding and Steve had accepted a job in Miami. It seemed he just wanted to get as far away from me as possible. Within weeks I was regretting the hasty decision but I didn't hear from him again until yesterday. Anyway, the result of the encounter is that the wedding is very much on again."*

*I decided to take a chance.*

*"So what was in the document, Miss Brownlow, that seemed so important to both of you?*

*"It was an advertisement for a house in one of the better areas of the city, the very area that I had suggested we dwell in as husband and wife after our marriage, and it stated that a deposit of at least five hundred dollars was required to reserve the property. Steve had made enough money in Miami to enable us to contribute jointly to a down-payment, and he had been successful in arranging a transfer to the San Francisco branch of the company where he worked. Despite my happiness at the way things have worked out Mr. Cawson, I realise that I am guilty of having wasted your time. As I say, I am willing to offer you compensation."*

*"That won't be necessary," I said. Hell, it wasn't as if I'd had anything else to occupy my mind over the past couple of days. Despite the outcome, I had*

enjoyed the temporary respite from the tedium of the past few months.

I got back to the office to find the plumbing had still not been attended to. However, rather than go through the ordeal of listening to an explanation from Laura I simply told her I'd be at home for the remainder of the day and to inform my partner of the situation if he called.

I thought long and hard on the way back to my apartment. The last couple of days had proved a big disappointment and I was becoming very disillusioned with my chosen path in life. Maybe it was time I turned my back on it all. There must be easier ways of making dough than this. I decided to sleep on it and make a decision in the morning. Just what that decision would be I had no idea. Perhaps I might even take up the saxophone.

# CHAPTER TWENTY

The week following the demise of the Speedwell Detective Agency held little joy for me. It wasn't only the fact that Susan Brown had acquired a boy friend. I supposed I would get over that eventually. However, on the Wednesday my mother had proudly announced that she had obtained a ticket for me for the Jubilee Working Men's Club Annual Children's Christmas Party which was to take place at the weekend, despite the fact that the festive season was still three weeks away. The truth was that each year I went I hated it more than the previous one. I knew both Billy and Nicky would be going but it didn't make me feel any happier. I'd been going since I was about five years old and I just couldn't see the point of it any more.

"Don't be silly," said my mother when I told her I didn't want to go. "You know you'll enjoy it."

That meant that I had virtually no option, but it seemed to me to be a total waste of a Saturday afternoon. When the day in question arrived I went round to Billy's immediately after breakfast.

"What time are we going?" I asked him.

"We're supposed to be there about two o'clock, I think. Nicky said he was coming round at quarter to."

"I'd rather not be going," I told him. "I think it's a waste of time."

"Why? What's wrong with it?"

"Well, we don't really do anything interesting, do we? I mean, we go in, take our coats off and sit down. Nearly everybody from school's there and they're all talking at once. Nothing happens for a while. Then somebody comes round with a jug of tea, dips a mug in it and puts it in front of me. I don't even like tea, Billy. Then after that someone else appears and hands out bags of buns. Within a few minutes all the kids start popping the bags and some of them start having bun fights. At first nobody seems to do anything to stop it and it's all just a mess. Eventually someone attempts to take charge and tries to get us all to sing Rudolph The Red-Nosed Reindeer.

Billy started laughing, but I hadn't finished.

"In the middle of the afternoon some woman called Cissie, or something like that, goes on to the stage and starts singing and it's awful because she must be one of the worst singers I've ever heard. Then she tries to make us all have a sing-song which never works because nobody wants to. From then on it's bedlam with everybody yelling and running around until they eventually manage to take charge again and send us all home. I hate it all, Billy. I really hate it."

What I didn't know at the time was that I would be leaving the club in a much better frame of mind than when I entered it

When the three of us walked through the door everything was as I had imagined. The room was already half full and we immediately recognised several of our schoolmates. All the tables contained four seats and we made our way to an empty one which was adjacent to one occupied by Alan Bartle, Ken Stacey, Ernie Peyton and Phillip Thatcher. We spent the next ten minutes or so discussing the dismal performances of the rugby team, having played four games and lost them all. We were each making various excuses when Billy tapped me on the arm.

"Look who's just walked in," he whispered.

I turned to see Susan Brown come into the room and make her way to a table at which were seated Sally Cheesedale and Wanda Aspinall.

"I'm not bothered," I said rather unconvincingly. However, it didn't stop me noticing that she had entered alone. There was no sign of a boy friend. I decided to direct the conversation back to rugby matters.

"What do you reckon the chances are that we might win a game before Christmas?" I asked, directing the question to no one in particular.

"We've only got one game left," said Nicky, but the way we've been playing it's not likely is it?"

"We haven't been losing by as big a margin as we were at the beginning though," offered Phillip Thatcher. "I mean we only lost 17 - 6 last time, didn't we? Surely, we must win one soon."

"I don't think I'm too worried about playing anymore," said Billy, whose lack of enthusiasm lately was beginning to be noticed.

Alan Bartle looked at him. "We never will win anything with that attitude," he said.

"I know what Billy means though," I told him. "It's not much fun when you lose every game, and I've always got to explain it to my dad when I get home."

This topic continued for a few minutes until Nicky decided to change the subject. "It looks like Susan Brown's got a boy friend," he said. "That lad who's just come through the door has gone to her table and it's her he seems to be talking to." Neither Billy nor I had told him about my observation on Woodhouse Moor.

We all turned and looked at the table in question. Wanda Aspinall and Sally Cheesedale were talking to each other but Susan was in deep conversation with the boy I had seen her holding hands with a few days earlier. I pretended that I was not interested and attempted to steer the discussion back to its earlier theme.

"Who are we playing in the next game anyway?" I asked.

Nobody replied. Billy was explaining to them how I came to see them together and how we had arrived at the same conclusion. Fortunately, he did not reveal the devastation I had felt at the time. I remained quiet for a while, allowing them to ramble on. My discomfort, however, did not last long as a plump, jolly lady with bags of buns had arrived at our table.

"There you are, lads," She said amiably. "Get stuck into those."

I looked inside the bag she had placed in front of me. It was the usual assortment. Two iced buns, two current ones and a jam tart.

"All the jam and icing's stuck to the side of the bag," observed Ken Stacey, peering inside.

"It always is," I said. "It's the same every year."

Following the plump, jolly lady was a skinny, miserable one with a face like a wet weekend in Filey. After dipping seven tin mugs into the bucket on the trolley she was pushing she banged each one onto the two tables sloshing a brown, muddy liquid loosely resembling tea all over the surfaces.

"Crikey!" said Billy. "I hope she doesn't come round again. I don't think she'd be out of place in the

Chamber of Horrors at that Madame Tussaud's in London."

"I'm going for a pee," announced Billy, turning towards me. "Are you coming?"

"I might as well," I answered, suspecting that Billy wanted to discuss the question of Susan Brown's boy friend. I knew that he was aware, despite my constant assurances that I didn't care, that I was really upset about it."

No one else volunteered to come, and as soon as we were through the lavatory door my suspicions were confirmed.

"Look," he suggested, as we began urinating. "Why don't I just go up to Susan and ask her if it's her boy friend she's talking to, because I know you can't do it."

"She'll want to know what you're asking for, that's why, and then she'll probably think it's you that's interested in her instead of me."

Our discussion on the subject, however, was soon interrupted.

"Oops! Sorry, lads," came a female voice from behind us. I thought it was the ladies,"

We recognised the voice immediately. Neither of us turned around.

"What's she doing at the party?" I said, with some annoyance. "She's thirteen. If I'm still coming here when I'm that age, I think I'll go mental."

"It wouldn't surprise me if she's still barging in on unsuspecting lads when she's twenty, said Billy.

As Mary Pearson departed and the two of us squeezed out the last few drops our conversation returned to its earlier theme.

"Why don't we ask someone else? There are two other people sitting at her table."

I thought about Billy's suggestion. Maybe we could find out from Sally Cheesedale or Wanda Aspinall, but I was still reluctant to ask the question myself.

We rejoined our companions who by now had ceased talking, as each was busily chewing away. It was not long before we were doing the same. Eventually, the sound of empty bags being popped was heard from every corner of the room. I tried hard to concentrate on my dilemma regarding Susan. As the noise grew progressively louder I heard a male voice from immediately behind me.

"Come on, Cissie. Let's entertain 'em."

So the time had arrived; the time when ear plugs would have been a welcome early Christmas present for everyone in the room. This year, however, instead of a solo performance it seemed we were about to be treated to a duet.

"Oh, no," said Alan Bartle as the two of them climbed onto the stage. "I don't think I'll be able to stand this."

.We watched as they approached the pianist who had, until then, been playing the occasional festive tune. The expression on his face portrayed what he thought of the lack of appreciation his efforts had so far received. After they had glanced through his music sheets and we were treated to two woeful renditions of Christmas songs, it was evident that the female half of the duo had not improved on the previous year's performance and her partner was little better. Their combined efforts in no way helped to quell the unrest which by this time was well out of order. However, quiet was eventually restored when a club official walked onto the stage and made an announcement using the microphone in a more professional manner, thus making sure that everyone heard.

"I'm sure you would all like to applaud Cissie and Barry for entertaining us," he said deafeningly," So let's hear it shall we?"

There was a very faint ripple of applause, after which the announcer continued.

"Every child leaving the party," he said, "Will, as usual, be given a packet of sweets to take home. However, we have decided on an additional surprise for this year. Six of you will be given something much more substantial. We have gifts for three boys and three girls. The names of all those who have attended today have been placed into two drums and I will very shortly be drawing three names out of each. When I call out the name on the card I would like that person to come onto the stage to receive his or her present."

"This is new," whispered Billy. "They've never done this before."

"There must be a hundred kids in the room though," I reminded him. "None of us are likely to be picked are we?"

"I'm going to draw a boy's name out first," went on our announcer, who by now had everyone's attention. "I don't believe in girls first and all that rubbish."

A cheer went up from most of the lads at the party.

"I bet he'd have been really useful if he'd been on that Titanic when it went down," observed Alan Bartle.

The club official placed his hand inside the blue drum and drew out a card.

"The first name is John Brent," he announced.

The name meant nothing to us. He certainly didn't go to our school. However, the person in question duly went up to claim his prize of a very large Meccano set.

"Hey!" said Nicky. "These presents aren't bad. I wouldn't have minded winning that."

"Me neither," I said.

The announcer was selecting the second card, this time drawn from the pink drum.

"Norma Clayton," he said, waving the card about in his hand.

Now that name did ring a bell, first one for our school.

We eagerly awaited the name of the second boy, even though we knew there was little chance of it being one of us. Again, it was a name we didn't recognise but he still went away with a Monopoly game and what looked like a comic book annual.

Helen Thomas was the next name called.

"I don't suppose there's much chance of her doing a handstand in the excitement," suggested Billy, mischievously. His supposition, unfortunately, proved to be correct. I couldn't make out what her present was but I knew that it would be something suitably girlie.

We listened intently for the name of the third and final boy, realising it was the final opportunity for one of us to head home with something worthwhile.

"Robert Brown," called out the announcer.

Again, it was a name we didn't recognise but both Billy and I were astonished to see Susan's companion, the one who had been causing me such misery over the past few days climb onto the stage.

"He's not her boyfriend," observed Billy, excitedly. "It must be her brother. You've been worrying for nothing."

I remained unconvinced. "It can't be," I said. "I know she's only got one brother and I think he's called Peter. Anyway, he's about six years older than Susan. Look at that lad on the stage. He can't be more than twelve or thirteen. It's just a coincidence that he's got the same name."

"Well, that's that then," said Phillip Thatcher as a hand reached into the drum to draw out the final girl's name. None of us are going to get anything."

The club official scrutinised the card. "Nelly Cawson," he announced.

There was deadly silence.

"Come on," he said. "There must be a Nelly Cawson here because all these cards have been verified against all those attending. Don't you want your present? Which one of you is Nelly Cawson?"

I leaned forward over the table with my head in my hands as dozens of fingers pointed in my direction. Everyone was in hysterics. Even Billy, I couldn't help noticing, was cracking up.

"Why are you dressed like a boy?" asked the announcer at first looking puzzled, before laughing along with everyone else as he realised there had been some error over the printing of the card.

"Well, let's see what you've won then," he went on, unable to conceal his delight at this turn of events.

He walked over to the side of the stage and emerged with a doll's house and what looked like a copy of School Friend Annual.

I was devastated. How was I ever going to live this down, especially at school? I noticed that Tucker Lane was laughing louder than anybody. Was everybody going to start calling me Nelly?

The announcer looked thoughtful as he waited for the laughter to die down.

"Well then," he said. "Now what do we do with this situation? We don't have any more presents for boys so I reckon we'll just have to draw out another name."

As he was doing just that I decided that the best way to deal with this humiliation was to join in the fun and to make out that I found it just as amusing as everyone else. Surprisingly, once I got into my stride I found it very easy to do. I was beginning to see the funny side of it all and I knew that if I made it appear that I was not upset about the situation then it was less likely that I would get ribbed so much when I got back to school. I did not recognise the name of the girl who was awarded the gift and I was anxious that the subject should be quickly forgotten. With this in mind I leaned over to Billy and whispered into his ear.

"There's no way that Susan could have a brother that I didn't know about, is there?"

"You should have taken the doll's house," he said, "And given it to her. Then you could have asked her, couldn't you?"

I sat back and tried to think of something else to say. However, Billy stood up.

"Hang on a bit," he said. "I'll be back in a minute."

I watched him walk over to where Sally Cheesedale, having temporarily left the table occupied by Susan, had joined one occupied by two of the other girls from our school. He was soon engaged in conversation with her. I had an idea what he was trying to find out and I waited eagerly for his return, though I was hoping that he would not divulge my interest in the proceedings.

"What have you been talking to the girls for?" asked Phillip Thatcher as he rejoined our company. "Are you fancying one of them?"

"Don't be daft," chided Billy. "I was trying to found out who this Robert Brown is, that's all. I mean, has she got a boy friend or what?"

"What did you find out?" asked Nicky.

"He's her cousin, that's what. He lives at the far side of the moor and he was taking Susan to visit his father. That's her uncle."

"It doesn't really explain why he was holding her hand though, does it?" persisted Nicky.

I remained quiet during the conversation pretending to be uninterested.

Billy was speaking again. "Well he's about two years older isn't he? Maybe he was just trying to be protective like an older brother or something like that. I mean it's a bit lonely on Woodhouse Moor, especially near the old bandstand. I bet Susan's father asked him to."

By this time Sally Cheesedale had returned to Susan's table and I could see that the two of them, plus Wanda Aspinall were giggling profusely and gazing in our direction. I couldn't see the expression on her cousin's face as he still had his back towards us.

I was very relieved by the way things had turned out and with the realisation that I was still in the running if ever I had the courage to do anything about it.

As the announcer on the stage, with the assistance of the pianist, was attempting unsuccessfully, amid the increasingly deafening noise, to encourage all of us to sing Rudolph, The Red-Nosed Reindeer I knew that the afternoon's festivities were about to draw to a close. I had been awarded a gift that I didn't want, had it taken away again and then, at the very end, been given the best present that I could have hoped for, and as I passed Susan on the way out she turned towards me, put a hand in front of her mouth and giggled.

# CHAPTER TWENTY-ONE

As I stood at the back of the queue in Doughty's off-licence I waited for the confrontation taking place at the front of the queue to subside. Unfortunately, there seemed no sign that it would do so. Neither Mrs I-Make-No-Wonder nor the proprietor seemed in a mood to back down.

"And what's this item here?" enquired the former, agitatedly, while tapping the note book with her finger, "Polony, one and six. I didn't even know you sold polony. I've usually got it from the pork shop near the bus stop in Woodhouse Street. I mean to say, you can't make any wonder that I've waited till Monday to settle, because I don't make any wonder at it."

It was a tradition with most of the owners of the corner shops in the area to allow their patrons to pay for the week's groceries on the day that their weekly wage packet arrived. The shopkeeper would list what had been purchased, along with its price, in a small notebook brought in by the customer. This was known locally as buying on 'tick' and the notebook was usually referred to as a tick book. At the end of the week each item would be ticked off and the required amount handed over. On the following day the whole process would begin again.

"Well, are you sure you didn't send someone else in for it?" asked Mrs Doughty.

"Now who else would I send? I've done all my own errands since I've been living alone, and anyway you've got sixpence listed here for a quarter of liquorice allsorts. Now, I stopped eating those years ago and you won't make any wonder why when I tell you that they always made me spend half the day sitting on the lavvy."

"Well, I don't see how we could have got it wrong. Are you sure you never had 'em?"

"Now, come on Edith. I wouldn't lie over a tanner. No, I reckon some of the items listed here belong in somebody else's book, and I don't make any wonder when I think what it's been like in here lately."

She didn't explain what she meant by the latter statement but I got the impression, looking at her face, that the person to whom the remarks were addressed clearly did. I could see, however, that Mrs Doughty, aware of the size of the queue and the gossip that she knew would take place between the neighbours afterwards, was desperate to resolve the matter and move on.

"All right then, Annie" she said, breathing out a long sigh. "Let's look at it again, shall we? You've no need to pay anything today and I'll straighten it up to your satisfaction the next time you're in."

As I left the shop a few minutes after Mrs I-Make-No-Wonder I observed a young couple walking up Speedwell Street. Each one was busily eating fish and chips from a crumpled up newspaper. I watched them walk past the empty fish and chip shop opposite Doughty's and turn left onto Melville Road.

As I entered my house I could sense immediately that something was wrong. Nell approached me with her head held down and her tail between her legs. A man I didn't recognise who was wearing a postman's uniform was standing by the fireplace. My mother walked over to me and took hold of the few groceries I had brought and placed them on the table. Then came the bombshell.

Your grandad's in hospital," she announced, "And it appears to be quite serious. He's had something called asthma for quite a few years now, though we never told you about it. It's an illness that makes it very difficult to breathe. Well he had a very bad attack of it this afternoon, so bad that he had to be taken away in an ambulance. This gentleman has kindly called on his way home to let us know."

"When can we go see him, mam?" I asked, really concerned.

"Well, after I've told your dad about it when he comes home from work, I expect that he'll suggest we go tonight, but I think he'll be too poorly today for you to go. Visiting time is seven to eight, so I'll see if you can go to your Auntie Molly's till we get back."

"I'll really have to be going now Mrs Cawson," said my grandfather's work colleague. "I do hope Sam's all right. At least he'll be getting some decent care while he's in the Infirmary."

My mother thanked him as he let himself out.

Every Monday teatime my mother would make a stew from the remains of the Sunday joint. However, because of the latest developments she felt it necessary to change her plans.

"You'll have to go to the fish shop," she announced, after obviously giving the matter a little thought. "There won't be much time left after your dad gets home from work so I haven't got time to be preparing vegetables today. We'll have to have fish and chips. If you go now you should be getting back at about the same time. Mind you make sure that you don't go to the one——"

"I know, mam. Make sure I don't go to the one opposite Doughty's."

I immediately went over to Billy's in the hope that he would accompany me to Jubilee Fisheries. He opened the door just as I was about to knock.

"Grandad Miller's been taken to hospital in an ambulance," I informed him, hurriedly.

"Why? What's happened to him?" he asked.

"My mam says he's got something called asthma that makes it hard to breathe and that he's had it for a long time, but it's got much worse."

"That's rotten luck," said Billy. "I like your grandad."

"I've got to go to the fish shop," I continued. "I was hoping you might come with me."

"Are you going to the one opposite Doughty's?"

"No."

"My mam won't let me go there either."

"I'm going to Jubilee Fisheries."

"If I come with you can I pinch a couple of chips before she wraps 'em up?"

"If you're quick enough, but no more than that or my mam'll notice, and I was going to pinch a couple myself."

"Hang on then. I'll just put my coat on."

The shop was almost full but it looked, on this occasion, that no one would be buying excessive amounts. There wasn't a cardboard box in sight. It was, however, not moving as quickly as I would have expected.

"We need some more chips, Eddie," shouted the lady behind the counter. There was no answer.

"Have you ever seen Eddie?" I whispered to Billy.

"No have you?"

"No. I bet there's no such person. I bet she makes all the chips and brings 'em in herself."

"More chips Eddie," she repeated. Again there was no answer. "Don't know what's the matter with him today," she went on. "I shan't be a minute."

She went into the back room and emerged a short time later holding a tray of newly-cut chips and emptied them into the boiling pan. A loud sizzling noise announced their arrival.

"Now, where were we?" she asked, looking round, before her eyes came to rest on the middle-aged lady at the front of the queue. "Three times and a fish, wasn't it?"

You see that lad near the front of the queue?" asked Billy. "He only looks about four years old."

I looked at the boy in question. He did look very young to be given the task of buying fish and chips. "I don't think I ever went on my own at that age," I said.

He was fourth in the queue but looked very insignificant between the three people in front of him and those immediately behind. It was quite obvious that he did not belong to any of them.

"He's so small," said Billy. "I don't think his hand will reach the counter."

The queue had started moving again. We both watched as he got nearer the front. Eventually, when it became his turn to be served, he tried to reach his hand up to the counter but it fell a few inches short. I noticed that he was holding a crumpled note.

"What can I do for you?" asked the server, addressing the man who was standing next to him.

"Just twice and a few scraps, please love," came the reply.

"She doesn't know he's there," said Billy, and I bet everybody else in the queue thinks he's with somebody."

As the man who had just been served collected his paper of fish and chips and made his way outside, the young lad tried once again to place his crumpled note on the counter.

"Two fish and a bag of chips, please," said the lady behind him.

"The fish isn't quite ready yet," said the owner of the establishment, "But it'll only be a couple of minutes."

Ten minutes later she was given her order and left the shop. The young lad tried again to place his order onto the counter.

"I don't think anyone's noticed." I said. "If it happens again I think we'd better say something."

"Four times and a fish please," came the female voice from the next in the queue.

Before either of us had time to say anything there occurred the most terrible wailing sound. The poor mite had evidently suffered as much as he could take and he tried to speak between huge sobs. "No one wants to serve me because I'm only four and I'm too little to reach the counter, and I've been standing here for ages, and my mam's waiting for me to go back with some fish and chips, and I think I want to wee now."

"At least three people have been served before him," I volunteered.

Everyone in the queue was now most distressed to witness his plaintive cries, most of all the owner of the establishment. "I'd no idea you were there, love," she said, guiltily. Can one of you pass his note up?"

Immediately, the most dreadful wailing began all over again. "It's gone," said the boy. "It was wrapped inside the note. I've lost my two shilling piece now. What am I going to do? What am I going to tell my mam?"

Everybody tried to calm him down but he continued sobbing: "I've lost my two shilling piece. It was wrapped inside the note."

"We'd better do something. Alice," suggested one of the customers addressing the lady behind the counter. "We can't send him home like this. I don't know his mother's name, but I think she lives in the street round the corner somewhere."

An unsuccessful search of the floor was made for the missing coin. "He must have dropped it outside," suggested one. "Can't we have a whip-round or something?"

"Nay," said Alice, "There's no need for that. I think he deserves to get his fish and chips for nowt on this occasion."

As he was handled his precious bundle this seemed to satisfy everyone in the shop, but not apparently the lad himself. He looked very close to tears again.

"There, there," said the shop owner, soothingly. "There's no need for any more tears. I know you've been kept waiting a long time but you've got your fish and chips now, haven't you?"

"But I haven't been given any change," he wailed. "I have to take sixpence back or my mam'll think I've spent it on sweets."

By this time Alice had resigned herself to making a substantial loss on this particular transaction, and with the eyes of everybody in the queue fixed on her, she reached into the till and handed down to him a bright, shiny sixpence.

The boy mumbled a tearful 'Thank you very much mrs. and, as he reached the door, he paused and looked back, his small face brightening noticeably. "Look!" he said, excitedly. "I've found my two shilling piece. I must have put it in my pocket." He looked back with a big smile on his face and then, with everyone gaping, he was out of the door.

"I think I know why his mam sends him by himself," said Billy, smiling.

Immediately after we had eaten our fish and chips my mother and father left and I went next door to my Auntie Molly's leaving Nell alone in the house, her protests at this treatment being to no avail.

"You can play Subbuteo with us if you like," said my Cousin Raymond, almost as soon as I'd walked through the door. "We've got it set up in the back room."

Subuteo was the most wonderful table football game I'd ever seen, but this was the first occasion on which I'd been invited to play. My cousin had invited two friends round of his own age and they seemed to be reluctant to have me take part in the proceedings. Raymond wasn't having it though.

"We're supposed to be doing the F.A. Cup aren't we? If we want the results to be realistic Neil can play for the weaker teams."

I had no objection to this. I was just keen to be involved and take my mind off Grandad Miller's illness. A list of matches had already been made and this was carefully being scrutinised.

"Look! Here's one that Neil can play," announced my cousin, "Arsenal against Halifax Town. Neil can be Halifax."

It was all the same to me, just as long as I was involved. Raymond started to explain the rules of the game to me and how to flip the figures with the tip of my finger.

"Now this is the third round of the F.A. Cup," he said, and we had just made the draw before you came in. Now because you're a lot younger and haven't played the game before, you can play for any team that's not expected to win. Bear in mind though that you always get some surprises in the F.A. Cup, so you could end up just winning one if you pick the game up quickly. You don't play until the fourth match so you can watch how we do it for the first three games. The problem is you'll probably only be here until Auntie May and Uncle Tom come back from the Infirmary, so it doesn't look as if you'll get to play many."

With each game lasting only a few minutes it wasn't long before it got around to my turn. Sheffield Wednesday had beaten Manchester City, Portsmouth had beaten Coventry and Liverpool had beaten Chelsea. One of my cousin's close friends was my opponent and I had already decided that Halifax Town were about to provide the shock of the third round. What actually happened was that they were beaten seven - nil. Nevertheless, two whole hours passed pleasantly by before my parents arrived home and, despite having enjoyed immensely what I had been involved in, I was anxious to hear the news about Grandad Miller. I decided, therefore, not to linger. Thanking my cousin for the evening's entertainment I immediately returned home.

I could see at once that the news wasn't good. It was fairly obvious that my mother had been crying and I waited for someone to say something.

"Your grandad is very very poorly," she eventually managed to say. "He didn't speak the whole time we were there and he had to wear something called an oxygen mask. It won't surprise me at all if he has to spend Christmas in the Infirmary."

I was really upset by the news. "Can I go see him with you the next time you go?" I asked.

"I'm not sure. I'll have to think about it."

"Now, cheer up," said my father, seeing the sad expression on my face and deciding to join in the discussion. It's early days yet. We'll see what tomorrow brings, eh."

I immediately went round to Billy's to tell him the news. "Grandad Miller's very poorly and he has to wear an oxygen mask all the time."

"Crikey!" He replied. "That's what those test pilots wear when they're testing out those new jet planes. You know, we've seen them on the news at the Electra. They say they'll be able to break the sound barrier soon."

"He might not be home in time for Christmas though, Billy"

"That's rotten luck. When he does come home I wonder if they'll let him keep his oxygen mask."

When I went to bed that night I prayed that Grandad Miller would soon recover. The possibility that he might not be out of hospital for the Yuletide festivities was an upsetting one, and even worse was the thought that he might never came out at all. What if I never saw him again? By the time I went to sleep I was really depressed.

# CHAPTER TWENTY-TWO

"I'm writing a letter to Tim," said my mother, looking up from the writing desk as I announced my arrival downstairs, "To let him know about your grandad. There's some warm water in the sink and your Weetabix is already in the dish. The milk's on the cellar head like it always is. It should be all right. I don't think it's off today. Nell can wait for her breakfast until I've finished."

My canine companion always spent the night on a dog blanket at the back of the cellar door. This was so that she could immediately leap into action if a would-be intruder attempted to break into the house via the coal grate. So far she had not had the opportunity to show her heroics. Her countenance this morning, however, showed a distinct look of disapproval at the unforeseen change to her routine. It was a quarter past eight on Thursday morning and Grandad Miller was spending his fourth day in Leeds General Infirmary. He had shown little improvement and I knew that my mother was really worried. Even more worrying for me was the fact that I still hadn't been to see him. I washed my hands and face in half the time I usually took, secure in the knowledge that my mother was not watching me as closely as she otherwise would have done.

"Can I go and see Grandad Miller tonight, mam?" I asked as I started to tuck into my Weetabix and tried to ignore the accusing looks that Nell was directing my way.

"You'll have to do your own jam and bread this morning," she said, completely ignoring my question. "I must get this letter finished, and be careful of the bread knife. It's very sharp."

I decided to let her get on with it and to finish eating my breakfast in silence. I usually called round for Billy at ten minutes to nine, hoping he'd be ready but on this occasion, as I was about to leave, my mother got up from the writing desk and handed me a sealed envelope.

"I want you to give this note to your headmaster," she announced, "And make sure you don't open it before you hand it to him. I know he teaches in your class so you can present it before he starts his lesson."

"What does the note say, mam?" I asked, genuinely puzzled.

"That's not for you to know yet. Now get yourself off to school or you'll be late."

I knew it was pointless to pursue the matter but I remained most intrigued by what the envelope might contain.

"Look what I've got," I said to Billy as we passed the Electra on our way to school. "It's a note. My mam said I've to hand it to Old Rawcliffe before he starts the lesson."

"Crikey, did she really call him Old Rawcliffe?"

"Don't be daft. She just told me to give it to the headmaster."

"What does the note say then?"

"I've no idea. She wouldn't tell me. She sealed it up and told me I hadn't to open it before I hand it over."

I could see Billy was just as intrigued as I was.

"Have you done something wrong? Maybe your dad was supposed to give you a good hiding for something and he didn't have time so your mam wants the teacher to do it."

"Thanks, Billy. That's a really daft idea. If my dad wanted to wallop me for something he'd find time to do it. Anyway, I haven't done anything wrong, have I?"

Billy thought for a moment. "Isn't there any way we could open it without him finding out? I remember a film once about this boy who brought a letter home from school to hand to his father. He was dead worried about what was in it, so he held it over the spout of a kettle when it was boiling so that the steam would unseal it."

"And did it work?

"Oh yes, it worked O.K. but not before he'd scolded his hand and dropped the letter on the floor. Anyway, he picked it up, read the note then put it back in the envelope and it sealed itself, but it took ages for it to dry out again."

"I don't know where there is a kettle in school anyway," I said as we vaulted over the low wall into the schoolyard, "And apart from that there wouldn't be time. I'm supposed to give it to him after assembly."

We joined the line of boys just as the bell rang, and we all followed Mr Barnes into the hall.

"Wait until after playtime before handing it to him," suggested Billy, whispering in my ear. "It might give us time to think of something."

I thought about his suggestion as the headmaster mounted the platform. Could I get away with it? What if it was something he needed to know straight away? However, I was desperate to find out what it contained. I decided to risk it.

All through the morning lessons I was trying to think of some way to open the envelope without anyone knowing, but by the arrival of the morning break I had still been unable to think of anything. As I left the room Billy came up alongside.

"Let's go into the cloakroom and try the radiator," he suggested. "Maybe the heat will be enough to melt the glue."

Although the idea did not really seem feasible to either of us we gave it a go.

"It's no use Billy," I said, after having held the envelope in close proximity for several minutes with no success whatsoever. "We might as well go outside and play for a while. There's still ten minutes left. I'll just hand over the note when we come back in and tell him I forgot to give it to him earlier."

I made sure I was the first to enter the classroom.

"Excuse me, sir," I said, announcing my presence as he was studying a book.

"What is it, boy? Can't you see I'm busy?"

"I forgot to give you this note from my mam, sir. I was supposed to hand it to you when I arrived at school, but I forgot."

He glared at me over his spectacles. "Well, you'd better give it to me now then, hadn't you?"

"Yes, sir." I handed it over.

It was obviously a very brief note as he spent no more than a few seconds scrutinising it.

"You should indeed have handed me this note as soon as you entered the premises. It would have been much more convenient."

"Sorry, sir,"

"You're not to return to school this afternoon. I think your mother would be the best person to explain the reason to you. Leave at the normal time this morning and I don't expect to see you back until tomorrow. There's one other thing you should know. Your mother writes a very neat and persuasive letter. You would do very well to take a leaf out of her book. Right, you can go to your seat now."

"Yes, sir. Thank you, sir."

I walked over to my desk feeling really puzzled just as the other pupils in the class were starting to arrive, Billy in the lead.

"Did you hand it to him?" he asked straight away. "What did it say?"

"I'm not coming back to school this afternoon. That's what he told me, but he wouldn't say why. He said I'd have to ask my mam when I get home."

"Crikey, I wish it was me."

"I think my mam must be taking me to see Grandad Miller this afternoon. Maybe he's feeling a lot better and started talking again."

"I can't see Old Rawcliffe letting you off school for that, Neil. I mean you could just go at night time couldn't you?"

What Billy said made a lot of sense, but it was obvious that I would not discover the reason for my having the afternoon free until I got home. I eagerly awaited the end of the morning's lessons and admit to paying little attention to the headmaster's efforts at making the teaching of geography interesting enough to hold the attention of a class of ten and eleven year olds.

As soon as the bell announced the end of the first half of the day's activities I shamefully totally ignored my constant companion and closest friend and ran home as if I were an Olympic sprinter. My mother had the dinner on the table as I breathlessly entered the house.

"Where are we going mam?" I gasped out eagerly. Why don't I have to go back to school?"

"Eat your dinner first," she replied, "And I'll explain when you've finished, and don't bolt your food down. You've plenty of time."

That was easier said than done. When you're desperate to hear a piece of news how do you concentrate on enjoying your food while eating in a leisurely and dignified manner?

"I'm taking you to see your grandad this afternoon," announced my mother as soon as she saw the clean plate in front of me.

"I wondered if that might be it, but Billy thought that wouldn't be enough to get Old Raw—, I mean Mr Rawcliffe, to give me the afternoon off."

My mother looked across at me with a sad expression. "He let you off school for a very good reason. Your grandad has taken a turn for the worse and you have to face the fact that this may be the last time you ever see him."

I said nothing for a while, taking in the full implication of what she was telling me. Was the thing I had dreaded most about to happen?"

"Visiting Time is two o'clock to three o'clock," she went on after giving me time to recover from the shock. "So we'd better set off as soon as you've had a wash."

The bus journey into town was a very quiet one and we were well into North Street before either of us broke the silence. My mother spoke first.

"We were given the news last night while we were at the hospital and I was talking to your dad after you'd gone to bed about what we should tell you. He agreed with me that you are old enough now to be told the truth, and we thought it was only fair, knowing how close the two of you are that if, God forbid, things go as expected, you should be given this last chance to see him."

I knew I certainly didn't feel grown up but I managed to stop the tears from flowing. However, as I entered the ward, my mother taking my hand and directing me to his bed, I was totally unprepared for the sight that met my eyes. My grandfather was deathly pale and, though he was still wearing the oxygen mask, his laboured breathing sounded dreadful.

As I stood there looking at him, the nurse took my mother to one side. I could tell from the expressions on their faces as they spoke in whispered tones that there had definitely been no improvement since the previous day. It seemed to me that the conversation taking place between them might even be indicating that he was much worse. Shameful as it seemed to me afterwards, at that particular time I desperately wanted to be out of the place.

We stayed beside him for about twenty minutes before my mother seemed to realise that it was serving no real purpose and was only making me more distressed.

"I think we'll leave him sleeping now," she whispered and guided me out of the ward.

The journey home was very similar to the earlier one with neither of us speaking much.

"Billy should be home from school by now," said my mother after we had safely arrived home. "You need to cheer yourself up a bit. Go see if he's playing out, and try to take your mind off your grandad for a while."

I wasn't really in the mood to do what my mother suggested. Despite this I soon found myself knocking on his door and opening it at the same time. Mrs Mathieson was the only occupant of the room.

"Our Billy's not come home from school yet," she said.

I looked at her clock on the shelf above the fireplace. It read twenty past four.

"Oh, thanks Mrs Mathieson. I'll see him later then."

As I left the house I remembered that I had run home from school at twelve o'clock instead of walking back with him like I had always done before. I couldn't help wondering if it had made him annoyed. I stepped outside and began walking towards the schoolyard in case he was still hanging about there. As I reached the Electra and paused momentarily with the intention of looking at the poster on the wall which advertised the weekend's film I happened to glance briefly to my left and was relieved to see Billy walking up the ginnel opposite. He held an ice cream cone in his hand and was engaged in his usual habit of sucking its contents through from the wrong end.

"Better watch out, Billy," I shouted as I rapidly approached him, "Or the top might drop off."

"You left a bit quick Neil," he replied, looking up, while at the same time heeding my warning and restoring the cone to its more natural upright position. "I never even noticed you go out of the door. After school finished and I was walking home I found a threepeny bit on the floor. I was going to buy a Knockout comic with it but I heard Tony shouting and it seemed to come from Craven Road. So I decided to get an ice cream instead."

"Isn't the Knockout that one with Our Ernie, where he says 'What's for tea, ma?' and his dad always says 'Daft I call it'? Anyway I think it's fourpence so you wouldn't have had enough."

"I didn't know that. What happened when you got home?"

I realised that I owed him an apology and an explanation.

"I'm sorry, but I just couldn't wait to find out what was so important for old Rawcliffe to let me leave early, and when I got home my mam told me she was taking me to the Infirmary. When we got there I saw the nurse talking to her and she looked really sad. I think my grandad's dying Billy."

My closest friend remained silent and stared at the floor. Billy wasn't usually lost for words. He even seemed to be losing interest in his ice cream. Eventually he looked up.

"He's not forced to be though, is he? I mean he's in the Infirmary and they might get him better."

I really wanted to share Billy's optimism but I knew that he hadn't seen him lying in the hospital bed like I had and, no matter how hard I tried, the image would not go away. As we walked back home together I just felt in my heart that I would never see my grandfather again.

# CHAPTER TWENTY-THREE

Things weren't going right. This was hardly surprising as they hadn't been going right all season. However, this was the last game before Christmas and we had been very keen to make a good show of it. Unfortunately, we were nine points down before we knew what had hit us and our situation was about to get much worse. Nicky was racing for the line when he was tackled around the ankles. He went down very heavily and just about everyone on the pitch must have heard the crack. He was clutching his right arm and rolling on the ground in agony. As we all anxiously watched, Mr Barnes and the teacher from the other school raced onto the pitch and joined the referee who was trying to take command of the situation.

"It looks like it's broken," said our coach as he took hold of Nicky's arm and scrutinised it. The noise that came out of its owner's mouth as it was being examined bore witness to that fact.

"We'd better take him into the warmth of the changing room," suggested his opposite number.

Tucker Lane stood with his arms folded as he observed the proceedings, his face betraying signs of impatience.

"Do you think they'll have to send for an ambulance, Neil?" asked Billy.

"I think he'll probably have to go to the Infirmary but somebody might just take him on the tram."

As soon as I mentioned the word 'Infirmary' my thoughts immediately drifted back to the sight of my grandfather lying there helpless. I realised that Billy was speaking again.

"I think they usually put it in a pot when it's broken."

I suppose we'll all have to sign it then when he gets home."

"It's taking a long time getting the game started again," said Tucker as he walked over to join us.

"I think Nicky's broken his arm," I informed him.

Tucker continued undaunted. "I mean it must be five minutes ago since we stopped playing,"

"They'll probably have to take him to the Infirmary to put a pot round it," Billy added.

Tucker wasn't listening. "We're only nine points down. We can soon get back into it."

"I bet it hurts something rotten," I said quite forcefully.

His face finally betrayed a glimmer of understanding. "What are you talking about?"

"We've been trying to tell you," said Billy, "That we think Nicky's broken his arm and they'll probably have to take him to the Infirmary to get it fixed."

"It'll most likely mean that we won't be able to finish the game," I added.

We could both see that Tucker was far from happy. "Well that wouldn't stop me. Why can't they just strap it up and let us carry on playing? He could shove the ball under one arm and he can still run." He thought for a moment. "I suppose it wouldn't be easy to catch it though," he conceded. "I think I'll go and have a word with the ref and see what he thinks."

Despite Tucker's eagerness for the game to continue and his reluctance to accept that a broken arm was a valid reason for leaving the field of play the outcome was that the match, as we had expected, was abandoned. The father of one of the boys of Burmantofts School, who had been our opponents, owned a car and he kindly took Nicky and Mr Barnes to Leeds Infirmary. The rest of us had a choice of how to get home. It was a case of either two trams, one to the Corn Exchange in the town centre followed by one from there to the Primmy, or a short walk to the number sixty-one bus, which left another short walk at the other end. As it happened only five of us accepted the bus option, and Billy and I were joined on the journey home by Leonard Horsey, Ernie Peyton and Johnny Jackson.

"I can't see Nicky playing again for a long time," said Ernie Peyton, as we sat at the back of the bus on the top deck."

"Me neither," volunteered Billy. "But Tucker thought he should have carried on playing this morning so that the game wouldn't have had to be abandoned. He said that if it had been him he wouldn't have let the side down like that."

"That's stupid," said Leonard. "Nobody could play with a broken arm, not even Dickie Williams."

My thoughts inevitably turned towards my grandfather probably dying in one of the wards upstairs while our team-mate was having his arm set in the accident and emergency section below. "We'll just have to see how things work out," I mumbled, "But it's tough luck on Nicky."

When I arrived home, much earlier than expected, I hastily informed my mother of the morning's dramatic events.

"They'll have to put his arm in a pot," she announced. "I suppose it's because the ground would be so hard with all this frost we've been having. I'm surprised the game ever got started."

I realised that my mother's point of view was quite a valid one. It was a gloriously sunny morning, but extremely cold and at the time we had kicked off the ground was still frozen in places. All of us, however, had been keen for the game to go ahead.

There was still half an hour to go before my father arrived home from work and we were able to sit down to dinner, so I went round to Billy's.

"Do you think Mrs Whitehead knows about his accident yet?" I asked him.

"I hadn't thought of that. Maybe we should go round and ask," he suggested.

However, just as we were approaching her door the same car that had carried Nicky to the Infirmary brought him back home again.

"Barnesy's still with him," observed Billy.

"Are you all right, Nicky?" I asked, as he was helped out of the car by our team coach and the father of the boy from the opposing team.

Nicky's face beamed with delight. "Look, I've got it in a pot," he said delightedly. "I'm going to get everybody I know to sign it. I bet I won't have to go back to school for ages."

"Well, we'll have to see about that," said Mr Barnes, not looking particularly pleased with the situation.

"I think we'd better leave him to talk to his mam and dad," said Billy as we watched Mr Barnes thank the driver of the car before accompanying Nicky into the house. "We'll call round to see him this afternoon."

I left Billy and went back home as I knew my father would be arriving soon.

"Me and your dad have something to tell you but it can wait until we've finished eating."

Nell's ears pricked up suggesting that she expected to be included in the conversation.

"I feared it might have been the bad news I had been expecting about my grandfather, yet my mother's face did not convey that impression. I had been told that it was likely that he would die in hospital but no one seemed to be able to say how long he might linger.

My father duly arrived and we sat down to eat. When the meal was over my father turned towards me. "We're taking you to see your grandad this afternoon. We had some good news when we went to the Infirmary last night. He's still very poorly but the nurse told us he's out of immediate danger. They're going to keep him in for a few days more but he should certainly be out of there before Christmas. Now, that's good news isn't it?"

It certainly was and I could hardly believe it. I could now look forward to the festive season with the same excitement that I always had.

"Have I got time to go and tell Billy?" I asked.

Yes," said my mother, "But don't be too long. We'll have to leave very shortly and you'll need to get washed and smarten yourself up a bit up before we go."

"Right mam, but I'll just pop round to see if Nicky's all right as well."

I had no intention of delaying things as I was extremely keen to see my grandfather looking a little more like I remembered him. My sight of him on the last occasion we had met had been quite a shock. I could tell immediately that Billy was also delighted by the news and as we knocked on Nicky's door a few minutes later I just knew that things were going to be all right now.

"We called round to see how Nicky is," said Billy as Mrs Whitehead opened the door and beckoned us inside.

"Oh, he'll get over it I reckon," said his father, from the armchair. "You've got to expect these things occasionally when you play a man's game. Isn't that right, lad?"

He turned towards Nicky who had just walked in from the adjoining room proudly holding out his encased arm for our inspection, which already included a couple of signatures.

"Yes, dad," replied our injured team-mate.

"I'm not so sure," indicated his mother. "Surely it should be a boy's game he should be playing."

"Aw, mam," objected Nicky, obviously feeling a little embarrassed that she failed to see the importance of taking part in what could on occasions be a very rough game.

"Now, come on ma," said his father, what do you want the lad to be doing, playing netball with the girls?"

A disagreement then developed between his parents as his mother attempted to persuade her husband that netball, which was the game she had played when she was at school, could be every bit as rough as any boy's game. Making my excuses, and anxious to see my grandfather, I left Billy talking to Nicky and walked back along the street. Half an hour later my parents and I walked to the bus stop in Woodhouse Street and boarded the number sixty bus which took us, via Hyde Park and Mount Preston, to Leeds Town Hall in The Headrow. From there it was a short walk along Calverley Street to the Infirmary.

As we entered the building the Town Hall clock struck twice. We were just in time to take advantage of a full hour's visiting. The first thing that struck me as we entered the ward was the fact that Grandad Miller was sitting up in bed and was no longer wearing the oxygen mask that had contributed to his looking so ill on my previous visit. On this occasion, as soon as he saw us, he smiled. It was good to see.

"Now then, lad," he greeted me. "What do you reckon today then, eh?"

I was really pleased to see him sitting up and talking with no sign of the laboured breathing which was so pronounced on my previous visit, and I told him so. It was as though he'd had nothing more life-threatening than a slight cold.

My parents had little more time than to greet him before one of the nurses approached. "Mr Miller's doctor would like to have a word with one of you," she said.

"Why don't you both go?" suggested my grandfather. "Me and the lad have got a lot of things to talk about. I don't reckon he'll keep you very long."

"If you're sure you don't mind dad," said my mother. "We'll be back as soon as we can then." She turned towards me. "Now don't you be tiring your grandad out by asking too many questions. I know what you can be like once you get started."

"Nay, leave the lad alone, lass. We're just going to have a brief conversation that's all, and catch up with what's been happening, as you might say."

As both my parents were being escorted out by the nurse I couldn't help wondering why the doctor had asked to see them. Was he, after all, going to tell them that my grandfather was still dying despite the obvious improvement he was showing?

"Now don't worry lad," said Grandad Miller, noticing my look of concern and making a successful interpretation of the cause of it. "I'm going to be all right, at least for a year a two, and if you're prepared to listen I'll tell you how I know."

If he said he knew he was going to be all right with such certainty then I was quite happy to accept what he had told me. I leaned forward eagerly to hear what he had to say.

"Well. I might not look so bad now," he began, "But it's been a rum do, I can tell you. When I first came in here I thought I was on my last legs and that's no mistake. I've had attacks like this before mind you, though I suppose your mother never mentioned them, eh. No I suppose she wouldn't have. Anyway, what I mean to say is that I've never experienced anything as bad as this, no, not ever. I just couldn't get my breath you see, no matter how hard I tried. I was just gasping all the time, but the worst thing is it just didn't wear off like it had done before. I was constantly struggling just to stay alive."

"What about the oxygen mask they gave you?" I asked. "Didn't that help?"

"Ay, I suppose it did for a short while, but they're damned uncomfortable things to wear."

"When did you start to feel better than, grandad?"

"Well, like I said I was just lying there trying to breathe in the best way that I could without making any real progress. Eventually, I just decided that I'd had enough. I just stopped struggling and allowed myself to fall into a deep sleep. I knew I was dying but I no longer cared. You see, the pain I was getting from all my strenuous efforts to stay alive was starting to recede.

After a while it seemed to me that I had started to float through a long tunnel, but I felt very calm and relaxed. All the pain had gone and I had no bodily sensations at all, and I think I must have stopped breathing altogether. Anyway, I felt quite contented that I was going to meet my maker. After all, I felt I'd had a decent life. So I had no qualms about it. However, after a short while, and I was feeling quite at peace with myself you understand, I saw a bright light in the distance. It was tiny at first, but it gradually got bigger, and a wonderful warm feeling swept over me and I knew I desperately wanted to reach that light. Then as I got nearer to it I thought I could see a figure standing in the middle and it was calling to me. I recognised the voice immediately. It was my Ethel and she looked just the same as the day we got married, even though she was turned sixty when she was taken from me. I couldn't hear what she was saying though, not at first, but she seemed to be shouting some sort of warning. Now you must understand that I was really looking forward to reaching this light because I had it in mind that it must be Heaven, but when I got closer I could make out what my wife was shouting to me.

"What was she saying, grandad?" I interrupted, fascinated by what he was relating.

"She was yelling at me, telling me to go back. She said she'd had a look at the book and she knew they wouldn't let me in because I was still a few points short. That warning struck me like a bolt of lightning and before I knew it the pain had returned and I realised I was still lying in the hospital bed struggling for breath again. It was then that I realised that if I could set the record straight, so to speak, by giving myself a little more time and getting myself a few more points in the book of reckoning at the same time then I had no need to fear the thought of dying anymore because I knew that the wonderful place that I had had a brief glimpse of was beckoning. After that it seemed so easy to relax and begin breathing normally again, and that's why you see me like I am today, but it's been a rum do and no mistake."

My mother and father returned shortly after Grandad Miller had finished telling me how he had returned to the land of the living. They told me that all the nurses and doctors were astonished at his recovery, but took great pains to point out that he was still very poorly and that he could have another attack at any time. They had decided to keep him in for a further few days, but if his condition remained stable they promised to discharge him in time for Christmas. As the bell sounded for the end of visiting time and we said our farewells and made our way to the door my grandfather beckoned my mother over.

"I want you to do something for me lass on the day I come out of here. I want you to call at a florist in Leeds market and buy a large bunch of flowers. I'll give you the money for them later. Then I want you to attach a 'Thank You' note and write on it 'A big thank you to all the doctors, nurses and general staff of Ward 17 for the kind care and attention you have given me during my recent illness.' Will you do that for me, May?"

"Of course I will dad, if that's what you want."

At that moment we took our leave of him and as I was about to walk through the door my grandad looked at me and winked, and I knew that he was well on the way to gaining the extra points that he felt he needed.

# CHAPTER TWENTY-FOUR

Mr Rawcliffe was looking most indignant as he stood in front of the entire class immediately after the morning break in lessons, more indignant I think than I had ever seen him.

"Under no circumstances," he bellowed, "Do we fasten rude notices to the bottoms of young ladies of this school."

"It's all right if they come from a different school then," whispered Alan Bartle in my ear.

I laughed, hopefully not loud enough to be heard. It was the last day of the term before the school broke up for Christmas and, as far as the pupils of our class were concerned, it could not have begun in a better fashion.

"This sort of behaviour will in no way be tolerated," continued the headmaster, "And when I find the person responsible their will be serious repercussions for the individual concerned."

We had all seen the notice that morning pinned to the dress of Pauline Dixon over her posterior which proudly proclaimed in large bold letters, 'I ALWAYS WEAR FRILLY BLUE KNICKERS', though to the best of my knowledge, no one had attempted to check the validity of the statement.

No one in our class seemed to know who was the subject of the head's wrath, and fortunately for the culprit, neither did he. If anyone did know they were certainly keeping quiet about it. The notice must have been attached to the victim for quite a while because it was not noticed until she rose from her seat at the end of the first morning's lesson. As she left the classroom it had been spotted by just about everyone except the headmaster who already had his nose stuck into one of his books. Pranks of this nature, however, never survive for very long without the victim becoming aware of what is going on and on this occasion her attention had been drawn to her predicament by the eagle eyes of Miss Hazlehurst who was, at that precise moment, leaving her own classroom. Obviously, in her eyes, the headmaster would have to be informed immediately. Pauline Dixon, much to her credit, thought the whole thing was extremely funny and had developed a fit of the giggles. Mr Rawcliffe, however, had taken a totally different view of the proceedings.

"I don't suppose anyone would like to own up," he suggested, hopefully. "I thought not," he went on after surveying the faces that stared back at him, each one looking equally guilty. "Right then, I want all the boys to stand."

When we did as he asked, Ken Stacey stood head and shoulders above everybody else. The head stared directly at him as he seemed a much easier target than anybody else.

"Was it you, boy?" He asked, venomously.

"No sir," stuttered Ken. "I don't know anything about it."

"It could have been a girl, sir," suggested Tucker Lane, rather bravely in view of the circumstances. I mean it doesn't have to have been one of us, does it?"

"Nonsense, boy," admonished the Headmaster. "It's one of you. I'm sure of it. I've seen this sort of thing many times in my teaching career. It's always a boy, someone who thinks up some malicious lie, writes it on a sheet of paper and plants it on the back of another pupil."

"But it's not forced to be a lie, sir, is it?" came a voice from the back of the class.

"What isn't?"

"What it said on the notice, sir. It might be true."

Everyone was laughing, Pauline Dixon as much as anybody.

"Who said that?" said Mr Rawcliffe, gazing around the room and scrutinising each face. He was beginning to look decidedly uncomfortable and was probably beginning to regret deciding to pursue the matter so forcefully. I wasn't sure whether the reason his face was turning scarlet was because his blood pressure was rising or because of the potentially embarrassing direction in which his enquiry was heading.

"Perhaps we should find out," a girl's voice this time.

"Yes, but the notice said that she always wore them, so we'd have to check every day."

The headmaster looked around trying to locate where this new voice had come from but by now he was desperately trying to regain control of what he had originally seen as a simple matter of enforcing school discipline, but it was becoming obvious that he was losing the battle. Whether it was the fact that it was the last day of term that was responsible for this sudden outbreak of bravado among the class I had no idea, but it provided a welcome change to the kind of teacher-pupil relationship that we had been used to. There was, of course, no way that it could continue in this vein. Our inquisitor was at that moment rescued from his predicament by a knock on the door followed by the arrival of Mr Barnes.

"Right, you may all sit down again, "said the headmaster, his face regaining its more normal colour. The two of them spoke in low voices presumably regarding some unconnected school matter while the pupils, realising that the morning's jollity had probably terminated, assumed a more customary demeanour.

"I thought that was great," I whispered to Alan Bartle. "Did you see his face? I thought he was going to explode."

"I wish I knew who'd put that notice on Pauline's bum," he said. "I'd like to give him a medal."

The remainder of the morning was an anti-climax and the dastardly deed was not alluded to again by any member of the staff.

When I walked back to school with Billy after dinner neither of us was particularly looking forward to the afternoon session.

"I wonder if she really does wear frilly blue knickers," he said.

"I don't think we'll ever know Billy," I replied, "But I bet this afternoon's dead boring after what happened this morning.

"It doesn't have to be though, does it?"

"How do you mean?"

"Well. It's the last day at school before Christmas. Why don't you just tell Susan Brown that you like her and ask her if she'll be your girl friend?"

I could feel my face starting to burn again. Before I had chance to say anything Billy continued expounding his idea to brighten up the afternoon, at least from his point of view.

"I mean she might be waiting for you to do just that. I bet she knows you like her anyway."

"But I couldn't. I'd be too scared she'd say 'no' and then everybody in the class would know about it and I'd be a laughing stock. I'd never live it down. At least this way I can believe that there's a chance that she might feel the same way about me."

Nevertheless I was still thinking about Billy's suggestion as we entered the classroom, yet I could think of no way that I would actually be able to ask the question.

As we sat down Mr. Rawcliffe began to speak. Seemingly having abandoned his earlier theme, probably with the realisation that it was getting him nowhere and only causing him embarrassment, he spoke of another matter entirely.

"Right," he began, "As this afternoon is the final session of this term I have decided that it would be highly appropriate to do something a little different and I have decided, therefore, to close the term by instigating a Christmas quiz. This will consist of questions on some of the things you have been taught since school resumed in September. I shall divide the class into several teams and you will confer with the other members of your team to decide on your answer."

I quickly realised that this might prove much more interesting than the usual stuffy lesson, and I found the competitive nature of it rather appealing.

The headmaster hadn't finished. "As there are twenty-eight people in the class today each team will consist of four pupils. At the end of the contest the winning team will be allowed to go home one hour early. Hopefully this will encourage you all to pay attention and to do well. The remaining members of the class will gather in the hall with the rest of the school for the final assembly."

Everyone knew that that meant listening to his usual lecture about the importance attached to school attendance, why early learning was so imperative in life, what we would be expecting to learn in the new term and a final long explanation about the true meaning of Christmas. If ever an incentive to do well in the quiz was needed, this was it. I wondered who my fellow team-mates would be. I did not have long to wait, and had no option but to greet the declaration with mixed feelings.

"Jenny Unsworth, Tommy Lane, Neil Cawson and Susan Brown," announced the headmaster.

I noticed Billy was bracketed with Johnny Jackson, Norma Clayton and Lorna Gale, who by now seemed to have totally forgotten, if indeed she had ever been aware of it, the total humiliation that she had made me endure several weeks earlier.

As we moved around the room to settle into the seven designated groups I knew that the fact that I would be working in close proximity to Susan more than compensated for any problems that having Tucker included in the same group might bring. Still, I always enjoyed seeing his reaction whenever he was referred to as Tommy.

"Right then," he said as soon as all the members of our team were seated and deciding to immediately take charge just as we all knew he would, "We're going to win this quiz. I can just do with going home an hour early."

"We don't know how it's going to work yet," I offered. "Old Rawcliffe hasn't told us anything yet."

No sooner had the words left my mouth than the headmaster resumed speaking.

"Now that you are assembled into your teams I'll explain to you how this contest is going to operate.

The team at the front on my right will be known as Team A and each succeeding team, moving in a clockwise direction will take the following letter of the alphabet. This means that the last team will be Team, er Team—-." He did a quick calculation on his fingers before proudly announcing that the last team would be called Team G.

"We must be Team D then," observed Tucker. "Why couldn't we have had a proper name like Tucker's Tornadoes?"

"Or Jenny's Jets," suggested Jenny Unsworth.

Tucker scowled at her.

"Or Susan's Scorpions," I said, hoping I wasn't winding him up too much.

"Or Neil's Nomads," offered Susan.

Whether it was having been forced into close proximity with Susan in this way I had no idea, but I felt much more comfortable in her presence than I had ever done before. A warm glow was sweeping over me and I knew that I wanted us to win this quiz just for her sake even if it did mean Tucker getting an hour off school as well.

"Look," said our self-elected captain. "It wouldn't be any good having daft names like that because none of them sound as good as Tucker's Tornadoes do they? Anyway we can call it that whether Old Rawcliffe wants us to be known as Team D or not."

So that was that. I certainly wasn't going to argue with him. The headmaster began speaking again.

"I will ask each team a question in turn. It will be a question that I expect you to know the answer to providing you have been paying close attention to your lessons over the past three months. You may confer with the other members of your team for one minute, and then one of you must stand up and give me the answer. Everyone else in the room must remain quiet during this period. If any team gets a question wrong it will be out of the quiz. The last team remaining will be allowed to leave the premises one hour early. Now, is that perfectly understood?"

"Yes, sir," we all cried in unison.

Mr Rawcliffe peered over his spectacles as he glared at Team 'A', of which Billy was a member. "Right, Team 'A', which popular fruit would you associate with Brazil, California, South Africa and Spain?"

Before any member of the team had time to confer Lorna Gale rose from her seat. "I know the answer to this, sir, because my Uncle Peter was in South Africa during the war. He didn't stay there long though, because he sailed on from there to Burma. That's where most of the fighting was, you see. There wasn't much happening in South Africa at the time. Well. I mean not many things happening to do with the war, not with anything else. I suppose it was a very busy country in other things."

"Yes," attempted the headmaster, "But———-"

Lorna was in full flow and wasn't going to be interrupted. "Anyway, he used to tell me things about the short time he was in South Africa and he told me all about Table Mountain and what a wonderful place it was."

"Miss Gale," said the headmaster.

Lorna would still not be interrupted, and I couldn't help noticing that Billy was having hysterics as were several of the other pupils. She continued. "He used to tell me all about the different kinds of animals there. They have lions there, you know and lots of other dangerous animals."

The headmaster tried for a third time. "What about the question, Miss Gale?"

"What question, sir?" She put a hand in front of her mouth. "Oh dear, I've forgotten what it was."

Billy rescued the situation. "Oranges, sir, it's oranges," he said, rising to his feet and obviously realising that his team's chances were receding if he didn't do something about it.

"Thank you, boy. You may both sit down. That answer is correct."

He was about to move on to the next team but decided to make an announcement first. "I've decided to change the rules slightly otherwise we're not going to finish in time to let anyone go home early. Each team may still confer but I will decide which pupil stands up to give the answer."

The first three teams all gave correct answers. We were next.

"What was the name of the war between England and France in which Joan of Arc was burnt at the stake? Jenny Unsworth, you can give the answer."

"I know that one," I whispered to the other members of the team. "History's my favourite subject. It's The Hundred Years War."

Tucker wasn't convinced, but the two girls backed me up.

"O.K. but you'd better be sure," he said, still a little peeved that he wasn't the one being asked to present the answer.

"The Hundred Years War," announced Jenny.

"Correct," said the Headmaster.

The question and answer session continued and I think the he must have been pleasantly surprised by most of the answers he had been receiving. Eventually, however, only three teams remained; namely Team 'A', which was Billy's Team, Team 'D', which was ours and Team 'E', which consisted of Phillip Thatcher, Keith Battle, Sally Cheesedale and Dorothy Steedman.

"We think it's an oak tree, Sir," offered Dorothy on behalf of her team in response to a nature question which I was glad we didn't get as I certainly didn't know the correct answer.

"I'm sorry, that is incorrect. The proper answer is the sycamore tree. That means there are now only two teams remaining. Teams 'A' and 'D' have each correctly answered six questions, therefore the first team to fail from now on will be the loser and the team that remains will leave school one hour early. If both teams answer a question wrong then I will ask further questions until we have a winner. Is that understood?"

"Yes, Sir, "we all answered eagerly.

"Right then, this question is for Team 'A'. In which ocean would you find the island of Ceylon?"

I could see straight away that Billy's team were undecided about the answer and Lorna was, as usual, attempting to do all the persuading. Eventually, Billy stood up and announced rather unconvincingly that they thought the answer was the Pacific. He looked crestfallen when the headmaster stated very firmly that Ceylon lay in the Indian Ocean. Now it was up to us. I desperately hoped it would be a history question.

"I want you to tell me," said our quizmaster which of the following expressions is grammatically correct. *It was the best thing that ever happened to me and John. It was the best thing that ever happened to John and me. It was the best thing that ever happened to I and John.*

*It was the best thing that ever happened to John and I.*
Neil Cawson, you can stand up after you've conferred and give the answer.

"I would always say *me and John,* I whispered to the other members of the team, but I don't think that's right, is it?

"No, said Tucker. He's always telling us to say *John and I,* isn't he?

I thought about it. "Yes it sounds right, doesn't it?"

"I think so too," said Jenny.

Tucker looked at me. "Right then, that's it. Tell him it's *John and I.*"

"I'm not so sure," volunteered Susan looking doubtful. "It's something to do with subject and object isn't it?

"What do you mean?" snarled Tucker' beginning to look angry.

Susan bravely persisted. "I think it should be *John and me.*"

"Don't take any notice of her," he said, addressing me. "What does she know?"

"But she might be right," I offered, not too convincingly. I seem to remember something about subject and object as well."

"Look, if I lose this quiz, and miss the chance of going home early because of you you're likely to find yourself splattered against the school wall later. Though this was said in a whisper there was no hiding the menace it contained. "Tell him the answer is *John and I.*

"Come along," said the headmaster. "We can't wait all day.

I stood up, aware that every eye in the room was on me.

My mind was racing ahead. What if Susan was right? *It happened to John and it happened to me. It happened to John and it happened to I. It happened to I.* That didn't sound right, did it? "We think the answer is *It was the best thing that ever happened to John and—-, John and— , John and me,* Sir," I finally manage to splutter out.

Jenny Unsworth immediately put her head in her hands, but it was the reaction of Tucker that concerned me most. He had a face like thunder. "What on earth have I done?" I thought to myself. "I'm going to be splattered against the school wall just before Christmas. Why did I do it?"

"Well done," said the headmaster. That is the correct answer. I therefore declare that the winner of the quiz is Team 'D'. So Jenny, Susan, Tommy and Neil may now get their coats and be on there way home. A merry Christmas to you and we'll see you back at school at the beginning of the new term."

Three of us needed no second bidding but Tucker Lane just sat there looking completely baffled. "Was that the right answer then, sir?"

Mr. Rawcliffe stared at him over his spectacles. "Why, lad, didn't you agree with it? Do you want to suggest another one?"

"No, sir. Thank you, sir," he said hurriedly, panicking in case the headmaster changed his mind. He swiftly followed us out of the room.

As we were putting on our coats he walked over to me. Surely he didn't intend to carry out his threat after I had given out what proved to be the correct response to the question.

"I knew that was the right answer all the time, you know," he announced with a smug expression on his face.

I couldn't understand how he had the nerve to say that. I didn't say anything but just looked astonished.

As the four of us made our way out into the street it was just starting to rain. Tucker Lane began running towards Woodhouse Street and Jenny Unsworth was walking unhurriedly in the same direction. I could hardly believe my luck. Not only was I leaving school an hour early but I was also walking alongside Susan Brown with my head held high as we made our way home, both of us ignoring the rain. My boldness in standing up to Tucker, despite his threat, had left me feeling not as shy and tongue-tied as I normally would have been in this particular situation. Before either of us had a chance to speak, however, the sky darkened considerably, the rain turned to hail and we began to run. By the time we had gained the sanctuary of the Electra doorway the hailstones were the size of pebbles and both of us were soaked to the skin.

Before we had a chance to shake ourselves down my eyes were drawn to the hailstones in Susan's hair. The words, for once, came easily. "They're just like diamonds," I said; "Like diamonds in your hair."

It was probably the most romantic thing I ever said in my entire life, but I was unable to discover her reaction for as Susan smiled, removed the red ribbon from her hair and gave her head a shake, Mrs. Wormley chose that moment to arrive and decided to attempt to squeeze her considerable frame between us.

"I'm not having this," she announced, totally oblivious to the fact that she had brought to an end the most wonderful moment I had ever experienced. "I'm just not having it. You can keep your Mr. Atlee. I don't remember having weather like this when Winston

Churchill was Prime Minister, at least not without having some warning of it. Here I am soaking wet and stuck here while I've got a couple of oven cakes wrapped in a tea towel propped up against my door. They aren't going to be much good now, are they? Well I'll tell you, I'm just not having it."

At that precise moment Mrs. Wormley was the one person I hated the most in the whole world. Susan was squashed up against one wall and I the other with the object of my hatred presenting an impregnable barrier. How things might have developed if she hadn't interfered I would never know. What I did realise was that the confidence that had swept over me just a few short minutes ago had now vanished.

"I think I'd better go now," said Susan as the weather became less severe. "I'll see you at school after Christmas, Neil."

As I watched her head home, leaving my antagonist still sheltering in the doorway, I followed behind feeling thoroughly deflated. I knew she lived somewhere near the ridge but had never been sure of the exact street. I had only a few yards to walk, and as I watched Susan disappear around the corner it took a great deal of effort on my part to stop myself from hurling Mrs. Wormley's sodden oven cakes into the midden.

For the remainder of the evening I was annoyed about the way she had intervened in what to me had been a sublime moment, but later, as I settled down in bed and reached under my pillow to touch the red ribbon that Susan had dropped, I knew that the Electra doorway would henceforth, to me, always be a magical place and one which would often feature in my dreams.

# CHAPTER TWENTY-FIVE

When my mother received a letter from Tim informing her that he'd been invited to spend Christmas with one of his newly-acquired army friends at his home in London she was, to say the least, rather unhappy about it. However, she made him promise that he would come home for a couple of days before the New Year. This news was balanced, however, by the fact that there would be a bed available for Grandad Miller to stay with us over the holiday period, and I eagerly looked forward to greeting him for the first time since his discharge from hospital.

"Now don't you be tiring your grandad out," admonished my mother rather prematurely as we sat having breakfast. "Just because he's out of hospital it doesn't mean that he isn't still poorly. He almost died in there, don't forget."

This latter statement was totally unnecessary as I knew only too well, and there was never any possibility of my forgetting it. As Grandad Miller wasn't due to arrive until mid-day I went round to Billy's immediately after breakfast. Both Billy and I knew, of course, that we were much too old to believe in Father Christmas but fortunately, for each of us, things hadn't changed much from those fairy-tale days, at least with regard to the receiving of presents. We were lucky, I suppose to have parents who were quite happy to continue the illusion and we always awoke in the early hours of Christmas morning to a pillow case full of wondrous objects of delight. I was very surprised, therefore, to find Billy, on this occasion, looking a little despondent.

"What's the matter, Billy?" I asked him. "You look as though you've talked yourself into having a scrap with Tucker Lane and can't find a way out of it."

"They haven't bought me anything," he moaned, despairingly.

"What do you mean?"

"I mean they haven't got me anything for Christmas, that's what."

"Well, how do you know? There are two days to go yet."

"I know, because I always find out where they've hidden everything. I always have, ever since I stopped believing in Father Christmas."

I knew Billy was right in that respect but I could never understand why he did it. While I was experiencing the sheer pleasure of rooting through my pillow case on Christmas morning and delighting in discovering something new and unexpected which had not been on my list, my closest friend would have already inspected every nook and cranny that he could think of where presents might have been hidden and, as far as I was aware, he was invariably successful. This meant, of course, that the surprise element of the big day, which to me was the best part, was missing. I know I would have hated to know in advance everything that I was going to receive.

"I bet they've found out that you always discover the hiding places and they've put them somewhere where you couldn't possibly think of," I suggested.

"No, there isn't anywhere else," he said, still despondent. "There aren't any other places to look. No, they haven't got me anything. I know they haven't."

"Do you know what I think, Billy? I think they've got them stored at someone else's house. They might be with one of your aunties."

Do you really think so?"

"Well, they've always got you something before, haven't they? Yes, I bet that's what they've done. Maybe it was something so big, they couldn't even bring it into the house without you noticing."

Billy seemed to brighten up at this suggestion. "The day before yesterday," he said, "As I came downstairs I saw my mam chatting to my Auntie Betty outside the front door and as soon as I opened it, they started talking in whispers. Yes, I bet that's it. Thanks, Neil. I bet all my presents are over at Auntie Betty's. I'll have to wait until Christmas morning though to find out won't I? Crikey, do you really think they might have got me something that's too big to bring into the house?"

I didn't think that was really a possibility, but Billy's mood had improved considerably and I certainly had no desire to see him returning to his earlier one.

The remainder of the morning passed fairly quickly and when I returned home it was to find that Grandad Miller had already arrived

"Now then, lad, you'll be all ready for Christmas then, I expect," he said as I took off my coat and walked over to the armchair he was seated on

"Yes, grandad, I'm really looking forward to it."

He looked better than I had seen him look for a long time, but I asked him how he felt, just to be sure.

"Oh, I'm all right now lad, I reckon. I don't plan on having any more rum dos for a while yet, touch wood." He wrapped the wooden arm of the chair with his knuckles.

"I've made a bit of stew for dinner, dad," announced my mother as she walked in from the other room. "Is that all right with you?"

"Oh aye, lass, that'll do fine. Not too much mind, I don't want to be over-burdening myself before Christmas Day, do I?" He winked at me.

"Did you always get presents at Christmas when you were my age?" I asked him.

"Aye, lad, I always got something. It wasn't a lot, mind. Money was even scarcer in those days than it is now. But my parents always managed to get me something, no matter how small. But I was never disappointed, you understand."

"Billy thinks his mam and dad haven't bought him anything because he can't find where they've hidden it."

"Well, it would just serve him right if they hadn't. That's all I can say. Finding out what your presents are before the big day would spoil the surprise. Anyway, he should really face the possibility that his parents may not have much to spend this year."

He paused for a moment as if he was thinking about something.

"Yes, I reckon today would probably be the best time to do it," he said eventually, with a faraway look in his eyes. He seemed to be addressing the remarks to himself rather than to me.

"The best time to do what, grandad?" I asked, rather puzzled.

He looked at me as if he had suddenly come to a decision.

"Did I ever tell you about a schoolboy friend of mine called Harry Crabtree? No, I don't suppose I will have done."

I decided not to enlighten him, as I was looking forward to hearing another of his escapades.

"Anyway, Harry was the closest friend I ever had. We were just like you and that Billy up the street that you were telling me about just now. Well, around the turn of the century when me and Harry were just nippers money was even scarcer than it is today. Both our fathers worked in the mill and really struggled just to find enough money to put some food on the table. Mind you, it was as much as any family in our locality could expect, you understand. Despite the hardships, both of us would always hang a stocking up on Christmas Eve and it didn't hold anything like as much as that pillow case that I expect you'll be putting at the side of your bed. Anyway, One year, and I reckon we'd just about be the same age as you are now, about a couple of weeks before Christmas, we were walking along Hunslet Lane heading towards some spare ground where we sometimes hung around with some other lads and we were discussing how times were hard for most of the people in our neck of the woods compared to those who lived in some of the more well-to-do areas of the city, and how it was a pity that we hadn't been able to think of any way how to make some extra money in time for Christmas. Well, call it, divine intervention or whatever you like, but within a few seconds of making this observation we approached a tram stop just in time to see the last man in the queue climb on board. As he fumbled through his pocket, no doubt looking for some change to pay the conductor, something seemed to fall from his hand onto the pavement. The tram then immediately resumed its journey, clattering along the lane on its way to Leeds city centre."

Grandad Miller's story was getting interesting and once again I was hooked. "What was it that he dropped?" I asked.

"Well, it could have been a sixpence or a shilling but it wasn't. It was a penny, and Harry pocketed it after we tossed for it. Like me, he thought it was a pity that it wasn't a larger coin that he'd dropped, though looking back on it now, if the man who had dropped it had been as poor as we were he could ill have afforded to lose even that much. At our age, mind you, we never looked at it in that way. Anyway, it set Harry thinking. He was always a great one for coming up with ideas and he put it to me that he wouldn't be surprised if people were always losing money at tram and bus stops while fumbling for change. He suggested that if we walked up one side of Hunslet Lane and back down the other we might find dozens of lost coins."

"And did you find many?" I asked, rather impatiently.

"Well that's just it lad, we never really took up the suggestion. Before we could discuss it further we were on the spare ground that I told you about and surrounded by about a dozen other lads. If we'd have mentioned it to them the whole gang of us would have been involved, which meant that if we did find anything it wouldn't have gone very far, and anyway there was a game of Touch and Pass in progress when we arrived."

"What's Touch And Pass, grandad?"

"Well it's like a game of rugby, but not like the way Hunslet play at Parkside, you understand. The ground was much too hard for that. Some of the kids wouldn't have minded but constantly having to go home with a grazed knee or a torn shirt always brought harsh words or a possible beating from your parents. None of us owned a proper rugby ball either. We always made do with a bundle of old rags squashed tightly together and fastened up with string. Instead of tackling someone you just had to touch them, and then the person being touched had to either pass the ball or give it away to a member of the opposing team. We never did investigate Harry's idea properly, but I often wondered what we might have found if we had. What made me think of it is because today is the last shopping day before Christmas and it would probably be the best day to do it, what with so many people going into town to buy last minute presents. Yes, I reckon there will have been countless people standing at the tram stops in Meanwood Road and the bus stops in Woodhouse Street all with money in their pockets to spend in the shops."

My mother chose that precise moment to come in from the other room and lay the table for dinner. My father would be having his in the special canteen where he worked. He would be arriving home earlier than usual with it being the last day before the festive holiday.

"I hope you haven't been tiring your grandad out," she said, rather unnecessarily I thought, as she had said virtually the same thing ever since he had been ill."

"No, mam"

"Aye, the lad's right, lass," said my grandfather. "We were just having a friendly natter so to speak, weren't we son?" and he gave me one of his winks.

It was as if he knew that I would be going straight round to Billy's as soon as I had finished my dinner to relate to him Grandad Miller's latest story and to see what he wanted to do about it.

I hated stew, but my mother always insisted that I eat every mouthful before being allowed to leave the table. On this occasion, however, she must have been surprised to see me rapidly devouring every morsel on the plate as if I hadn't eaten for days.

"Your grandad's always getting these great ideas," enthused Billy when I related Grandad Miller's story. "I wish I had a grandad like that. Is he better now then?"

"My mam keeps telling me that he's still poorly, but he looks all right to me. He certainly doesn't seem any worse than before he went into hospital."

"Well, what are we going to do about it then?"

"Do about what?" I asked, rather puzzled.

"Are we going round all the tram and bus stops looking for lost coins? Didn't he say that there'll be a lot more money in people's pockets today?"

"Right then, let's start at the Primmy and walk as far as the Golden Cross on North Street, then we can walk back on the other side of the road."

The agreement was made and we headed down the hill towards the Primrose public house with eager anticipation of what rewards our latest venture might bring.

"Don't forget, Billy, Grandad Miller's ideas don't always work out the way we expect them to," I said as we crossed Meanwood Road to get to the tram stop. I had suddenly recalled the unfortunate outcomes, for me in particular, of our escapades on Mischievous Night and the day we were following imaginary suspects, though I couldn't imagine how any misunderstandings regarding Susan Brown could result from this particular adventure.

When we reached the first tram stop we weren't really sure what to do. There were five people in the queue. Should we pretend to join the queue and seem to change our minds when the tram arrived, or just hang back and invite anxious glances from travellers who would no doubt wonder if we were up to some sort of mischief? We surveyed our prey which consisted of one elderly lady, a child of about five years old in the company of an attractive, youngish woman and two other women of middle age who were engaged in constant conversation, though a little one-sided, perhaps.

"Well, I told him straight, Phyllis," said woman number one. "I said you're expecting me to put all this food on the table and all I've got to last me till Christmas is ninepence. I'll be lucky to get a roll of black pudding with it. I tell you, I gave it to him straight, Phyllis. I did."

"Ooh, you did right, Edna. You did right."

"I know I did, Phyllis. I know I did. Well, I tell you, he didn't know where to put himself. 'Well, I do the best I can,' he said. Well I put it to him straight. Do the best you can? I said. Do the best you can? If it was her what lives next to the off-licence in Craven Road you'd have done the best you can. Well, I tell you Phyllis, I've never seen a man look more guilty in my life. Did he know where to put himself? He did not."

"Ooh, he wouldn't Edna. He wouldn't."

"I wouldn't care, Phyllis, I wouldn't. I mean where have I gone wrong? Haven't I always looked after him to the best of my ability?"

"Ooh, you have Edna. You have."

The conversation continued in the same vein, so that I felt really sorry for Edna's husband. It didn't seem a surprise to me that he'd taken a fancy to 'her what lives next to the off-licence in Craven Road', whoever she was.

Billy broke my thoughts. "I can't see any point in targeting her," he whispered. "She's only got ninepence."

We watched them board the tram as it arrived at the stop.

"They were all women," I said to Billy, and none of them got their purses out before they got on board."

We looked around the vicinity to see if any coins had been dropped by any other passengers prior to our arrival, but found nothing.

"We can't expect too much at the first stop, can we?" said Billy. "Let's move on to the one at the Junction."

The Junction was yet another of the many public houses that lined Meanwood Road. It seemed to me that most of the tram stops seemed to be outside one. It meant, of course, that anyone who had had too much to drink would not have too far to stagger in search of transport home.

When we arrived at our destination we found that there was no one waiting for a tram. We had another good look around but it was equally unrewarding.

The next stop outside the Royal Picture House held more promise as it was on both the tram and bus route. As we neared our destination a bus was just pulling out of Cambridge Road, and we arrived at the stop simultaneously. Seven people were in the queue but only three were boarding the bus, the others deciding to wait a few more minutes for the tram. As the trio stepped onto the platform we watched keenly for any sign of a falling coin, but to no avail. Of the four that remained only one was a man. The women, as Billy had observed earlier, tended not to open their purses until they were seated inside. The bus arrived shortly afterwards and the remaining four climbed on board.

"I think we're wasting our time," said Billy as we diligently searched the surrounding area for any lost coins. "We haven't found anything and it's getting colder. I'll be freezing in a minute."

"There are only two more stops before we reach the Golden Cross," I said, being reluctant to give up on the challenge, despite the fact that his observation on the decline in the temperature was perfectly correct and I was starting to feel uncomfortable in the chilly atmosphere.

"Let's run to the next stop then."

We reached Barrack Street, blowing out freezing puffs of air. There was no one at the stop which wasn't surprising considering that it was only a few minutes since a tram and bus had gone past. We decided not to hang around as it was patently obvious that there was nothing of interest on the ground. By the time we reached the Golden Cross we were both thoroughly miserable. There was only one woman at the stop and we had just about lost interest completely.

"I'm not walking all that way back on the other side of the road," said Billy, waving his arms about in a frantic attempt to get warm. "Let's get the tram back to the Primmy."

We walked across the road to the tram stop immediately outside the public house.

"How much money have you got?" I asked taking a threepeny bit from my pocket. "This is all I've got."

"Well that's enough. I bet it's only a penny from here. You can go right into town for tuppence. Anyway, I've got seven pence, but the next time your grandad comes up with one of his ideas I'm not going to listen," moaned Billy.

"Well it seemed like a good idea. Look the tram's coming, so let's just forget about it, eh."

As the traffic lights turned to green our transport duly arrived. The relief we felt as we stepped on board and climbed the stairs to the top deck was immense. The fact that nearly everyone was smoking didn't bother us. All that mattered was that we were out of the cold. As the tram rattled on we talked about what we might be getting on Christmas morning, Billy having now accepted that his presents had simply been placed somewhere out of his reach.

"Tickets, please," boomed the conductor, arriving at the top of the stairs.

"I bet it's only a penny, "repeated my companion, taking one from his pocket. As he turned towards me he could see the look of consternation on my face. "What's the matter?" he asked.

"It's gone," I said, "The threepenny bit. I took it out to show you while we were standing at the tram stop. I must have dropped it when I tried to put it back in my pocket. I've no money to pay the fare."

"What? You mean we've spent all this time looking for money that people might have lost at tram stops and you've gone and lost some yourself. I can hardly believe it."

"Tickets please," said the conductor as he arrived at the front of the tram where we were seated.

Billy replaced the penny he had removed from his pocket with a sixpence. "Two to the Primrose please," he said.

When I arrived home, cold and thoroughly disgruntled, and explained to my grandfather what we had been doing and how things had turned out, I was totally unprepared for his comments.

"Well, I always thought it was a daft idea though I never said so to Harry. I mean I certainly never fancied walking all that way in the hope that there just might be some small financial reward at the end of it. Still, you did manage to prove that people do lose money while boarding a tram, didn't you?"

If it had not been for the fact that Christmas morning, with all the pleasure that it would bring, was only two night's sleep away, my feeling of discontentment would probably have lasted the rest of the day. However, by tea time I had recovered all my earlier enthusiasm for the festive season and I knew that the following day was the one day in the year when I eagerly looked forward to bedtime.

# CHAPTER TWENTY-SIX

"You have won second prize in a beauty competition. Collect ten pounds." read out Grandma Cawson before placing the card at the bottom of the pack. "And what are you laughing at, young man?" she added, addressing me. "I'll have you know I could have had my pick of a lot of the most handsome men when I was a young woman. So don't you forget it."

The traditional Christmas afternoon game of Monopoly was well under way and I was enjoying every minute of it. At least to my mind, the day was progressing in the same splendid fashion that it had begun. Ever since I was about five years old, the first thing I invariably did on Christmas morning was look at the pillow case at the side of the bed to make sure there was something in it. The second thing I did was to walk over to the window and draw back the curtains to see if it was snowing. Even though on this occasion Grandad Miller had been asleep in the bed usually occupied by my brother Tim when he was home, I had seen no reason whatsoever to change this routine. It was still dark as I had looked out of the window yet I had been able to see that there was no sign of any snow, despite the freezing cold weather. I had heard my mother say sometimes that it was too cold to snow, but I could never understand that and, whenever I had pointed out that it must be much colder in Antarctica and that it snowed there, she never had a satisfactory answer.

"I thought you'd be up early today," said my grandfather, obviously awakened by my sudden movements. "What are you hoping to see by gazing out of the window so intently?"

"I was hoping it might be snowing, grandad."

"Oh, it'll come in its own time, Lad. It'll come in its own time. I would have thought you'd have enough to occupy yourself with on Christmas morning. Why don't you have a look under my bed? You might find something interesting."

Instead of exploring the pillow case full of presents I looked under the bed occupied by my grandfather. I pulled out a large, but rather dusty, box.

"What is it?" I asked, intrigued by the size of it. It was a plain, brown box bearing no label.

Grandad Miller rested his elbow on the pillow, leaned over and peered down at me. "Why don't you open it and see?"

I did not really need his encouragement as I was already hurriedly working my way through the various knots that held the string together. The things I extracted from the box were nothing like what I had imagined. They consisted of a perfectly formed replica of a steam locomotive, three Pullman carriages, a signal box, two station platforms and a large assortment of track. I could barely conceal my delight.

"It works by electricity," expounded my grandfather. "Mind you, it's not brand new, you understand. No, there's no way I could have afforded that. Still, I know it's in working order because I tried it out myself."

"Thanks, grandad," I said, unable to conceal my delight. "Will you show me how it works when you get up?"

"Of course I will, lad, but aren't you going to see what else you've got?"

This was the first Christmas morning ever that I had delayed, even for a few minutes, rooting through the contents of my pillow case. When I did so, immediately after my grandfather's prompting, I was not disappointed. There the usual comic annual and lots of other smaller things, but the object that gave me the most pleasure was a real, full-size rugby ball. I revived in an instant my fading interest in the performance of the school team. A few moments earlier I had been keen to get my grandfather to construct the electric train layout, yet now I could hardly wait to get in some practice. I assumed that Nicky, because of his recent injury, would not, at this stage, get permission from his mother to engage in anything she might regard as too strenuous.

Immediately after breakfast I had called round to see Billy and I quickly realised that my assumption that his parents had not forgotten him was correct. We spent a few minutes discussing what each of us had received. Then we were outside for a passing session and kick-about, which only ended when I spotted my father arriving with Grandma Cawson, and knew that Christmas dinner would be only a few minutes away.

The Monopoly board was set in place immediately after the table had been cleared and all the plates and utensils had been washed and put away. The meal had been a great success, a fact which Nell bore testimony to by contentedly settling down on the clip rug in front of the fire and immediately falling asleep. This was fortunate as it meant that we did not have to witness her displeasure at not being allowed to participate in the afternoon's activities.

"I wonder how much the winner got," said Grandad Miller.

"What do you mean, dad?" asked my mother, moving her piece along the board at the same time.

"Well, if second prize in the beauty competition was ten pounds, how much did they give to the person who won it?"

"My property!" shouted my father as the iron landed on Regent Street, immediately relegating my grandfather's question down the list of my mother's priorities.

"When did you get that? I didn't know you had any of those light green ones."

The rent was duly paid, and the game continued. It was very light-hearted and from my point of view it was just what was needed after the substantial dinner to prevent Grandma Cawson and Grandad Miller from each settling in an armchair in the back room and going to sleep for the duration of the afternoon.

"I was talking to Mrs what lives in Cocoa House Hill with a funny arm the other day," said my mother, taking the two hundred pounds she had received for just passing Go and placing it on top of what had hitherto been an ever decreasing pile, "And she reckons that Mrs-At-The-Back-Of-Glover's has been having trouble with her lad, and that he might have to go to prison."

It doesn't surprise me," said Grandma Cawson. "There's bad blood in that family if ever I saw it.

"Why what has he done, mam?" I broke in.

Everybody stopped talking and stared at me. Even Nell awoke from her slumber and glanced across. I realised they were going to tell me that I shouldn't have been listening again

"That's not for you to know," my mother said eventually. "Concentrate on your game."

The truth was that there wasn't much game left to concentrate on as it was heading towards its inevitable conclusion with my father about to bankrupt everybody.

"Why does everybody call it Cocoa House Hill, mam?" I said, moving on to what I hoped might be a safer topic. It's not its proper name, is it?"

"Well, everybody in Woodhouse seems to have called it that for as long as I can remember, but if you look at the name on the wall at the top of the street I think it says Speedwell Mount, or something like that. Does anybody else know?"

I had created an interesting talking point which took us to the end of the game, but after everybody around the table had contributed to the discussion and various theories had been put forth, the result was that no one had the faintest idea.

As the Monopoly board was being folded up and placed into its box, where it might conceivably wait until the following Christmas. The front door opened and a familiar voice asked "Are you there, May?"

"Come in, Mr. Senior. Come on in," invited my mother.

"I'm sorry to be disturbing you today, with it being Christmas Day and all that but I was wondering if you happened to have any nutcrackers. Phillip, that's our Doreen's husband, do you see, has brought this packet of nuts round and they've all still got their shells on, and we haven't got anything we can use to crack 'em open."

"Tom, can you pass me the nutcrackers? I think they're in that drawer behind you. By the way, how are you today, Mr. Senior?"

"Oh, I'm just fair to middling lass, just fair to middling, but best not to grumble on Christmas Day, eh."

As my father handed him the required object, our neighbour mumbled his thanks, apologised again for disturbing us and went out the door.

"I bet you didn't know that Mr. Senior's never been to Dewsbury, grandad" I said.

"I thought he used to be in the Merchant Navy. He must have travelled to more countries than I can think of."

"Yes, but he's never been to Dewsbury. He told me himself."

"Mind you, I don't think I've ever been either, come to think about it."

"Yes, but you haven't been all round the world, have you? So it's not really the same."

"Aye, lad, you're right there, I suppose."

With the game of Monopoly over and still an hour or so remaining before tea I was about to ask Grandad Miller if he would lay out the track for my electric train set, but before I could ask him he had already announced that he was going into the back room for a short nap. I decided instead to call round at Billy's.

"We've been playing Monopoly," I said as he opened the door. "What have you been doing?"

"I was just reading the Beano Annual before you walked in. Have we to get the rugby ball out again?"

I thought we might go see how Nicky's doing."

"Good idea, but I need to go for a pee first."

I waited for him next to the midden at the top of the lavatory yard, keeping lookout in case Mary Pearson had seen us walk past her house and taken it into her head to make an appearance with the intention of causing maximum embarrassment.

"Right!" he said, emerging from the cubicle. "Let's go see what Nicky's got for Christmas"

As we made our way towards the far end of Cross Speedwell Street Billy became quite serious. "You know I really did think that they hadn't got me anything. It was great waking up this morning and seeing all the presents there. Even if I didn't get a bike at least everything was a surprise this year. I don't think I'll go searching for them next time. I'll wait until Christmas morning."

We knocked on Nicky's door, which was opened by his mother. "I'm afraid you won't be able to see our Nicky this morning. He's got a very bad cold. He hasn't even been able to open any of his presents yet."

"That's rotten luck," said Billy as we looked in Mrs. Ormond's sweet shop window, which was next door. "What a horrible time to get a cold. It's not as if he's been able to play out much either, is it?"

"I think his mother might have been bothered about him playing anything too rough until his arm's healed properly," I suggested.

"I wonder what your girl friend got for Christmas," said my companion, mischievously.

"She's not my girl friend, Billy. I only wish she was." I had told him nothing about us sheltering from the rain in the Electra doorway, and I had no intention to.

"Look, you can't go on like this all next year," said my companion, showing what appeared to be genuine concern. "We've still got a week left of this one. Why don't you tell her you like her before it runs out, and just see what happens?"

"I can't just knock on her door on Christmas Day and tell her I like her, can I? I mean she might laugh. Anyway, we don't know which is her house, do we?"

"We know it's on one of the roads at the side of the ridge though, don't we? Come on, we might just see her playing out."

"No," I said, rather forcefully. "Let's get the rugby ball out again like you suggested."

We spent about fifteen minutes passing and kicking before it started to rain, thus bringing an end to our activities. When I re-entered the house it was to find some kind of dispute taking place.

"I'm not sure we should be doing that on Christmas Day," said Grandma Cawson, now seated along with Grandad Miller at the dining table awaiting the evening meal which would consist of ham sandwiches followed by trifle.

"I don't see what difference it makes what day it is," added my father. "We did it quite a lot in the army. It was quite a popular pastime when things were quiet. Mind you, we found a few things out that we hadn't bargained for."

"What are we going to do, mam?" I asked, my interest aroused.

"We were thinking of doing The Mirror and the Glass after tea," replied my mother, "But we're not sure if it's the right thing to be doing today."

"Oh, good," I said, "I like The Mirror and the Glass. Please, can we do it?"

"I can't really see any harm in it," said Grandad

Miller, "But let's not ask any questions that we don't really want to know the answer to, eh?"

And so it was decided. Immediately after tea my mother produced a large mirror from the back room while my father took a piece of plain paper and a pair of scissors and proceeded to create thirty-eight small squares on which he wrote every letter of the alphabet, all the numbers between zero and nine and the words YES and NO. Before long the mirror, which now had the small squares of paper arranged around its circumference, the affirmative at the top and the negative at the bottom, occupied the surface of the now empty dining table. We took up our seats around the table as my mother produced a drinking glass and placed it upside down in the centre of the mirror.

"Now, remember," She said. "If anyone laughs or crosses their legs it won't work, and no one must lift a finger from the top of the glass."

I immediately wanted to start laughing but managed to suppress the urge. I had heard these instructions many times before. I suppose what we were doing would have looked ridiculous to many people but I had to admit that the process we were about to be engaged in nearly always produced amazing results.

"Can I ask the first question, mam?" I urged.

"It depends what it is. I don't want anything silly."

"It isn't anything silly. I just want to know when it's going to snow."

"That's not a bad question to start with, lad," said Grandad Miller.

Nell barked her approval. She always loved a romp in the snow.

Everything went deathly quiet as we each placed a digit on the top of the glass.

"Spirit of the glass," said my mother, "We would like to know when it is going to snow."

The glass remained motionless in the centre of the mirror.

"Has anyone got their legs crossed?" asked my mother.

No one answered.

"It's stubborn sometimes," she went on, by way of explanation. "It might take a while to warm up."

No sooner had the words been spoken, than the glass began to move across the smooth surface, apparently of its own volition. This prompted the usual accusations

"Who's pushing?" demanded Grandma Cawson.

Denials came from all around the table. I firmly believe that all those present were, as far as they were aware, speaking the truth. Was it possible, therefore, for someone to set the glass in motion without realising they were doing it? To deny that possibility meant accepting that the object we were all focussing on was a conscious entity capable of self-mobilisation, or that there was, indeed, some kind of spirit lurking inside it. It was puzzling, yet I had seen remarkable results with my own eyes on several occasions.

The glass came to rest immediately in front of the number three, then returned to the centre and remained motionless.

"Three what?" I said. "It hasn't finished."

"I think that's all it's going to tell us," said my mother. "It could mean three days, three weeks or even three months."

"I think you'd better have a look outside," suggested Grandad Miller, with a grin, "Just in case it means three minutes."

After providing us with its first answer there was no stopping it.

"Should we be doing this on Christmas Day?" asked Grandma Cawson.

"NO," said the glass.

We continued anyway.

"What is Tim doing now?" asked my mother.

"E-A-T-I-N-G," spelt out the glass.

"Who'll win the Rugby League Cup this season?" asked my father.

"W-I-G-A-N," spelt the glass.

"Who are you?" asked my grandfather.

"G-L-A-S-S," spelt the glass.

We continued in this vein for about a further half hour with no one admitting to directing the glass to an appropriate answer. Eventually Grandad Miller came up with a question that set my cheeks burning.

"When Neil gets married, what will be the name of his bride?" asked Grandad Miller.

My face burned as the glass began to give the answer.

"S," said the glass.

Before it could complete the word, Nell chose that moment to jump up at Grandma Cawson, causing her to turn around, startled, and knock the glass with her arm. Before anyone could prevent it the object dropped to the floor and shattered. There was then pandemonium with everyone first trying to prevent Nell from walking onto the broken pieces and secondly everyone crawling on hands and knees attempting to locate them all and gather them up.

"I knew we shouldn't have done this today," admonished my mother. "It's a sign. I'm sure it is."

"Well that appears to be that," said Grandad Miller a few minutes later when everything had been tidied up.

"I reckon we're destined not to find out who your lady friend's going to be," he added, turning to me. "I mean the letter 'S' isn't going to tell us much, is it?"

It told me a great deal, however. No one in that room could have known the significance of what the glass had attempted to say. Was I really going to marry Susan Brown? It was certainly a wonderful thought to take to bed with me.

# CHAPTER TWENTY-SEVEN

Three days after Christmas the snow came. Grandad Miller had by this time returned to his own house and, Tim having not yet arrived, I had the bedroom to myself. The sight that met my eyes as I gazed out of the window on that wonderful morning was truly magnificent. It must have been snowing for several hours. The clock on the chest of drawers read ten minutes past seven. It should have still been dark, yet the ground was covered by a white, fluffy blanket. The flakes, which were still falling, were huge. I looked up at the sky and I knew that there was a lot more to come. The snow clouds were bright as day.

Breakfast was just a blur, but before I had even finished it Billy was already knocking on the door. It was a good job it opened inwardly or no one would have been able to get in or out. The snow was already above the threshold.

"Are you coming?" asked Billy, excitedly. He was attired in a thick coat, wellington boots, a thick, woollen scarf, knitted gloves and a cap.

"Crikey!" I said, grinning. "You look as if you're going to the South Pole."

"My mam made me put all this stuff on. All I really needed was a coat. I'm going to shove the gloves in my pocket, though. You can't make snowballs properly with these. The snow just sticks to 'em."

"You'd better come in, Billy," suggested my mother. "Neil isn't going anywhere until he's finished his breakfast." She looked down at my companion's wellingtons. "On second thoughts, you'd better just stand inside the doorway for a while," she added.

Nell, suddenly realising what all the excitement was about and knowing that she'd already finished her breakfast without having to be asked to do so, decided she wanted to make it a threesome.

Before long all three of us were outside, but not before my mother had insisted, much to my annoyance, on clothing me in a very similar fashion to Billy.

"Let's throw snowballs to Nell," he suggested, paying regard to his earlier promise and tucking his knitted gloves into his trouser pocket to provide company for all the other mysterious delights that he always kept hidden in there.

"You'd better be careful when you take 'em back out of there Billy," I warned. "You might lose all sorts of treasures."

I suddenly realised that the gloves that my mother had insisted that I wear were equally as useless when it came to the construction of an effective snowball, so I did the same. The only difference was that my pocket was empty.

We spent a pleasant ten minutes watching, with some amusement, Nell's vain attempts to catch a snowball in her mouth. There was no doubting her enthusiasm but it soon became clear that she would have to be taken back inside. Her hair had become so knotted with snow that she could hardly walk.

"If she stayed out any longer," laughed Billy, "She wouldn't be able to move."

"I knew it was going to snow today," I told him, after we had taken Nell in to dry off. "The glass said so."

I explained to him what we had been doing on Christmas Day and some of the things that the glass had revealed.

"We tried doing it at home once," said Billy, unimpressed, "But nothing happened. The glass never moved."

"Maybe your mam had her legs crossed, or somebody laughed," I suggested. "Anyway, it was right about the snow today. And there's another thing I didn't tell you. It said I was going to marry Susan Brown, and no one could have been pushing it because nobody at the table would have known who she was."

"What, do you mean it actually spelt her name out?"

"Well, no, it just moved to the letter 'S', and then Nell jumped up and the glass got knocked over before it could spell out the rest of it, but it has to be her hasn't it?"

"How do you know? It could have been anybody." He started laughing. "It might have been going to spell 'Sophie Morton'. Yes, that's it. I bet that's who it was."

I wasn't amused by Billy's remark and decided to change the subject. "Let's get the sledges out," I said, eagerly.

Billy needed no more encouragement, and we both disappeared into our respective houses, emerging almost simultaneously a few minutes earlier, with each of us dragging behind the object of our excitement.

"It's a pity Nicky's mam won't let him go sledging," said my companion. "She won't let him do anything where she thinks he might have an accident. I hope she changes her mind when he's got the pot off his arm."

My Cousin Raymond chose that precise moment to step out and begin clearing the snow outside my Auntie Molly's house, using the coal shovel.

"I see you're going sledging then lads." He said. "It looks to me as if it might snow all day, and you know what that means don't you? Conditions will be absolutely perfect tomorrow for attempting The Long Sledge."

"What's that?" asked Billy, just beating me to it.

"What! Do you mean to tell me that nobody's ever told you about The Long Sledge? Well I'd better enlighten you then, hadn't I? Mind you, you'll have to wait until I've finished clearing this snow. My mother's expecting me to shift it from in front of Mr. Senior's house as well. I'll tell you what. If you call round after dinner I'll let you know all about it."

"I've never heard of it," I said to Billy as we dragged our sledges towards the end of Cross Speedwell Street. "What do you think it is?"

"I've no idea. Why don't we ask Nicky if he knows?"

We halted outside his door and knocked.

"I saw you coming past the window," he said as he opened the door. I wish my mam would let me go sledging."

He looked a little down-hearted. "Don't worry Nicky," I said, attempting to cheer him up. "I bet this snow's here for ages, and I'm sure your arm will be better soon. At least you've managed to have all that time off school."

"We came to ask you if you've ever heard of The Long Sledge," said Billy.

Nicky looked puzzled. "No, I've never heard of it. What is it?"

"We don't know either, but Neil's Cousin Raymond thinks it's something special, and he's going to tell us about it this afternoon."

"Your Cousin Raymond knows all sorts of things, doesn't he?" said Nicky, looking at me.

"He went to Leeds Central High School," was the best I could manage by way of an explanation.

A few minutes later saw us round the corner outside Doughty's shop. There were a few other lads there with sledges, but it was obvious that the snow on the ground was so thick and soft that it was far from ideal for the purpose of sledging. There were a few half-hearted attempts but no one got very far. Before long, the other lads had all dispersed but not without our finding out that none of them had heard of the Long Sledge. We decided to give up and try again tomorrow by which time it should have stopped snowing and the ground would be much firmer, and anyway it was almost time for dinner.

"Don't forget," I said to Billy before he disappeared into the house. "We're going to see my Cousin Raymond later."

I think we must both have hurried our midday meal, for we emerged into the street within a few seconds of each other. He was obviously as keen to hear Raymond's story as I was. A few minutes later we were seated in my cousin's front room waiting for him to begin.

"This Long Sledge," I said, before he had a chance to speak, "We asked some of the lads about it this morning, but none of them knew anything."

"How old were these lads?" he asked.

"I think they were about nine or ten."

"Well, that's why then. You see it hasn't been done since 1947. That year, although you might not remember because both of you would only have been about seven, when the snow came the ground froze very quickly. It was bitterly cold for months and the snow never cleared in all that time."

"Well, what is The Long Sledge then?" asked Billy, impatiently.

"Anyone my age could tell you," said Raymond, and then paused for a moment as if searching for the best way to put it across. "Do you know which is Delph Lane, near the top of the ridge?"

We both nodded.

"Well then, The Long Sledge starts around the corner from the end of that street. It's quite a gentle slope at the beginning, so you have to take a bit of a run with it before getting on. With a bit of luck it will keep going until you get to the steep part. Before long you're whizzing down past the entrance to the ridge and it gets very difficult to steer properly. Don't forget that at the speed you're going it's very easy to hit the side of the road or even turn the sledge over completely. Mind you, this isn't the hardest part. Eventually you come to Melville Road. It's highly unlikely that there will be any vehicles using the road with all this snow about. Even so, there'll be a couple of lads stationed there to make sure there are no obstructions. Once you've crossed into Cocoa House Hill the track becomes even steeper, and then when you get to the end you have to swing round to the left and head towards Meanwood Road. If you carry straight on from there you'll finish up on the tram lines. So there should be another couple of lads there to make sure that you don't. To avoid doing that, what you have to do is swing to the left again at the last minute and go into Ridge Road. That's where the run ends. You couldn't go any further anyway because after a few yards it starts to slope the other way. That's where The Long Sledge finishes and you'll get a pat on the back at having achieved what not many kids have done before"

"Crikey!" gasped Billy. That must be about half a mile long."

"As far as I know nobody your age has ever done it. I never attempted it myself but I know the last person to succeed was Nipper Brennan who lives in the street at the back of ours, and that's nearly four years ago. I think he was thirteen at the time. Quite a few lads before him had completed the course, but so many of the others who tried never even managed to get across Melville Road."

I looked across at Billy. I knew he was thinking the same as I was.

Raymond looked at us. "You're thinking of having a go at it, aren't you? Well, if it snows all day and freezes during the night, conditions will be just about perfect, I should think. I might even be one of the marshals. You have to have them in four places to make sure that nobody cheats. You need two at the top of Delph Lane at the beginning of the course, two in Melville Road, two at the bottom of Cocoa House Hill and several more at the finish in Ridge Road. If anybody stops on the way down they are disqualified and have to do it all again. That's if they still want to try, of course. Don't forget, there aren't that many lads who are successful. If you two manage it I think you'll be the youngest ones ever."

"Hasn't anybody tried in the four years since Nipper Brennan did it?" I asked.

"We tried getting one together a couple of times since then, but the conditions had never been really right for it I reckon tomorrow should be just about perfect though."

"Do you think we've got a chance of finishing it?" asked Billy.

"Well, you'll certainly have more chance then anyone who doesn't try."

By the time I left Billy and entered the house it had stopped snowing and it immediately felt a lot colder.

"I'm glad you've come in now," said my mother. "I was just going to call for you."

A feeling of dread hit me as I gazed at the piles of wool in a basket on the floor. I knew immediately what was coming.

"As soon as you've taken your coat off," she continued, "I want you to sit on that chair opposite and help me to wind some wool."

Nell, who had been lying in front of it, obligingly moved away and settled down on the clip rug in front of the fire.

"Aw, mam, I hate doing this," I objected. "My arms always hurt for ages afterwards."

"Don't be so silly. It can't be as bad as that. Anyway, your arms will deserve to ache after what I've got to tell you."

"What's that mam?" I asked with some trepidation, while at the same time adopting the dreaded position with hands outstretched.

My mother proceeded to wrap the first hank of wool around each hand. She gave me a very stern look.

"I was talking to Mrs Three-Doors-Away this morning, and she told me that she had heard you and Billy calling Mrs In-The-Next-Street, Mrs I-Make-No-Wonder. Now you know you shouldn't be giving people nicknames like that. That's not the way you were brought up. So it had better stop."

"Yes, mam," I managed to say, though my mother's statement sounded grossly unfair.

"Now, let's have this wool wound up properly. Make sure you move your thumbs at the right time, and I don't want to hear any moaning about your arms aching. It's not as if I'm asking you to do anything hard, is it?"

I had been through this ritual many times before, but never once without the feeling that my arms were going to drop off.

After enduring ten minutes of it there was a knock on the door and a familiar figure walked into the room.

"Are you there, May?" he announced. "I was going to call earlier, but I was waiting for Raymond, the lad next door do you see, to kindly clear the snow from the front of my house."

Well, it's very cold today," said my mother putting the wool down, but not telling me to lower my hands. "You've got to be very careful when you go out today."

"Well, that's why I decided to pop round, do you see? I fancied a bit of jellied tongue for my tea, and I just wondered whether your lad might be going over to Doughty's this afternoon. I daren't go myself, not with all this snow about."

"Don't you worry about it Mr. Senior. As soon as I've finished winding this wool I'll get him to go for you. He can bring something back for me at the same time. How are you today, anyway?"

"Thanks very much May. That's very good of you, and in answer to your question I don't suppose anybody can be more than just fair to middling in this sort of weather, can they?"

Despite my mother's agreeing to Mr Senior's request it in no way reduced the interminable length of time that

I had to sit with aching arms outstretched while attempting to ensure that my thumb didn't become entangled in the wool. Eventually, however, the hated chore came to an end and I slipped on my coat and scarf and ventured outside in search of Mr Senior's jellied tongue, plus a couple of other items that my mother had asked for. After I had completed my errand and was leaving Doughty's shop the sky was beginning to darken and though it had stopped snowing the temperature had fallen considerably and it was obvious that the following morning was going to produce ideal conditions for The Long Sledge.

I was not the only one to notice the worsening conditions for as I went to bed I was provided with a hot oven plate wrapped in a sheet, the sort of luxury that I usually had to beg for. Before settling down I opened the drawer in the bedroom which contained my pyjamas among other items of clothing and felt underneath them. It was still there, exactly where I had placed it each morning after having awoken. As I walked over to the bed and placed Susan's red ribbon under my pillow I knew that I would not be returning it to its daytime location on the following morning as it seemed to me that I might have another use for it entirely, and it did not take me long to fall asleep.

# CHAPTER TWENTY-EIGHT

When Billy called round during mid-morning I was just beginning to obey my mother's strict rules for going outside on such a cold, frosty day. I was even more thickly attired than on the previous day as she had insisted on my wearing an extra pullover.

"Make sure you wear it on the inside of the other one," she said, "Then no one will be able to see the holes in the sleeves."

By the time I was completely dressed I felt distinctly uncomfortable, and did Nell have an amused expression on her face or was I imagining it? As soon as I stepped outside, however, I was very grateful for my mother's insistence on my wearing the correct apparel for the extreme conditions.

Billy and I had agreed that we would not take out the sledges immediately but would spend the first half hour or so surveying the area to see if there was any activity which would suggest that the event we were so interested in was going to be staged that morning.

"Crikey, it's freezing," he gasped. "I bet it can't be any colder than this at the North Pole."

"I don't think I ever want to find out," I told him. "At least the ground is going to be just right for sledging on. Let's go see if we can find out what's happening."

We knew our hopes had been realised when we stepped out onto Melville Road. There seemed to be quite a lot of activity at the top of Cocoa House Hill.

"I told you Cocoa House Hill wasn't its proper name," I said, as I looked at the street sign which boldly displayed the name SPEEDWELL ROAD.

"It still doesn't tell us why everybody calls it that though, does it?" replied Billy, looking puzzled.

"So you two decided to give it a go then, did you?" said my Cousin Raymond as he watched us approach.

"Is it on then?" I asked him, eagerly.

"It looks like it. We're just trying to get everything ready. We'll need to have it over with before the gritters get here though, or nobody will be able to cross Melville Road to get onto Cocoa House Hill."

"We've been trying to find out why it's called Cocoa House Hill," volunteered Billy. "Do you know?"

"Well, that's just its name isn't it? Why shouldn't it be called that?"

"Because according to what it says there it's Speedwell Road," I informed him, pointing in the direction of the street sign. "That's why."

"Well, blow me," said my cousin. "I never knew that."

"When do you think everybody will starting doing The Long Sledge?" asked Billy, no doubt considering that the mystery of why just about everybody in Woodhouse called Speedwell Road, Cocoa House Hill, rather boring and a distraction from the really exciting event of the day.

"I think we're nearly ready to start now. There's already about half a dozen lads making their way up the hill towards Delph Lane. In fact one of them is about your age, so he probably goes to your school."

I just hoped it wasn't Tucker Lane. If Tucker completed the course there'd be no living with him. I looked at Billy and I knew he was thinking the same.

"Do you think it might be Nicky?" he asked, hopefully.

"Don't be daft, Billy. He's hardly likely to go sledging with his arm in a pot, is he?"

"I'd forgotten about that. I wonder who it is then."

"Well, if you two intend doing it then, don't you think you'd stand a better chance if you had a sledge?" said Raymond. "Don't forget if you slide down the course on your bellies it won't count."

We both laughed. "We're going back to get them now," I said.

We turned around and made our way back, being very careful not to slip, injure our backs and ruin our chances.

"Don't be too long, Neil" said Billy, as he entered his house, "Otherwise we won't get a run in before dinner."

He needn't have worried. I was just as keen to get back out again as he was. However, it very quickly became obvious to me that my mother had other plans.

"We'll be having our dinners early today," She informed me as soon as I walked through the door. I have to go out this afternoon. Mrs. Along-The-Way is taking her cat to the vet because it's got a serious illness, and she thinks he might have to put it to sleep. I can't let her go on her own because I know how upset she'll be if he does. So you might as well take your things off. The dinner's nearly ready. You can always go out again later."

Billy was not as sympathetic to my predicament as I had hoped he might be, and it took a lot of persuading on my part to get him to wait until we had both completed our mid-day meals, as he appeared ready to tackle the course on his own. However, my appeal to his strong sense of loyalty was successful. Unfortunately, the situation became worse as Billy's dinner was delayed and he didn't begin eating until an hour after I had finished.

When we did finally emerge it was almost mid-afternoon and I couldn't help informing Billy of my apprehension.

"What if they've stopped doing it?" I asked him as we hauled our sledges towards the end of Cross Speedwell Street. "There can't be all that much daylight left and I'm sure they won't continue with it in the dark. What then? We might never get another chance. As it is we'll be lucky to get two or three goes at it."

"Well, we can still do it on our own. There doesn't have to be anybody there."

"If they've all gone home there wouldn't be any point finishing it because nobody would believe us when we told them."

Billy was right, but by the time we reached Doughty's shop our mood brightened considerably as it was obvious from the noise that some sort of frantic activity was still taking place, and as we rounded the corner we were greeted by my Cousin Raymond.

"I thought you two must have changed your minds," he said. In fact, the way things have been going it might have been better if you had."

"Why? asked Billy. "What's been happening?"

"Well, apart from having a break for dinner we've been here for well over four hours and only three people have completed the course in all that time and there have been quite a lot of accidents, though nothing really serious. Some just fell off and some crashed into other lads hauling there sledges back up the hill. So when you set off to the Start Line make sure you walk on the right hand side of the road. That's what we've got everybody doing now."

"You said there was a lad about our age who might be from our school. Do you know if he finished it?" I asked him.

"No, all the three successful ones were about thirteen." He pointed towards the ridge wall at the end of Melville Road. "If you want to know how he got on you can ask him yourself. He's over there."

"You two aren't thinking of giving it a go, are you?" was Johnny Jackson's greeting as he saw us walking towards him. "You must be barmy if you are. Look what happened to me. We stared aghast at the severe grazing on his upper arm and his leg. There was also some bruising above his right eye."

"Crikey!" exclaimed Billy. "What on earth happened to you?"

"I crashed, that's what, twice. "I've got a spell in my finger from this sledge as well. I'm going to see if my dad will get me a metal one next year."

"Is it that hard to do then?" I asked him, with some trepidation.

"It's nearly impossible. I've tried five times and I only managed to get across Melville Road once, and each time I failed I had to walk all the way up the hill again."

I was beginning to wonder if it was going to be worth going through with this and the look on Billy's face suggested he was thinking the same. However, as I took off my glove and placed my hand into my jacket pocket I found the encouraging feel of Susan's red ribbon, which I had placed there that morning. It filled me with renewed vigour and I knew that it would mean so much to me to complete The Long Sledge.

"Good luck!" said Johnny Jackson, as we started to make our way up the hill. "Don't say I didn't warn you though."

"Do you think we're doing the right thing, Neil?" asked Billy, the doubt plainly etched on his face. "I mean we could just spend the rest of the afternoon sledging somewhere else, couldn't we?"

"Well, we could at least try to do this once, and then if it doesn't work out right it doesn't mean that anyone's going to force us to climb all the way back to the beginning and try again does it? Anyway, what if we just manage to complete it first go? We'd be able to tell everybody about it at school."

"Yes, maybe you're right Neil. We'll sledge down once and if it goes wrong we should know by then whether we want to have another run at it."

With a little more purpose to our step we trudged up the steep incline. As we passed the entrance to Woodhouse Ridge we watched three hopefuls, each appearing to be about a couple of years older than Billy and me, whizzing past in rapid succession. I was taken aback by the speed at which they were travelling, clinging onto their mounts in a manner that suggested that they had very little control over their intended destination. I felt that the looks on their faces showed apprehension rather than determination.

When we eventually reached our destination I could understand why many of the participants were reluctant to endure the climb to the starting point several times over.

"That was harder than I thought it would be," said my companion. "I'm all out of breath now."

"Never mind Billy, before long we'll have the thrill of hurtling down the hill together." My sense of bravado had returned and the adrenaline was flowing again. I was surprised to see two older girls amongst the hopefuls waiting to start and it seemed to me that they were the only ones there that showed no signs of bruising.

After a brief wait of a few minutes to regain our composure after the long climb we got our sledges into position ready for what I hoped would be the adventure of a lifetime.

One of the older lads, whose sole purpose seemed to be one of ensuring that each participant began from the correct starting point and didn't try to steal a few yards, came over to talk to us.

"You two are a bit young for this," he exclaimed. "It isn't going to be easy, you know. However, if you're determined to have a go I'd better give you some advice. There isn't much of a slope at the beginning, so make sure you take a really good run at it before getting onto the sledge. Don't forget that if you stop you'll have to come back to the beginning. If you manage that all right, by the time you get to the entrance to the ridge you'll be going really fast which means you might start to lose control. If that happens try to slow it down by steering into some of the softer snow at the sides of the track, but not so much that you stop altogether. If you're lucky to get across Melville Road without a mishap, and not everybody has done that, then it becomes even steeper and you might have to try the same manoeuvre. If you manage to get to the bottom of Cocoa House Hill you have to be going slow enough to steer to the left and then do the same again a few yards farther on to enter Ridge Road where the run ends. If you don't manage that bit successfully you could end up on the tram lines in Meanwood Road."

Despite the less than encouraging comments we had just received we were both eager to do the best we could. As we took up our positions at the start of the track I slipped my hand into my pocket, hoping that Billy didn't notice, and produced the red ribbon that had nestled there all day.

My companion and I began running and pushing our sledges at the same time, but Billy jumped on before I did. I thought he seemed a bit premature as the slope at that point was still a very gentle one. However, he managed to keep going and by the time I climbed on board my own craft he was already some way ahead. Just as I was about to gather speed as the incline became a little steeper Susan's ribbon, which I had tied loosely around my arm unwrapped itself and fell to the ground. I knew if I told anyone of my reason for turning into the deeper snow and stopping while it still seemed safe to do so I would almost certainly have been laughed at, but I was determined that my prize possession would accompany me all the way down the slope. As I gathered it up and shoved it back into my pocket I realised that the possibility of just starting again from the point where I had stopped was never really a valid option for I could still be seen by the boys who were looking after the starting position, and even if I did manage to complete the course from there unobserved I would still have the knowledge that I had not really accomplished what I had been so eager to do. No, the only way forward was to go back to the beginning. Fortunately, I did not have too far to walk and as I reached my destination and was about to set off on a second run Billy's head came into view on the crest of the hill. As the remainder of his body emerged I could see that he looked a little the worse for wear, and as he got nearer the expression on his face showed that he was extremely displeased. I decided to wait for him.

"What happened, Billy?" I asked as he walked over to join me.

"I think it's impossible Neil. The sledge was going so fast when I reached the entrance to the ridge that when I tried to slow down by steering it onto the softer snow at the side it turned right over. Look, I've torn my shirt and grazed my arm as well."

I examined the unfortunate consequences of his accident.

"I bet your mam's more bothered about your torn shirt than your grazed arm," I offered helpfully. "You're having another go though, aren't you?"

"I might as well. I'll get a right telling off anyway. So it won't make any difference."

"Honestly though, Neil, we've got to be able to slow it down without falling off."

As soon as he had finished speaking we were joined by an older boy of about fifteen.

"You can follow me if you like. I'll show you how to avoid falling off."

We thought with those words that he must have completed the course but he told us that, although he'd reached the end of Cocoa House Hill he'd never actually reached the finish line, but that he was determined to do it this time.

We set off for our second attempt immediately behind him, and jumped onto our sledges at the same point that he did. As the steepness of the incline gradually increased so did our speed, and as we approached the entrance to Woodhouse Ridge the person whose actions we were supposed to mimic turned into the deeper snow piled up at the side. As we both attempted the same manoeuvre we were just in time to see our tactics advisor's sledge turn on its side and throw him off before virtually the same mishap befell Billy and me.

"You see, that shouldn't have happened," he shouted to us as we sat in the snow assessing the extent of our wounds.

Our journey back up the slope on this occasion was undertaken with even more disillusionment than the previous one. At least Susan's ribbon hadn't come adrift this time. I looked across at my companion and saw that the look on his face reflected my own.

"I'm only going to have one more go at this, Billy" I announced. "If it doesn't work this time I'm packing it in."

"It'll be dark soon anyway," he said. "I think it's a lot harder than we expected it to be, isn't it?"

When we eventually found ourselves back at the start line we realised that we did not have any other option than to make this our final run.

"We're all packing up in ten minutes lads," announced the boy who had been giving us advice earlier. "So this will be your last chance."

I looked at Billy and without either of us speaking we knew that it would be better if we both failed rather than for one to succeed and the other not. I decided to lessen the risk of the ribbon coming loose and tied each end to the two extremities of the vehicle which I hoped would propel me all the way to the finishing line. We wished each other Good Luck and began running with the sledge. There appeared now to be no other competitors. It looked as though we had the whole track to ourselves.

296

I only hoped that if we did make it all the way, that there would still be someone there to record our achievement.

Billy jumped on first and I quickly followed. We soon gathered speed as the incline became steeper and as we neared the entrance to Woodhouse Ridge I knew that I had travelled further than on the two previous attempts. I watched my companion effectively slow down his velocity by turning into the softer snow at the side of the track without going too deeply into it on this occasion. As I passed him I was aware that he was successfully steering himself back into the centre of the road without having stopped. I was full of admiration for his expertise, and I knew that if I didn't attempt a similar manoeuvre soon I would be travelling so fast that I would undoubtedly lose control. The track, because of all the activity it had seen that day, resembled a sheet of glass. With Melville Road approaching rapidly I steered my sledge just sufficiently away from the centre to slow it down. A few seconds later, as I went back onto the main run the adrenalin was really starting to flow and as I gazed at Susan's ribbon I felt, for the first time that day, that there was a definite chance that Billy and I might complete the course without any serious mishap.

There was only one observer at the crossover point into Cocoa House Hill so it certainly seemed, as we had been told, that this would be the final opportunity of the day for anyone to complete The Long Sledge. There was a temporary slowing of velocity as the incline ceased as we traversed the more horizontal Melville Road only for it to become even steeper as we entered the other side. Billy was immediately in front of me and seemed to be clinging on for dear life as we picked up speed again. It soon became obvious, however, how few of the lads had completed the course. What had hitherto resembled a solid sheet of ice because of all the frenzied activity over the past few hours gradually became a little softer and therefore enabled us to decrease our speed a little. As the bottom of the hill approached we knew we faced a sharp left turn to take us onto a gentler slope towards Meanwood Road. At this point there was no obvious track to follow this close to the finish line. As I was about to attempt the manoeuvre I was distracted as the ribbon chose that precise moment to disengage itself from one side of the sledge. After having travelled so far I was anxious that it should remain attached for the entire journey. With one side of my memento blowing freely in the wind I accomplished the difficult task immediately behind my companion and we both found ourselves hurtling towards the tram lines. Sensing an impending triumph Susan's ribbon was waving frantically in the breeze as we took the final turn into Ridge Road. Billy took it a little wider so that when our mounts came to a stop as the incline began to change direction we finished side by side.

While we were in a state of euphoria we were approached by a lad of about sixteen.

"You two must be about the youngest to ever complete this," he exclaimed with a look of surprise on his face. "Are you sure you managed to do it without stopping? "

We both began to protest our innocence.

"Never mind," he said, producing a notebook and pencil from his pocket, "I'll be able to check with the others later. It's the first time I've seen anyone finish with a red ribbon tied to his sledge though. What's that for? Is it some sort of good luck charm?"

I looked down at the ground and couldn't think what to say.

"Anyway," he went on, not pushing me any further, "You're the last ones today. It'll be dark in a few minutes. I need your names and the name of your school if you want the other lads to know that you've completed the course."

He jotted down the information in his notebook before replacing it in his pocket.

"My sister goes to your school," he observed, "And she's about your age. You might know her - Susan Brown? Anyway, I'll tell her about you two, though I bet she'll think it's a bit odd when I mention that one of you had a red ribbon tied to his sledge for good luck."

When Billy and I completed The Long Sledge together I believe it cemented our friendship more firmly than any other single event could have done, and as we made our way home in a celebratory mood one thought just refused to go away. What on earth was Susan going to think when she heard about the ribbon?

# CHAPTER TWENTY-NINE

"Do you think we'll still be alive in the year 2000, Neil?" asked Billy as we stood outside Mrs. Ormond's sweet shop.

"Well, we'll only be sixty so we should be," I answered, after thinking it over, "But you never know, do you? I mean we might walk in front of a tram and be knocked down."

Nicky Whitehead chose that moment to step out of his front door and join us. "I thought I heard you two talking," he said, cheerily. We both noticed immediately that the pot had been removed from his arm.

"When did you get that off?" asked Billy.

"It was only taken off yesterday. The nurse said it was healing very well. The only trouble is that I'll probably have to go back to school next week when the new term starts. I thought I'd probably have it on for another fortnight." He sounded disappointed.

"There was a film on at the Capitol at Meanwood a couple of months ago," I told him. "It was all about everything that had happened in the first half of the century, and Billy and me were just wondering if we'd still be alive in the year 2000. We thought we might because we'll only be sixty."

"That means I'll be fifty-nine then," responded Nicky. "I wonder what it'll be like. I bet rockets will have landed on Mars by then," he said, enthusiastically.

"What if there's another war?" suggested Billy. "It could be the Third World War, or even the Fourth or Fifth with atom bombs dropping all over the place."

"If that happens," I told him, "There might be nobody left when it had finished. Everybody would be wiped out."

"By the way," said Nicky, "Did your brother come home from the army yesterday like he was supposed to?"

"Yes, he arrived just before bedtime."

My thoughts immediately went back a few hours to when I awoke on this final day of 1950. Tim was already getting dressed, despite the late hour that he had arrived on the previous day. He had already drawn back the curtains even though it was still quite dark outside. "There's not much chance of sleeping in when you're doing National Service, Neil," he had said. I had hoped he would be getting into his soldier's uniform but he had opted for the street clothes he had worn before having joined the army several months earlier.

I had gazed out of the bedroom window to see that the street outside was still covered by snow, but the fact that I could see through the glass at all was a contrast to the previous few days when it had been decorated by various patterns of frost. This had suggested to me that a thaw was on the way. I realised that, surprisingly, I didn't really mind this. After the euphoria that Billy and I had experienced after our achievements of just a couple of days previously the prospect of sledging down some inferior slope to that which we had successfully negotiated did not seem to hold the same attraction

My mind was brought back to the present time the moment I heard Susan's name mentioned.

"What did you say, Billy?" I asked him.

"I said that there's not a lot of this year left. Why don't you tell Susan Brown that you want her to be your girl friend so that you can start next year without moping about it all the time; well, nearly all the time anyway?"

"If I could do that, Billy, I'd have done it ages ago, besides I still don't know which is her house, do I?"

We had, of course, informed Nicky about our achievement in successfully negotiating the Long Sledge immediately after completing it, but I was totally unprepared for Billy's next comment.

"I bet you didn't know he fastened Susan Brown's hair ribbon to his sledge."

With my face burning fiercely I attempted to offer a valid reason for my action.

"Well, it's only like those knights did at tournaments in medieval times," I reasoned. "They used to point the lance at some lady they liked and she used to fasten a silk scarf on the end of it. "We've seen them do it at the pictures."

"Yes, Neil," countered Billy, "But Susan didn't even know you had her ribbon, did she? I mean, it's not as if she gave it to you herself, is it? So it's not the same."

"Well she'll know now, won't she? Her brother said he was going to tell her, didn't he?"

"Maybe he forgot," said Nicky. "I bet he never mentioned it at all."

"Why don't we all go up to the ridge?" suggested Billy. "We can have a snowball fight. It won't be all slush up there because there won't have been as many people walking on it, and anyway we might just bump into your girl friend on the way."

"I'm afraid you'll have to go without me," countered Nicky. "I have to go back inside. We're going to visit my

Auntie Maureen soon. I only came out because I heard you talking."

As Nicky re-entered his house, Billy and I began making our way towards the ridge. Just as we were about to cross Melville Road I hung back and whispered in his ear.

"Those two women standing next to that lamp post, do you recognize them?"

"I think so," he said, after thinking about it for a few seconds. "Aren't they the ones we saw at the bus stop in Meanwood Road when we were looking for lost coins?"

They were both staring, rather apprehensively down Speedwell Street. As soon as we started eavesdropping on the conversation, while pretending to be examining the contents of Doughty's shop window, we were left with no doubts

"It's looking a bit hazardous down there, Phyllis," said the larger of the two ladies. She paused for a moment before seemingly coming to a decision. I can't see as how God would take it personal if we missed out on going to the Sunday service for once. I mean he's not the sort who'd want us to go breaking our legs trying to get to the church, is he?"

"Oh, no Edna, he's not."

"Although I was going to have a word with him today, try to set things right, so to speak."

"How do you mean, Edna?"

"Well, it's like this, you see, Phyllis. Would you say I was a wicked woman?"

"Oh no, you're not, Edna. You're not."

"Well, I'm beginning to feel like one, Phyllis, and it's all the fault of that worthless husband of mine. He was round there again yesterday, you know."

"Oh, Edna, I am sorry."

"When I challenged him about it, do you know what he said? Just one word, 'mushrooms'"

"What did he mean, Edna, 'mushrooms'?"

"Oh, I knew what he was getting at right enough. He was making me suffer for when we were in digs in Scarborough."

"Why, Edna, what happened?"

"Well, I'll tell you, Phyllis. I'll tell you. We'd just arrived and been shown to our room. It was the usual sort of room, a double bed with a jerry underneath, marble washstand and a water jug. Anyway, while he decided to try out the bed I went back downstairs to have a word with the landlord. Well, you could have knocked me down with a feather, Phyllis, when he told me his name was Nigel. Now, I'm used to landlords in digs being called Fred or Jack or Sid. I mean your Nigels are strictly hotels or posh guest houses. Anyway, Nigel it was. So, he then asks me what we wanted for breakfast on account of how he'd got some fresh mushrooms and if we fancied having some with our bacon and egg. Now, I want you tell me something, Phyllis."

"What's that, Edna?"

"If, after what I'm going to tell you, you think I'm a wicked woman, I want you to come right out and tell me."

"Oh no, Edna, you're not a wicked woman."

"Ah, but I haven't told you what happened yet, Phyllis. You might think differently in a minute. Now my other half is very partial to mushrooms, though I can't abide them myself, and I thought 'Right lad, this is where I get a bit of my own back'. I was so incensed you see, about him spending half his time with her what lives next

304

door to the off-licence in Craven Road. So do you know what I did, Phyllis? I told this here Nigel straight out that he didn't want any mushrooms for his breakfast and that he didn't like them.

"Oh, Edna, you didn't."

"Oh, I did, Phyllis, I did. Mind you I still don't know how he found out about it. So there you are, I am a wicked woman, but it was him that made me so."

"That was a mean thing to do," said Billy as Edna came to the end of her story and we watched them head back along Melville Road, while Billy and I left the vicinity of the shop and began walking towards the ridge.

As we made our way up the hill which had played such a large part in our triumph of a couple of days previously we couldn't help but notice how much the slushy conditions we now witnessed contrasted with those of a couple of days earlier.

"Do you remember that history lesson Old Rawcliffe gave us just before Christmas?" I said as we arrived at the entrance to the ridge and leant over the railings surveying the snowy scene before us. "You know, that one about The Anglo-Saxon Chronicle."

"What, you mean what those monks wrote, where they listed everything that had happened in each year since the Anglo-Saxons landed in Britain?"

"Yes, that's it. Anyway, Billy, I've decided that I'm going to start my own chronicle, beginning tomorrow, but instead of one entry each year, I'm going to enter something for every day, and I'm going to call it THE WOODHOUSE CHRONICLE. I'll record all the different things we do." This had been on my mind ever since we'd had this particular history lesson, and I knew that the start of a new year would be the best time to begin it.

"Oh, I couldn't be bothered doing that, Neil. It'd be just like being back at school and being forced to write a composition. I bet after three days you get fed up with it and don't write any more."

"I wonder what we'll get up to," I remarked, ignoring Billy's lack of faith in my determination to see it through. "For instance, do you think we'll win a rugby game before the end of January?"

"I don't know, Neil, but I hate playing when the weather's so terrible, don't you?"

"I don't think it would be as bad though if we actually won a game occasionally."

After a couple of minutes silence while we considered whether the conditions which existed on the ridge were more conducive to forming proper snowballs than the slushy mess which covered the streets, Billy decided to make an observation.

"How can it have thawed so quickly, Neil? I mean everywhere was frozen two days ago."

"I don't know, Billy, but I don't think I'm all that bothered now. At least we completed The Long Sledge together, didn't we?"

The damp atmosphere was doing nothing at all to raise our spirits and I was starting to feel cold.

"I think we might as well go back down," I said. "I don't fancy going onto the ridge now."

I could sense that Billy's mood was the same as my own and we started to make our way back down the hill.

"It doesn't look anything like it did a couple of days ago, does it?" he said. "I bet all the snow's gone by the middle of the week."

As we approached Melville Road, we could hear what to most of the other lads in the area was a very familiar sound, and both of us knew immediately that it was the sound of a football being driven against a wall. As we turned the corner we were surprised to see Johnny Jackson, and a couple of lads we didn't know, attempting to enjoy an effective kick-around in the dismal conditions.

"Hiya, Johnny," shouted Billy. "It's not the best sort of day for a game of footie, is it?

"Hiya," he said turning round. "There's not much point getting the sledge out, though, is there? The snow's nearly all gone. Anyway, I heard you two both finished The Long Sledge. I wish it had been me. I bet I'd have done it if I hadn't hurt my arm." I couldn't help noticing that the other two lads were now giving us envious looks. I couldn't help feeling even more proud of our achievement. Then Billy decided to say something that put me in a more anxious frame of mind.

"Yes, in fact it was Susan Brown's brother who was looking after the finish line when we completed it. Susan lives round here somewhere, doesn't she?"

"Yes, I saw her this morning. She was going to her grandmother's near the top of the hill. Are you joining in, then? We can play two and a half a side."

Billy laughed. "No thanks, trying to kick a ball in this stuff we'd be soaked through in five minutes."

We left them to it and continued walking towards home. As we reached the beginning of our street Billy stopped, grabbing my arm at the same time.

"The first half of this century ends in a few hours time," he said. "Now's your chance to ask Susan Brown to be your girl friend before the second half starts. We know where she is now, don't we?"

"I can't do it, Billy. She'll just say no and it'll make me feel silly, especially now that she probably knows about the ribbon."

"Come on, Neil," he said, turning back towards the ridge. "Let's do it." Without thinking much about it, I found myself reluctantly following him back up towards the ridge.

"We'll wait round the corner from her grandmother's house like you did on Mischievous Night, then when we see her come out and start walking down the hill we can follow behind and tell her we just came off the ridge. She'll have to be going home soon for her dinner, so we shouldn't have to wait long."

"Look, I don't think I can do this, Billy and I certainly won't be able to if you're there as well."

I managed to get Billy to agree to stay hidden behind the corner while I would follow Susan down the street. My mind was frantically weighing up the various options which were open to me. Eventually, I realised that the only way I could really go through with it was by deciding that I wouldn't actually commit myself to saying anything at all, except hello. Then, if she initiated a conversation other than just the reciprocal greeting I would see how it progressed from there, though I realised I'd probably be tongue-tied anyway.

We can't have waited for more than ten minutes before we heard a door opening and Susan saying farewell to her grandmother. I immediately felt my mouth go dry and every muscle in my body tense up. As soon as she started walking down the street, I followed a few paces behind. Then it all went horribly wrong. In order to catch her up I increased my pace. Unfortunately for me, and as it turned out for Susan, I became less careful in coping with the extremely slippery surface. My feet gave way causing me to slide the remaining distance on my backside and crash into the object of my desire, thus allowing her to accompany me in a similar fashion for a further few yards down the slope. For a few seconds, the two of us just sat there. Then Billy, who was obviously thoroughly enjoying the situation, chose that moment to announce his arrival, having obviously taken more effective steps to avoid the mishap that had befallen me.

"It looks like you two have fallen for each other," he suggested, mischievously, as we both rose to our feet.

"I'm sorry, Susan," was the best that I could manage in an attempt to rescue something from the situation. "I just couldn't stop myself. Are you all right?"

"I think so, but what were you trying to do? You scared the life out of me," she said, her voice slightly raised.

It occurred to me, however, that she wasn't as angry as she could have been. I knew, though, that, given this new set of circumstances my mission would have to be aborted. I was no longer in the right frame of mind, especially as Billy was now in attendance.

"I'm sorry, Susan", I repeated. "I saw you walking down the hill and I was just trying to reach you."

"Well, why were you in such a hurry to catch me up?"

"I just wanted to say hello."

I was beginning to feel really awkward and uncomfortable and I just didn't know what to say next.

Billy, however, as usual, wasn't stuck for words. "Me and Neil finished the Long Sledge two days ago," he announced, "All the way from the top of Delph Lane almost to Meanwood Road."

"I watched some of them doing it," said Susan, "But I didn't see you two. I saw Johnny Jackson though."

Relief swept over me. It seemed apparent that she hadn't heard about me using her red ribbon as a mascot. It in no way, however, gave me the confidence to ask the question that had been the whole purpose of the morning's activities. After having made such an unseemly arrival I would have felt incredibly silly. I realised that I just wanted to be away from there while I still had some shred of dignity left.

"Come on, Billy" I managed to stumble out. "I think we ought to be going now."

He looked surprised, but shrugged his shoulders and accepted the situation. "Bye, Susan," we both said, and began to resume our passage down the hill, leaving her to stand, rather dishevelled, looking down at us.

"You missed the perfect opportunity there," Billy whispered, in case Susan was still in hearing range.

"How could I say anything after I'd just knocked her over like that? No, the only thing I'm pleased about is the fact that, at least, her brother doesn't appear to have told her about what I had fastened to the sledge."

A few seconds later my skin went cold as Susan's raised voice carried down the hill towards us. "You can keep the ribbon, Neil, if you like."

That evening my mother surprisingly announced that she would allow me to stay up until midnight to celebrate the arrival of the New Year now that we were a complete family again, even though that state of affairs would only exist until Tim departed to resume army duties in a few days time. There was also the added attraction, for me, of bedding down on the sofa in the back room with the promise of a warm oven plate wrapped in a cloth to keep me company. This change to sleeping arrangements was to enable Grandad Miller to stay the night with us, which was also something that pleased me immensely, Grandma Cawson having already decided to stay with one of my aunts. One hour before midnight while my mother was busy making sandwiches there was a knock on the front door and, as it was opened, a familiar voice was heard.

"Are you there, May? Only it looked as if the light was on, so I guessed you must be staying up to see the New Year in."

"That's right, Mr. Senior, and you're more than welcome to sit with us if you like," responded my mother.

"Nay, lass, that won't be necessary as I've got my Doreen and her husband staying with me, though it's nice of you to ask No, what it is, do you see, I was wondering if you had any sticking plasters as my grandson's cut his thumb on a tin of beans that we'd just opened. I thought it was a bit of tomato sauce at first and I couldn't understand why he was making such a fuss. Anyway, as soon as we realised what had happened we searched high and low for a plaster but couldn't find one anywhere, though I did find a bit of soothing ointment to put on it."

My mother walked over to the sideboard, opened a drawer and triumphantly produced the required article, opened the packet and handed one over. "I bought some just the other day," she said. "You never know when you might need a sticking plaster."

"Aye, you're right there, lass." said the grateful recipient." It just goes to show doesn't it?"

"How are you in yourself then, Mr. Senior?" asked my mother as he made to step outside with his trophy.

"Oh, I'm fair to middling lass, just fair to middling, but we mustn't grumble, must we?"

My thoughts returned to my encounter with Susan. At first the realisation that she knew I had her ribbon and used it in the way that I had, made me feel despondent. However, as the evening wore on and I gave it more thought it occurred to me that it might not be a bad thing after all. At least she hadn't laughed when she told me about it. I even dared to think that perhaps she might have been quite pleased that it had been used in the way it had. With midnight fast approaching I found myself looking forward with renewed vigour to what 1951 might bring.

"You're looking very thoughtful," announced Grandad Miller, who had obviously been watching me staring quietly into space. "How about a penny for 'em?"

"I was just thinking about all the things that me and Billy had done during this year grandad, and the things we might be doing next year."

"Well, there's not much of the old year left now, is there? I'll tell you one thing though. You're very lucky that your mother's let you stay up to see in the New Year. Mine never allowed me to. Mind you, that doesn't mean that I never did."

"How did you manage to do it then, grandad?"

"Well, I've probably never told you this but my best mate was called Harry Crabtree. Now one New Year's Eve when, we'd be about the same age as you are, Harry came up with this brilliant idea for staying out until after midnight."

Suddenly I felt really contented. I knew that 1951 held even more promise than 1950 had. I felt that Billy and I were even more closely linked because of our achievements in completing the Long Sledge together and there was every possibility that we would have even more exciting escapades than before. Nicky had had the pot removed from his arm so he should soon be joining us. Grandad Miller seemed to have fully recovered from his hospital ordeal. Then there was the realisation that I might not feel quite so embarrassed about admitting my feelings for Susan Brown and after what had happened earlier I assumed that she was probably already aware of them. Things were going better with the rugby team and surely it wouldn't be too long before we actually won a game. Tim would not be returning to the army for another couple of days and I was about to see in the New Year for the first time ever, before sleeping in the downstairs room with the warmth of a hot oven plate wrapped in a cloth to keep me company. On top of all this, my grandfather was about to relate one of his enthralling stories. At that precise moment in my life everything seemed wonderful. I settled back in the chair with a smile on my face.

"Now then, lad, I'll tell you exactly how it happened," said Grandad Miller.